Nightfall

The bedroom door slammed shut behind her, and as she was coming up from the floor, turning, yanking the pistol from its holster, the lamp chimney was smashed, the flame leaped thinly and went out.

Anita made ready to shoot without having to think about it. Thumb the safety down, pull the slide back smartly, release it – a satisfying sound in the black trap of the room. She caught a runaway breath and held it, the automatic steady in her two hands. *Where was he?*

She listened, listened for the giveaway creak of floorboards beneath his heavy tread.

Instead, she smelled him. A morbid, spunky odor, collapsing on her like a spider's dense web.

Come at last, the Angel of Death.

'Not *this* time, Angel!' Anita fired the automatic, emptying the magazine into the suffocating darkness around her.

'John Farris has a genius for creating compelling suspense'

Peter Benchley author of Jaws

'Few writers have Mr Farris' talent for masterful devious plotting, the shattering effective use of violence, in-depth characterisations, and scenes of gibbering horror guaranteed to turn the blood to gelatin'
New York Times

About the author

John Farris is the author of THE FURY, THE
LONG LIGHT OF DAWN, KING WINDOM,
WHEN MICHAEL CALLS, THE CAPTORS,
SHARP PRACTICE, ALL HEADS TURN
WHEN THE HUNT GOES BY, SHATTER,
CATACOMBS and THE UNIVITED. He lives in
Puerto Rico.

Nightfall

John Farris

NEW ENGLISH LIBRARY
Hodder and Stoughton

Copyright © 1987 by John Farris

First published in the United States by Tor Books, 1987

First published in Great Britain in 1987 by New English Library Paperbacks

A New English Library Paperback Original

Grateful acknowledgement is made for permission to reprint lyrics from 'Wreck on the Highway', words and music by Dorsey Dixon. Copyright 1946, renewed 1973 by Acuff-Rose/Opryland Music, Inc. 2510 Franklin Road, Nashville, TN. International Copyright Secured. Made in U.S.A. All rights reserved.

Printed and bound in Great Britain for Hodder and Stoughton Paperbacks, a division of Hodder and Stoughton Ltd., Mill Road, Dunton Green, Sevenoaks, Kent TN13 2YA. (Editorial Office: 47 Bedford Square, London WC1B 3DP) by Richard Clay Ltd., Bungay, Suffolk.

British Library C.I.P.

Farris, John
  Nightfall.
  I. Title
  813'.54[F]   PS3556.A777

  ISBN 0-450-41729-8

For Peter John,

slayer of dragons
and all-around good guy

There is no night as deep as this
Inevitable mind's abyss,
Where I now dwell with foes alone.

From an untitled poem
by Olive Fraser

CHAPTER
ONE

Angel came back to life in the Watchtower on the
night of October 22, which, coincidentally, was his
birthday. He was thirty-four years old. There were a
few people left who cared enough to remember his
birthday, but no one had called or come to visit.
Angel was in the third week of a catatonic posture, a
long run for him, and the latest experimental drug he
was receiving from the head of Clinical Neurogenetics
at Silver Birches had failed to retrieve him from
beyond the rigid boundary of his affliction.

Almost before anyone knew he was back, Angel
killed again.

His victim was LaDonna Morales, a New Yorican
from Long Island City, who was in her first week at
Silver Birches, and less than a year out of nursing
school. Her brief orientation to psychiatric nursing
undoubtedly was a contributing factor in her death.
Also she had never been exposed to anything like
Angel (or *Ahn-hel*, as she persisted in calling him),

and had never been permitted access to his case history on the Institute's computer. All she knew about him was what she had learned from the departing charge nurse on the Watchtower's graveyard shift, a woman named Alma.

Alma had been scary enough in her summation. She was a thirty-year veteran of psychiatric wards. Silver Birches was the Garden of Allah compared to some of the state institutions Alma had worked in. She was sixty and tough, with dry, crisp, artificially yellow hair. She smiled as if her feet were always killing her, which was true; this was a major factor in her decision to retire and become a part-time missionary to the Indian tribes of the Southwest. Alma had scars from tooth and claw on her hands, forearms, and one side of her heavily freckled neck. She was one of those people you know are not prone to exaggeration after you've talked to them for a couple of minutes.

"No b.s., honey," Alma would say. "I don't b.s. nobody, and nobody b.s.'s me." She had taken a liking to LaDonna, and felt a little sorry for her. The Watchtower could be rough duty, even from midnight to eight A.M., when the four to seven residents (occupancy fluctuated in maxlock) were supposed to be asleep. But of course some of them had different sleep cycles (Mrs. Tashian, who had murdered an infant in a supermarket, impulsively squeezing the fragile skull as if it were a melon she was testing for ripeness, was, for therapeutic reasons, on a twenty-seven-hour day). And at least one, Angel, appeared never to close his eyes during his catatonic episodes.

That was how LaDonna encountered him on her first day at work: he was seated on a padded bench in the stark wedge-shaped room he had occupied for eighteen months, his back against a padded wall. He was all strung up in IV and catheter tubing, the EKG wires that were linked to an oscilloscope outside. And the first thing she noticed, was disturbed by, was his round, amber, glistening eyes—they seemed to give off light, not take it in. She was reminded of the eyes of piranha fish she had once seen in an aquarium. The second thing that struck her was Angel's near-nakedness. He wore only a short hospital gown that covered him about as well as a baby's bib. It was easy to tell that, despite the fact that he had been drip-fed for a while, he had a firm attractive frame, not narcissistically sculptured like a body-builder's, but naturally well-muscled. His skin was olive, his closely-shaved cheeks and chin glowed.

The third thing she saw was a hard-on. His penis was almost perpendicular in his lap, raising the hem of the shortie gown. LaDonna winced slightly; how could it get up so powerfully with a tube running through it, didn't he feel pain? She wondered what he was thinking about, or if he thought of anything, way back there in the mind where life and death were so tenuously linked.

"Don't pay attention to *that*," Alma said casually when she realized where LaDonna had fixed her eyes. "It's a side effect of the medication he's on."

"Priapism," LaDonna said, her tongue dry in her mouth. She just wanted to let Alma know she had learned a thing or two lately. She massaged her slim throat with one hand, an unconscious habit held over from childhood. Angel seemed to have shifted his gaze to look at the small unbreakable observation window beside his door where the nurses stood. He blinked a couple of times, looking—but had he focused on LaDonna, acknowledging her presence? She had no sense of soul inside that repository, the perpetual twilight in which he was kept.

Angel's forehead was furrowed. Like most rigid catatonics, he drooled, out of the left side of his mouth, and the cotton johnny was stained in ringed circles below the shoulder. His black hair, with little glints of silver, was cut short, and his hairline had receded well back from his temples. He had a high square forehead and sturdy chin. He would never have been called handsome, LaDonna thought; yet in passing she would have been compelled to look at him, perhaps to stare.

"He's bipolar, you said," LaDonna remarked, determined to be professional.

Alma nodded, adjusting Angel's lighting with the outside rheostat. LaDonna felt a twinge of relief, no longer needing to dwell on those bright and utterly savage eyes, the tortured erection, the energy throttled back in his stiffened body. He was, somehow, not like two other catatonics her class in nursing school had observed; his rigidity seemed self-willed. But wasn't that, in one sense, true of all of them? No one knew, and those who suffered from the rare disorder couldn't explain. Fascinating. LaDonna was a little intimidated, but she had been required to overcome intimidation all of her life. She knew she was going to like working here, although Silver Birches was a daylong trip from the neighborhood, from her family and friends.

"How does he come out of it?" LaDonna asked, with a glance at Angel's dark blue door.

Alma sighed. "We never know. This time he may

be gone for keeps. Dr. Bushmill's frustrated, no doubt about that.''

LaDonna followed her a few steps to the center of the round Watchtower, the nurses' station, where Alma reached over the counter easily, something the slightly built LaDonna could never do, and flipped the switch that double-locked the door to Angel's spartan room.

"One cardinal rule. Never go into a patient's room alone. Always have a male attendant with you, even if you have to wait a couple of minutes for one to come up from Main House. And if Angel recovers, he's never permitted off the floor unless he has a straitjacket on."

"Is Ahn-hel Latin? He looks like he might be."

Alma sighed again, with less forbearance.

"Honey, it's 'Angel.' Not Smith or Jones or Brown—just *Angel*. Like the Angel of Death."

LaDonna laughed uncertainly. "He's here kind of anonymously, is that it? What is his story, then?"

"I've heard a little bit of this and that," Alma said vaguely. "Enough to know there's nothing funny about Angel. If you take your eyes off him at the wrong moment, he just might kill you."

LaDonna didn't laugh this time, but held herself a little straighter. Intimidation, again. She had seen gang warfare and knifings in the street near her house, people crazed by dope threatening to throw loved ones from rooftops. A man had tried to rape her in a vacant lot when she was fourteen, but she was more than he could handle, wiry-tough, she had stuffed half a brick up his nose. She was ready for anything at the Watchtower.

On the night she died, LaDonna left her rented

room in the resort town of Kelmore, New York, at
eleven-thirty and drove in her new Buick Skyhawk,
her pride and joy, to Silver Birches. The luxury
sanitarium was on a nameless island in Lake George,
reached by a private causeway across a little bay.
There had been a storm earlier, the sky had cleared
midafternoon as she was waking up, now it was
raining again, a hard rain with thunder and wind that
tore what remained of the gorgeous fall leaves from
the thick woods; the foliage season was over.

She crossed the causeway, seeing the lake in whitecaps with each downstroke of lightning. The main
house was hulking stone, three stories, three wings; it
had once been the summer retreat of a Victorian-era
railroad baron. Now, perhaps, descendants of wealthy
friends of his paid several thousand dollars a month
to keep dotty or drug-destroyed relatives out of harm's
way.

Few of the patients at Silver Birches could be
considered dangerous. Those that were stayed in the
Watchtower, a separate structure that overlooked the
main body of the lake, on a promontory a hundred
yards from the house. The Watchtower was fifty feet
from ground level to the patients' floor where LaDonna
worked, but there was an elevator inside the circular
staircase, a blessing unless the power shut down. She
made it upstairs okay, getting off one level below the
patients' floor, as far as the elevator went. But as she
was climbing the remainder of the stairs to the top
she could hear disturbances through the thick stone
walls and steel exit door; the full moon and the
racketing thunder had everyone in rare form tonight.

Britta, the Swedish girl who worked the four-to-
midnight, looked a little bedraggled and happy to be

relieved a few minutes early. An elderly actor who had messed up his end of a suicide pact with his terminally ill wife was loudly reciting Goethe in his room, in German. Mrs. Tashian also was carrying on, tearfully, about the poor woodland creatures who were drowning in all this rain. Britta, according to Alma, who had known everybody's dirty little secrets, had a drinking problem, but if she'd been sneaking nips on her shift today it wasn't obvious as she went briskly through the charts with LaDonna, pointing out a change in medication here, an antibiotic there.

"They are an opera tonight; they are a chorus of demons," Britta said, thunder around their heads.

The charge nurse in Main House had assigned an attendant for the duration of LaDonna's shift, which she appreciated until she saw who it was coming out of Lacey Steegmuller's room. McSwain. One of those men who devote a lifetime to drifting from job to job where the hardest physical activity is an occasional lick with broom and dustpan. Violent blue tattoos on his forearms, a head full of old sick teeth. The couple of times they'd been around each other, he'd made a point of tugging and scratching at his balls, when he thought LaDonna was looking.

"The kid shit her bed," McSwain grumbled.

Britta gave him a hard stare. "Is what you are paid for, to clean up."

McSwain glanced at LaDonna. "Let the new nursie get her hands dirty, she needs the experience."

"My name is LaDonna, which you already know, and I have done plenty of scut work." Lacey Steegmuller was sobbing in her room. "All right just stay away from Lacey, I will look after her myself in a minute.''

McSwain didn't move. "Fifty million bucks," he said, speaking of Lacey Steegmuller, "and all she ever bought with it was angel dust and crack. So she ate part of her fingers, she's got the bowels of a baby and a mind like a kumquat.''

Britta said, still staring, "You like your job?'' McSwain shrugged. Britta said, "Maybe you would care to take a hike right now back to whatever mission they found you in. Yah?'' McSwain grinned. "Then go and strip the got-damned bed,'' Britta finished irritably.

"Kind of tight-assed tonight, huh, Britta? How about a nice relaxing enema later? I'd get my hands dirty for *you*. McSwain's your pal.'' He whistled softly to himself, turned and went back into the girl's room.

Britta looked at LaDonna, who waggled a hand deprecatingly. "That was choice.'' Then she glanced at a row of TV monitors, stopping at room number 6. "At least Angel is quiet. No change?''

"Nothing. He is clean, you should not need to move him. A shame you must be here all night with that prick McSwain.''

"He doesn't bother me. He's just mouth.''

"Yah. Well, I'll be going. I hope the causeway is not flooded again.''

"It was okay when I came across.''

Britta looked up unhappily at the lightning-illuminated dome of the skylight overhead, then retrieved her trench coat and umbrella from the nurses' lounge and said good night. LaDonna buzzed her off the floor, then went to Lacey Steegmuller's room. The girl needed a shower, a change of night-clothes, some soothing words, all of which took LaDonna twenty minutes. Then she put Lacey back to bed. McSwain was leaning against the nurses' station drinking coffee when LaDonna came out. He watched her make a slow circuit of the other rooms, looking in through the observation windows, pausing the longest at Angel's room.

"Know anything about the science of phrenology?" McSwain asked her.

"Do you?" LaDonna said, not looking at him. It occurred to her that Angel had changed position, subtly, since she had last seen him. His head was at a higher angle. He was looking LaDonna's way, and seemed startlingly alert in the sprays of lightning that lit him up from time to time.

"I know a lot of things. I got a couple of high-class university degrees, believe it or not."

"I don't."

"Now, that one in there, Angel, the goombah, he has all the classic contours, the cranium measurements, of a homicidal maniac."

LaDonna shrugged off a dusting of ice across her shoulders. "Why do you call him goombah?"

"Oh, I found out all about him; his mama was on the speaker phone to Bushmill the other day. Doc's door wasn't all the way closed and I kind of listened in. She sounded real emotional, old-country, Italian or Sicilian maybe. Anyway, his name's Barzatti. That give you ideas?"

"No. Why should it?" Talking to McSwain was a little distracting, and the low level of light in Angel's room, between skybursts, put a strain on her eyes. She closed them briefly, and when she looked again she could swear Angel had turned ever so slightly on his bench, toward the observation window. His gaze full and yellow and unearthly, it gave her an itch along the spine, excited dread, stimulated her curiosity. Maybe he was coming out of his catatonic state after all, her standing orders were to call Dr. Bushmill at any time of night if—

McSwain came up behind her silently on rubber soles and touched her elbow; LaDonna jumped and frowned.

"Take it easy," he said. "Like I was telling you, the mother lives down in Howard Beach, you know about Howard Beach?"

"I may have heard of it."

"Lot of Mafia in that neighborhood: *capos*, maybe even a big fish like, what do they call 'em, a don."

"And perfectly ordinary people too, I'm sure."

"Jesus!" McSwain said, peering in over LaDonna's shoulder, breathing rancidly on her. "I think he just moved. Didn't he move?"

"I don't know." LaDonna touched the rheostat on the wall and dialed up the lights recessed into the ceiling of Angel's room. Light spread across his dark brow, the thin rope of saliva hanging from his chin glistened.

"He's watching you," McSwain said. "Look at that big dick! I think he's got it on just for you, kid. Angel likes you. Angel wants you."

"Oh. Great. Suddenly my life has meaning."

"Think you could go for Angel? Maybe he's a real important man where he comes from. I mean, he didn't get into Silver Birches because his daddy's in the chickenshit business."

"*Bichote*, why don't we do some work now? I got

to give Mrs. Tashian her medication or she will never shut up.''

McSwain accompanied her to the drug safe and then to Tashian's room.

"I have some sweet lullabies for you, Mrs. Tashian. You need to get some rest now.''

Mrs. Tashian wanted to know the death count in the squirrel population, out there in the drenched wood. LaDonna assured her the SPCA had saved every last one. Mrs. Tashian was gratified, but then she began to talk about the Dupers, and the mean things Dupers did, like leaving a two-week-old infant with a crushed head in a perambulator, for which she got all the blame. LaDonna let her ramble on, plumping her pillow, fussing with the bedcovers, and presently Mrs. Tashian stopped tracking very well and her crinkled eyelids closed.

"I had a Puerto Rican old lady once," McSwain said when they had left the room. "She was only about four and a half feet tall, but she made good *chimichangas*. You know how to make *chimichangas*?"

"That's Mexican, not Puerto Rican.''

"So what do you know how to cook?''

"*Empanadias. Alcapurias.*''

"Maybe I'll let you make me up a mess of those sometime. I've always been partial to Spic food.''

"Such an honor," LaDonna said, too bored to put much of a delivery behind her sarcasm. She had eight and a half minutes to live.

LaDonna kept herself busy behind the counter of the nurses' station and, after making another attempt at conversation, McSwain went yawning off to the lounge to watch TV, pretending not to hear her request to swab down the patients' shower room. The rain had stopped for a while, but there were still little flashes of lightning, faint rumbles of thunder.

The pulse on Angel's oscilloscope suddenly began to jump as his heartbeat accelerated. LaDonna stared at the face of the scope, then at Angel's shadowy image on the TV monitor.

He was moving.

Keeping her eyes on him, LaDonna reached for the telephone, then shifted her attention to the listing of staff home numbers beside it. *Bushmill, Asa D*.

During the few seconds she was diverted, Angel went into convulsions.

The heart line of the oscilloscope was throwing up quick spikes, the machine beeping like crazy. LaDonna glanced at the monitor, seeing him on the floor, bare legs jerking. She turned and tripped the switch on the panel that opened the master lock on the door to Angel's room.

"McSwain!"

LaDonna was still holding the receiver of the telephone. Instead of ringing Dr. Bushmill, she dialed 1-2-3 for Medalert, which would set off an alarm at the nursing station in Main House and bring experienced help on the double.

That was when the biggest bolt of lightning she'd ever seen hit the Watchtower like a bomb, knocking out the power. LaDonna cowered. In the dazzling blue afterglow the battery-powered emergency lights, a pair of 150-watt floods, came on above the stairwell door. They cast stark shadows around the Watchtower floor. Lacey Steegmuller whimpered. The old actor in room 3 woke up and, thinking he had been cued, began singing "Some Enchanted Evening" from *South Pacific*.

LaDonna opened a cabinet and yanked out the medical kit.

"What's up?" McSwain asked, looking at her from the doorway of the nurses' lounge.

"It's Angel. He's having a seizure." The TV monitor was blank, the oscilloscope had quit. "Come with me."

"Hey, careful, LaDonna—"

She was already at Angel's door. She had the right key in her hand. She placed it in the second lock and turned it, opened the door. Some light from the glaring floods on the other side of the tower spread into the room. The soles of his feet looked very white. Blood was backing up in the IV tube that was still attached to the back of one hand. All of the EKG wires were loose, she heard him grinding his teeth. She looked for McSwain.

"He needs help! Probably swallowed his tongue. I don't know if I am strong enough—come on, McSwain!"

McSwain wasn't budging. "You better wait for the med team, LaDonna. That guy—no shit, he—"

"*Bichote*," LaDonna said contemptuously, and entered Angel's padded room.

She saw the glare slits of his eyes, the violent trembling. She was not afraid. She kneeled beside him and opened the double-decker medical kit, wishing she had more light. It began to rain again, a deluge.

In room 3 the old actor sang thrillingly of enchanted evenings, crowded rooms, and meeting strangers.

Outside, McSwain finally moved. He shuffled to

the door of Angel's room, glanced in, saw LaDonna take a metal separator from the medical kit. He turned and went quickly back to the nursing station. He had to paw through several cabinets, not sure of just where it was. But he had a hunch he was going to need it.

Angel's mouth was slippery with blood and mucus. LaDonna didn't think he'd swallowed his tongue after all. Forgetting about McSwain, LaDonna concentrated on getting Angel's jaws apart, sliding in the separator so he wouldn't chew his tongue any more.

Suddenly Angel stopped trembling. His mouth opened easily. Blood and vomit spurted into her perspiring face, setting her back on her heels with a cry of distress.

McSwain, hurrying to get the CO_2 gun loaded, heard her and thought, *Oh, Jesus.*

As she was trying to clear her face of the mess, a strong unshaking hand seized LaDonna by the throat.

Terrified, immobile, she saw that his eyes were wide open and understood that she had been tricked. Mrs. Tashian's pet word flashed through her mind, before the blackness came up: *Duper.*

Outside, McSwain dropped the cartridge he was trying to load into the tranquilizer pistol. It hit the tip of his white Reebok shoe and didn't break.

Do you love me?

There was nowhere LaDonna could look but into his eyes. His spoiled blood and vomit were on her lips, his strong blunt fingers put pressure on the hyoid bone. She had one of his shoulders deep by her fingernails, but her grip was slowly loosening. Her left hand, groping the air, came down and delicately stroked his hard penis as he pushed her head far to one side.

"Do you love me?" he asked her.

She had never known such strength, nor felt so lonely.

The U-shaped bone embedded at the root of her tongue snapped. Angel came up off the floor and LaDonna, eyes glazing, went with him, dangled in his grip, died.

Angel threw her body through the door of his room and, while McSwain was looking at it, the white dress riding high on her hips, her frozen face turned back at a dire angle over one shoulder, Angel flung himself over the counter of the nurses' station and knocked McSwain sprawling. The CO_2 pistol flew from his hand. McSwain's head hit the floor hard. He saw lightning flare on the domed skylight directly overhead, and a lot of sparklers. Injury only added to his terror; McSwain struggled to his feet. He was tipsy, couldn't stand without hanging on to something. When he tried to take a step his feet got tangled. The free-fall of sparklers continued, the starkly lit floor tipped and whirled. He saw something rise up between him and the emergency lights, blotting them out. He tried to scream and could only gargle a sob.

The CO_2 gun that Angel had retrieved fired, not making enough sound for McSwain to hear above the ringing in his ears. The stubby tranquilizer dart, freezing cold, popped him dead-center of his right eyeball. Half the lights in his brain went out, leaving it dead dark, but he felt no pain, just the stunning blow. He lost his grip on the counter, dropped down hard to his knees, hesitated there for a few seconds, made another, mournful sound, and keeled over.

Angel stepped over him and stood looking at the numerous switches that controlled access on the floor. He pushed several of them, rapidly, until he heard the buzzer of the stairwell door. Then he pulled McSwain upright, propped him in a chair, tilted him until his forehead depressed the switch that controlled the stairwell door. It buzzed continuously as Angel let himself out; it would operate for upwards of half an hour on the independent circuit fed by another nine-volt battery.

Angel heard the Medalert team toiling up the stairs toward the patients' floor, swearing because the elevator wouldn't run. There was an emergency light over Angel's head. He saw a fire extinguisher on the wall, ripped it down from its mountings, went quickly down the stairs toward the two men. They saw a naked muscular man with a hard-on suddenly rounding on them from above, and they had nowhere to go. Angel broke both their skulls with the heavy fire extinguisher and left them behind. He went hobbling down the remaining steel-clad steps, cramps in both his thighs now, a stitch in his side, remnants of hospital gown flying from one shoulder. He still carried his unyielding penis like a flagstaff before him.

He opened the door at ground level to a cold faceful of rain, saw lights in Main House but no one on the mist-shrouded lawn. He spent only a few seconds looking around. His body, unused to violent effort, tortured him. But he understood torture, believed in it. He forced himself to run. He was the Angel of Death, and he was on the loose again.

CHAPTER TWO

After his eight hundred and ninety-ninth—and worst—carrier deck landing, Captain Clay Tomlin stayed in the Navy for a few months longer; but when it became obvious there was no good way he could serve his country any more, he resigned his commission. He was forty-three years old, unmarried, and he had no idea of what to do with himself.

He did the usual things, ashore: he saw old buddies, took up with a lot of women, drank too much. He brooded when he was in his cups, and wasn't much fun. He tried, and failed, to put together a coherent picture of his future. Financially, he was all set. He'd been earning in the midfifties, with negligible expenses, and a former Annapolis shipmate, now with a solid Wall Street firm, had put him into bonds when nobody could give them away. Subsequently bonds had appreciated well past par. He wasted some of his money on civilian specialists, who told him what the Navy doctors at Bethesda had already told

17

him. He just wasn't going to fly again. But flying
was everything that really mattered.

Finally he got bored with himself and his predicament and decided to go home, because there wasn't
anyplace else to go. Also it would soon be winter;
and winter didn't suit his Southern bones.

Near noon on October 24, a cool clear day, Tomlin
drove into Port Bayonne, Mississippi, a Gulf Coast
town east of Biloxi. He parked his white Corvette
near the office of Mace Lefevre, counselor-at-law, a
small restored one-story building on the main drag.
There were orange mums in the window boxes. He
strolled in through the open door. Nothing much was
doing. The receptionist was on the phone to a
girlfriend. She was a pert little package, all of five
feet tall and eighteen years of age, but a pinhead
diamond was sticking up out of an engagement ring
on the appropriate finger. They still ripened fast and
married faster in this part of the country. Their hus-
bands were a year or two older, worked the shrimp
and oyster boats or the shipyards in nearby Pascagoula.
He felt a slight nostalgia, as if he'd passed the shade
of his own youth on his way in.

The receptionist put her hand over the mouthpiece
of the receiver.

"Yes, sir?"

"You got any homesick coonasses loafing around
here?" Tomlin asked her.

He heard the front legs of a chair hit the floor in
one of the back offices.

"Clay Tomlin! That you?"

"Get on out here, Mace."

Mace Lefevre filled his office doorway. He was
Tomlin's age and height, about six-one, but in far

worse shape, 150 pounds overweight. Tomlin detected a wheeze. Mace wore a powder-blue seersucker suit and a dark blue knit tie. And diamonds. Although he had a paralegal working for him, and a girl to do the word processing, it was basically a one-man office. But Mace had put together some lucrative deals up and down the coast.

"Well, doggone, there he is! What're you up to, wild man?"

Tomlin said, with a trace of a grin, as much smiling as he was apt to do, "Had a little time off. Thought I'd come home, do some fishing."

"So come on in here. God dog, we got us some catching up to do."

"If you're sure you're not too busy."

"Shitfire, when did I ever get that busy? Elizabeth, next time Perrine calls, tell him we're at the courthouse rounding up the appropriate documents, and he'll have his easement by four o'clock."

Elizabeth nodded and popped her chewing gum and went back to gossiping with her girlfriend. Mace Lefevre followed Tomlin into the spacious back office, which was much as Tomlin remembered it, all the sturdy oak furniture Mace's daddy had left him, along with the business. A couple of deep leather chairs, a desk with an inlaid green leather top. Blue and belligerent trophy billfish on the walls. Aerial survey maps of the county. A framed architect's rendering of a resort that had gone up on land Mace owned and leased to the hotel chain.

"Nice-looking girl," Tomlin commented.

"Oh, yeah, hell, I've employed maybe a dozen just like her; they last eight months, a year, then they go off to have babies. Sometimes I get their names mixed up, they all look the same once you reach our advanced age. If Elizabeth appeals to you, listen, she's got a tiny sister I could introduce you to, there's a few more years on her but it don't show yet. Real looker. Divorced last year, she's working hostess at the Sea Sprite. I'm assuming you didn't up and get married without letting the homefolks know."

"Confirmed bachelor, Mace."

"I know how it is. All that sea duty. And there was a girl, wasn't there, Bob mentioned her, nurse in Vietnam. But something happened to her." Mace took a seat by his desk, fingers laced on his upstanding belly, blue eyes serious in a darkly tanned face.

"Bomb at Cam Ranh Bay. Took out most of the tail section of a 707 ferrying wounded back to the States. Pat was just in the wrong place at the wrong time. She lived for two months after the blast, I don't know how."

"I sure am sorry to hear it," Mace said, judging by Tomlin's lack of expression that it was time to change the subject. "So you got yourself some leave. You're, what, wing commander of the *Saratoga* these days?"

"I was. They reassigned me to the *Vinson* after she was commissioned. But I've been out of the Navy for a year."

"Damn! Where've you been keeping yourself, Mr. Tomlin?"

"Here and there."

"Took your own time getting home. Last time we saw each other, we laid old Bob to rest. Three years ago?"

"About that." Tomlin was feeling down in the mouth; he had no taste for reminiscing, no sorrow for the dead brother who had been older, old enough to be a stranger to him all of his life. Bob, the naval historian; his wife had died childless in the sixth year of their marriage. The family had thinned out drastically. A few old-timers scattered here and there, great-uncles, aunts, no one in the vicinity to whom he had close ties. He began to wonder why he was in Port Bayonne. But as long as he was—

"Who's living out at the big house, Mace?"

"Couple from the New York area. They've been down here almost eleven months now. Hell, I just renewed their lease for another year! Had no idea you were coming. Clay, you know you're welcome to stay with Lorraine and me long as you want."

"That's okay, Mace. I think I want to be off to myself for a while. I'll find something."

"Take a drive with me. Been a few changes since your last time home. We'll have ourselves some lunch. New place opened down by the Bluebelle Marina, best blackened redfish I ever ate."

They took Mace's Cadillac, two weeks off the showroom floor, to the marina, parked there in the ample lot and walked a big right angle of sports fishermen and glossy blue-water sailers. Most of them belonged to locals. All but a few tourists were gone from the Gulf at this time of the year, prime hurricane season: there were a lot of vacant slips. They came to a double-cabin diesel Hatteras, forty impressive feet, and Mace's step slowed, his face creased in a smitten smile. The *Shady Lady IV*. Tomlin remembered a couple of other *Shady Lady*s, beginning with a homely well-traveled twenty-three-foot O'Day painfully acquired in the days when Mace's skinflint father was working him until he was ready to drop.

"Business been okay, Mace?" Tomlin said blandly.

"Hell, you know me, I'll wear the tread off my sneakers and starve the kids to keep myself in toys! Let's go aboard, I'll rustle us up a couple cold beers before we mosey on over to the Landlubber. Oh, yeah, and an extra set of keys."

Tomlin looked at him.

"She's yours. Anytime you want to take her out, Clay."

"Sounds like a winner," Tomlin said.

Somebody was playing Bob Seger's "Nine To-night" on a ghetto blaster three slips away. Tomlin saw a husky man with a deep red hide, more hair on his shoulders than on his head. He was down on one knee by the engine hatch of an 8.8-meter Fountain powerboat that was moored stern-to. Plenty of horses from a pair of inboard Mercs, a tough Kevlar-and-fiberglass hull. He was changing plugs, sweating a little in the mild October sun, pausing to slap his thigh rhythmically with a free hand in time to the rock music.

"Talk about toys," Tomlin said.

Mace shrugged. "You see a lot of those along the coast nowadays. I mean, guys you know couldn't scratch up a dime most of their lives, all of a sudden they're into seventy-five-thousand-dollar speed demons."

The husky man shifted his position slightly on the cockpit bench and, still kneeling, his plaid Bermuda shorts tight on his muscular thighs, he looked up and right at them. Because of the volume the speakers of his silvery blaster were cranking out, he couldn't have overheard them. He wore sunglasses, lenses like polished coal. He grinned acknowledgment of his fellow yachtsman Mace Lefevre, and went back to work.

Tomlin said, "Full tanks, haul ass down and back to Isla Mujeres or Campeche with no strain."

"Well, there's a lot of talk," Mace said, looking a little uneasy and anxious to be aboard his own boat. "Shrimping's hard, and it ain't always been steady. Dope looks easier, although I hear the Coast Guard manages to pick off one boat in three that comes up through the Yucatán Channel to the Barrier Islands."

Tomlin said, "There's a Navy Bronco squadron with FLIRs operating out of Homestead now; I think they use P-3s too. They can fly sixteen-hour missions and cover 95,000 square nautical miles in an hour." He was still looking at the husky man. "I know him, don't I? Excuse me, Mace, be right back."

He walked down the quay to the powerboat. The man in the cockpit, now using both hands, his lower lip between his teeth, worked with a socket tool on a stubborn plug. He got it loose. Tomlin took off his Revo sunglasses, wincing a little in the noon glare.

"Aren't you Wink Evergood?"

The husky man looked up, a little surprised. He stared at Tomlin, then reached out with a hand that had a skinned and bloody knuckle and turned down the volume on his ghetto blaster. He didn't say anything.

Tomlin introduced himself.

Wink Evergood nodded slowly and got to his feet, pushing his sunglasses to the level of his receding hairline.

"Yeah. What'ya say, man? Been a long time."

Tomlin nodded. "The Coast Conference championship game."

"Yeah, us and Farragut. I remember. Helluva game. You know, you busted my jaw in three places." He was grinning now. He needed a dentist. His teeth were white enough, particularly against the dusky red shade of his skin, but chipped and broken. And he had scars around the mouth. A brawler who could take punishment, Tomlin remembered. But soft-spoken now, almost amiable as he studied Tomlin.

"Got kind of rough there under the boards," Tomlin said.

"Damn if it didn't. You make it on up to the Academy?" Tomlin nodded again. "Remember reading something about you in one of the papers, you did a couple tours in Nam. Fly-boy, right?"

"Right."

"Well, good to see you again, man. Be in town a while?" Wink Evergood rubbed his chin and a day's growth of blond stubble, looked past Tomlin at Mace, waiting at the bow of his cruiser.

"A while," Tomlin said.

Wink dropped his eyes to Tomlin. "Drop around again, when I've got the time." He was rubbing his jaw now. Grinning. "Guess I owe you one."

"If you say so."

Wink shook his head slightly, amused. "No. I mean, a drink. Wasn't you the one sent me that quart of Jack Daniel's in the hospital? Thought so. Sure did appreciate it." He put the skinned knuckle to his mouth and sucked on it, happy, something unpredictable and a little dangerous in the gray eyes, one flecked with a serious bloodknot.

Tomlin said so long and walked back to where Mace was waiting.

"What was that all about?"

"We played against each other in high school. He didn't have much ability, he was just big and rough and dirty. He gave me some shots, and one time I got him back. I just wanted to see if I liked him any better than I used to."

"Do you?"

"No."

Mace showed Tomlin around his yacht and tried not to brag, and they had some beers. Then they went to the Landlubber, which had been called Something Fishy once upon a time, and ate the redfish and sides of oysters on the half shell, washing the meals down with Montrachet, and Tomlin mostly listened while Mace told him about his wife and kids and the real estate business; he made getting rich sound like a matter of lucky breaks, just opportunities dumped on his doorstep that he'd been too lazy to kick to one side. Tomlin had known Mace since they were kids, and knew what a competitor he was. He had a lot of affection for Mace, and it turned into a good afternoon, but by three o'clock Mace needed to get back to the office. Tomlin told him he would pick up the extra set of keys to the boat in a couple of days, and thanked Mace for his kindness. He was invited to dinner at Mace's home every night that week, and made excuses.

In the parking lot he told Mace he wanted to go out to the house on Lostman's Bayou, if it wouldn't be a problem for the people living there now.

"Hell, no, no problem, just say when and I'll set it up."

"How about tomorrow morning?"

"Should be okay; just give me a call before you go."

*   *   *

It was almost inevitable that, driving back toward his room at the Ramada Inn from downtown Port Bayonne, Tomlin would take a sudden right turn onto the road that went down to the bayou.

He was a little shocked to see how far the city had grown in the direction of the Sound, laying down tentacles of blacktop, erupting in clumps of trailer parks and strip shopping centers and ranch-style homes, all the way to the northern boundary of the national seashore. Then abruptly all habitation was behind him, the road divided, one branch angling across the northwest corner of the federal land and beginning to deteriorate, full of potholes, just past the faded sign that read "PRIVATE ROAD/PRIVATE PROPERTY/NO TRESPASSING." Flat land on either side, a dense tall mixture of southern hardwoods and loblolly pine, then mostly all pine. No water in view yet, but he had a glimpse of bright seabirds just before the steep roofs and topmost gingerbread of the white house appeared through a break in the woodland. On one side of the narrow blacktop road a marshy finger of bayou meandered; on the other side there was a sight so curious and unexpected Tomlin was past it before he put his foot to the brake.

He backed up twenty feet into the shade of the huge and solitary live-oak tree. On the grassless and dusty hardpan beneath the widespread boughs there were some wooden folding chairs, set there for a purpose but unoccupied. He looked up, following the rickety line of a staircase that encircled the black trunk of the oak to a roofed platform large enough to hold an upright piano and a shack that was about twice the size of an outhouse. There was a belfry on the metal roof, containing what looked like the bell of an old locomotive. A rope hung down from the belfry. Numerous cats lazed around and in the tree.

Tomlin got out of the Corvette and gave the bell-pull a couple of tugs. Presently the door of the tree house opened and a Negro man lowered his head as he stepped out, showing a bald crown with parentheses like grimy old wool around his ears. He was wearing a black frock coat and a pair of Duck Head khaki pants and jogger's shoes worn out at the toes. He had in his hands a tall black hat with a lot of little mirrors on it. Tomlin recognized the hat before he could name the man; it had been that long.

"What goes on here, Wolfdaddy?"

Wolfdaddy ceremoniously put his hat on, catching a lot of flash from the rays of the sun that filtered through the orange-streaked dying leaves of the live oak.

"All pilgrims and humble seekers," he said, "find a welcome at the Next-Thing-to-Heaven Church of the Right-Way Gospel. Donations be welcome. Now, I read you any ten verse from the Bible, that's a dollar. A prayer for your affliction, two dollars. Hymns, you name it, I plays and sings 'em all. Three dollar. Praise Jesus."

"No more blues, Wolfdaddy? Sure will miss that great baritone horn."

"Don't play the sinnin' blues no more. Just sing His praises, Precious Lord. Yes, sir, make yourself right t'home, Mist' Bob."

Tomlin said, "Bob's dead. I'm Clay."

Wolfdaddy fished in a pocket of his baggy pants for glasses, and put them on.

"Well, well. Filled out some, hasn't you? Bless

you, Mist' Clay. Reckon how long it's been since I last laid eyes on you?''

"A very long time."

"That's true."

For a little while Wolfdaddy just rocked heel to toe and smiled serenely, and neither man spoke. A rising wind stirred the boughs of the old hurricane-battered oak. Two of the lean cats had a brief spat. Tomlin felt the sun going down behind his head. He felt a little cold.

"I should ought to have told you, the healin' service is ever' Thursday night. We seen prodigious miracles come to pass here."

"What makes you think I'm looking for a miracle?"

"Oh, I got ways of knowin', Mist' Clay," Wolfdaddy said, serious but not smug. He turned his head, his hat flashing little blips of light across the hand-sized oak leaves. "You come. We'll pray for you."

Tomlin didn't say anything. He looked over his shoulder to see how much light he had left. Just enough, he thought; but it had been a mistake to come down this road today. Some of the bitterness he had forbidden himself to feel leaked from his heart. What the hell, maybe Wolfdaddy was right. Maybe that *was* the real reason he had returned to the bayou, in childish hope of being redeemed, if not by Jesus, then by—something. Someone. But they were all gone from the house. Mother. The old man. Brother Bob.

"See you around, Wolfdaddy," Tomlin said, and walked to his car, trying not to believe that he had come full circle in his life, only to trap himself.

CHAPTER
THREE

On the morning of October 25, overcast in upper
New York State with a wind that had begun to bite,
Lieutenant Barney Greenland of the state police parked
his car on the side of the road that ran parallel to and
above the busy thruway, and walked to the woodlot
that was the scene of considerable activity. Troopers.
Two ambulances. Investigators and a full field crew
from his own office. The medical examiner was there.
Greenland had been on another case, at Lake George,
and had driven sixty miles flat-out to get here.

The first body he looked at was a male Caucasian,
about six feet and probably more than fifty years old;
but that was all he could tell. The victim had been
bludgeoned repeatedly, and there were major injury
locations on the head. There were also large gaps in
the scalp, and the quantity of blood that had flowed
from those wounds had made a grim thick mask for
the dead man's face.

Nobody said anything to Greenland. There were

tire prints, but no car; they were making casts. He walked over to the second body. Female. Naked from the waist down except for one sensible, high-laced black shoe. She had been strangled. There were large bruises on thighs and abdomen. She had curly smoke-blue hair, like Greenland's grandmother. But repeated rapings had taken most of the curl out of her perm.

Sergeant Wilkowski was talking to two kids in plaid jackets who, along with the golden retriever one of them held on a short leash, apparently had come across the bodies. Troopers kept a small pack of TV news teams at a distance from the crime scene. Wilkowski came briskly to Greenland's side when the lieutenant caught his eye.

"ID?" Greenland said, listening to a big truck whining south on the thruway, to blackbirds in the trees around them. There was a tang of woodsmoke in the air, from a house just visible over the rise behind the woodlot. There was a barn. Cows in dun pasture. And dead people, brutally dead.

"Richard and Martha Pell. RFD Route 119. He's a retired farmer. They were both communicants of St. Stanislaus Catholic Church in Comstock."

"So what?"

"That may be where they picked him up, last night after mass. Take a look at what he did her with."

Greenland leaned over the elderly woman's body. There were smears of blood on her forehead; presumably, since he saw no cuts, the blood had come from her vulva. He took a business card from his wallet to lift the ornate silver cross of the all-but-invisible chain embedded in her dark throat.

"A rosary?"

Wilkowski nodded. "I'll bet you a steak at the Claridge House it's our boy from Silver Birches."

Greenland said nothing. He was looking more closely at the blood tracings on the woman's forehead. They seemed to be words. He reached for his glasses, then looked up as the medical examiner walked over behind two ambulance attendants toting a gurney.

"Barney."

"Mal. How long, do you think?"

"At least twelve hours. Probably longer. Just a guess, but I'd say the old man went right away. The killer took his time with the woman."

Greenland stood, the hem of his trench coat flapping in the wind.

"What's that on her forehead? Looks like he wrote something."

The medical examiner nodded. "Near as I can make out, it says 'Do you love me?' "

In her room in the house on 83rd Avenue in Howard Beach, Queens, Antonia Barzatti had awakened before six A.M., feverish, her chest still sore and her throat raw although she was over the worst of the bronchitis. It was just daylight outside, but gray, she heard rain. And the telephone, on a lower floor of the house.

She had dreamed about Angel, who had brought her a bunch of flowers; but the flowers had black spiders in them.

Early for phone calls. Too early. Something was wrong, she was sure of that.

She got out of bed, feeling a little light-headed,

and cold despite her full-length flannel nightgown.
Her son-in-law had to do something about the fur-
nace this winter, or they would all be dead. She put
on her Dior robe, a gift from her grandchildren last
Mother's Day; she was trying not to cough, because
coughing tore at her breast like barbs. Even barefoot
she was very tall; and Antonia wore her hair proudly
high, like a bishop's mitre. It looked set in place with
a tarbrush, scarcely disturbed by a night in bed.
There was nothing feminine in Antonia's hound-heavy
face; only the amazing cliff of her bosom served as a
landmark of her sex.

Antonia parted the blinds and looked down at the
small misty backyard, at the garden of withered flowers along the fence and the children's jungle gym and
a plain-looking sedan she didn't recognize, parked in
the alley just past the Sinagras' garage.

Through the years she had developed a keen eye
for police surveillance teams, and although she couldn't
see anyone in the sedan she knew they were there.
So. The house was being watched, but why? Her
son-in-law was a civilian who worked for the city,
her daughter was a highly respected professional
woman, why should they watch this house?

She heard a soft knock at her door. Antonia Barzatti
turned, a hand pressed to her chest just below the
throat.

"Mama?" Carol said softly. "Are you awake?
Father Tonelli's here."

In all the years since she had come to America as a
young woman, she had never missed early morning
mass, even when she was so sick in the hospital
following the birth of her only son. Named Dominic,
after his father; but she had called the baby "An-

gel.'' When he was first brought to her she had seen,
been the only one to see, a distinct golden aura
around his darkly furred head.

She opened the bedroom door and looked at Carol.
''There's something going on. Why don't you tell
me?''

''Oh, Mama. You haven't been feeling well, and—''

''Is Angel dead?''

There was a look in Carol's eyes for an instant that
she tried to hide from her mother. *If only he was.*
''No. He escaped. The night before last.''

''Ah.'' Antonia Barzatti released the painful breath
she had been holding. She was glad. She had visited
Angel at Silver Birches, and she hated the place.
''That's all? He escaped? They don't know where he
is?''

''Mama—he killed a nurse. And maybe some other
people.'' Carol looked depressed, and afraid.

Her mother nodded, solemn, but it meant nothing
to her. For all she knew, the dead nurse had been a
wicked woman, and cruel to Antonia's son. She had
never blamed Angel for his violence. She had never
really believed the stories she heard.

''Last night I dreamed about Angel. He brought
me flowers, like he always used to do. There were
nine spiders in the flowers, I counted them carefully.''

''Oh, Jesus,'' Carol said. It was too early, and she
had a headache already. The baby was crying. What
if Angel showed up here?

''Nine spiders,'' her mother said, with a slow
nodding emphasis.

''Well, what does that mean?''

''I'm not sure. I only tell you that I counted them.

Our Lady will explain the meaning of the *ragnos* to me.''

"Mama—" But she knew better than to argue about the visions of Antonia Barzatti, or question the close friendship she claimed with *La Virgene*. That just touched her off, made her more difficult to live with. Carol loved her mother, but. "Mama, I have to go take care of Varonne, and I have a very important shoot today; I need to leave by quarter of seven to get to Brooklyn. Go on now, Father Tonelli's downstairs in the rumpus room."

"Will you go to mass with me this morning, Carol? A little of your time, *carrissima*.''

"The baby's crying," Carol said resentfully, then attempted a smile. "Just go ahead without me, I'll try to be there in a few minutes."

"Also take a few minutes to eat breakfast this morning. You are too thin. Last winter you had so many colds."

"All right, Mama, breakfast." Joe was calling her, irritably. Antonia Barzatti's thin upper lip turned under in a familiar grimace of disdain. She had never quite forgiven Carol for marrying beneath her. A cost analyst, he worked in the borough comptroller's office. He brought home little money, half of what Carol herself, a writer and producer of television commercials, earned. But at least he came home, most nights. He had no *comares,* no wasteful vices.

Antonia Barzatti walked down three levels to the paneled basement, already smelling damp with the onset of fall weather. Father Tonelli, a young priest from Feast of the Assumption Catholic Church, was waiting for her in the alcove where Joe and Carol had installed a shrine to the Virgin, who, gazing with enameled blue eyes from her plaster pedestal, did not have to see the Ping-Pong table or Joe's collection of beer cans from around the world. Antonia Barzatti had refused to move out of her house and into theirs until suitable arrangements for the Virgin had been made.

She knelt ponderously to kiss the right hand of the statue, and the hand of the priest.

"This is kind of you, Father Tonelli," she said, a dismal rasping in her throat that hadn't been there while she talked to her daughter upstairs. She rolled her eyes woefully at the priest.

"*Nemmeno*. It's good to see you up and around." He looked expectantly past her. He had a wistful little crush on Carol.

"No, no," Antonia Barzatti said, struggling with his assistance to her feet. "There's no use waiting for my daughter. These children. It's work, work, they give no thought to the spiritual side of life."

Father Tonelli saw her to her chair, and prepared the mass. She responded when required and clutched her rosary, looking at the youthful face of the Madonna, wondering if she didn't need a touch-up again, it was the damp. One of her pink cheeks looked slightly scabrous.

Having been forewarned and fortified by *il sogno*, Antonia Barzatti was not surprised to see the statue brighten until all else in the alcove seemed dim and far away. Spirals of Celestial Light came at her from the center of the forehead, where all the witches said a third omniscient eye lay buried in the bone. Father Tonelli had to tap her rather forcefully on the shoulder when it was time to take communion; he looked concerned. She held the wafer on her tongue and relished it before swallowing. She made the sign of the cross and sat back limply. The appearance of the Celestial Lights, a phenomenon she had observed since early childhood, meant the Virgin would soon come to her. The more dazzling the lights, the bigger the news. When she had last seen such a fabulous display, the Virgin subsequently told her that her husband was going to die of cancer. "Big Marbles" had just begun a six-year term at Auburn State Prison for extortion and bribery, the principal tools of his trade. He laughed at his wife's revelation. He took his health seriously, and could bench-press three hundred pounds. Where was he now? Long in his grave.

"Are you all right, Mrs. Barzatti?" Father Tonelli asked her. "Let me call your daughter for you."

"No, don't bother her." She continued to gaze at the childlike Madonna, wanting more, impatient for what must come. "I'll sit here for a little while, and pray. Good-bye." He seemed reluctant to leave her alone, but she ignored him, and finally he went away. She had known it was futile to attempt to explain the Celestial Lights to him. Only the monsignor took the time to listen, and seemed to understand; but he was so busy these days, she could never get him on the phone.

Angel, yes, Angel realized what the Celestial Lights meant to her. She had first shown them to him when he was very young. They would sit for many hours in front of a madonna much like this one, silent together; similar in temperament, not needing to speak, their souls whispered intimately. When he grew older and restless, like any boy wanting to run outside and play with his friends, she had only to tighten her arms around him in the sunless room, in candleglow, hold him closer to her breast . . . their souls conversed, he would be still. Once in her rapture Antonia squeezed too tightly; her husband had come home to find her with a dazed look and the boy unconscious, nearly suffocated, in her embrace. Big Marbles made Antonia see doctors. She told them nothing about the Lights, the Divine Visitations. They gave her medicine, which she dumped in the toilet when nobody was looking. She had seen no more doctors.

CHAPTER
FOUR

Carl was already awake and had taken a couple of aspirin, chewing them dry, and the blond girl with the fading full-body tan and the word *Brazo* tattooed on one cheek of her behind was just waking up; he was looking her over and thinking about fucking her again when a perimeter detector went off, making a rapid high-pitched beeping like the sound of a fuzzbuster in his stateroom.

"Wassat?" the girl said, pulling a tangled mass of hair out of her eyes and giving him a vague grayish look that suggested she wasn't sure where she was.

"Company," Carl said, reaching out to the starboard port and pulling the pleated curtain to one side. He saw, two hundred yards away, a white Corvette with a guy in a blue shirt or windbreaker at the wheel, the Corvette rolling in past the gate now and going on down to the house. He frowned.

"Anybody I know?" the girl said. She was feeling herself all over, tentatively, as if she thought he might have swiped something irreplaceable while she was asleep, her left tit or an earlobe.

"Who do you know?" Carl answered idly.

"God, have I got a head! What kind of panther piss were we drinking?"

"Black velvets."

"God. No wonder. Where's the, uh, facilities, skipper?"

"Carl."

"Carl, sure. I'm Evie."

"Yeah, I know." He hadn't been sure what she called herself. He pointed. "The door with the mirror on it."

"Thanks. Right back." She sat up on the edge of the narrow berth, hunching her shoulders and rolling her head side to side.

"Uh, never mind," Carl said. "I might have a little business to attend to at the house. After you refresh yourself, why don't you pull your clothes on and schlepp on out of here? Leave your phone number, Evie, I promise I'll be in touch."

"How did I get here?" Evie said, rising, going up on her toes, upstretched palms flat against the ceiling of the stateroom, breasts pointing halfway to heaven. Oh, man. Invitation to grab something. Carl issued himself a restraining order. The guy in the Corvette bothered him.

"We came in your Chris-Craft. It's tied up on the other side of the dock."

"Oh, sure. I remember now. Well, bye-bye, Carl." She gave him a cute smile and a little wave over one shoulder before ducking into the head.

"Bah, honeh," Carl said, mimicking her considerable accent. He had another outstanding view of her unflawed back and long legs and admired his good taste, wondering how old she was. Then he got up and reached for a ragged pair of shorts to put on, decided it might be nippy out and added a fisherman's cable-knit cotton sweater.

The house in which Clay Tomlin had grown up was two stories of old brick and a third of ornate, Victorian clapboard, lightning rods sticking up everywhere. There were long deep covered verandas, shady except for very early in the morning and late afternoon, across the front and down the length of the west side of the house. They had been restored after a hurricane named Camille had done a lot of property damage in '69. A lawn of tough persistent Bermuda sloped seventy-five yards to the marsh grass that fringed Lostman's Bayou and the roofed, U-shaped boat dock and boardwalk, also rebuilt after the big blow.

Tomlin, waiting on the veranda for someone to come to the door, saw a classy sportfisherman with a fly bridge tied up at the dock, along with a small open-cockpit runabout and a couple of the battered old johnboats they'd always used for trolling in the marshes. Behind the house and spreading eastward across the rise on which the house was situated was near-wilderness, uninhabited, much of it covered in slash pine and new-growth hardwoods where blown-down trees moldered pungently. The old brick carriage house and a smaller pump house stood at the elbow bend of the paved driveway. Parked in front of the carriage house, on a concrete slab, was the luxury motor coach his brother Bob had bought to see some of the country in before his chronically weak heart failed him. As far as Tomlin knew, Bob never had had the opportunity to enjoy it. But someone was keeping the coach up, perhaps driving it periodically. The maroon and white paint job and the chrome looked spotless. Tomlin had forgotten that he now owned the thirty-eight-foot RV, probably worth at least a hundred depending on what Bob had ordered inside. He had never given Mace any instructions concerning this legacy. Maybe, Tomlin thought, adding to his small store of options, he'd hit the road in it after a while . . . yeah, he could just picture himself, sitting out under the long awning 'neath Technicolor western skies, trading tips on maintenance with the other retirees.

He was intrigued and baffled by some of the improvements the renters had put in at their expense. A satellite TV dish occupied its own slab. There were a hell of a lot of big floodlights that covered a wide area of the property. Television surveillance cameras had been installed over the front door and at each corner of the veranda. How much security did they think they needed, down here on the bayou? Few people came by, and the gators kept pretty much to themselves.

Tomlin heard a dog's deep barking, then the louvered outer door was opened by a lanky black girl who looked as if she'd just been costumed for a scene in *Gone with the Wind*—bandana-wrapped head, full apron. She had a long hang-loose body, a wistful expression as if she were waiting, like Bill Cosby's daughter in one of his routines, for the Breast Fairy to show up. She drew back a little, a double-take that ended in a shy smile.

"Why—Mist' Clay!"

Tomlin didn't know her.

"It's Opal, Mist' Clay—Chessie's niece."

"The one with the good left-handed hook shot?"

"That's right! Come in, come in, Mrs. Jeffords expectin' you?"

"Mace Lefevre called her this morning," Tomlin said, entering the house. The familiar sun-filled foyer, with the high window at the bend of the semicircular staircase. "How did you girls make out?"

"Oh, we went to the state semifinals two years in a row, but we never won nothin'."

"How's Chessie? My God, she was old when I left." He saw another TV camera below the stairs, looking straight at him. He took off his blue windbreaker; it was warmer in the house than it had been on the veranda.

"Chessie ain't complainin'—but you know, her bones. She don't do work no more. She'll be real pleased to hear that you're home again, and asked about her. Let me take that jacket for you."

Tomlin glanced at the mirrors, the paintings, the Chinese furniture picked up in Hong Kong and other exotic ports of call.

"Everything looks the same."

"Mist' Bob, he never changed nothin'. He loved this old house."

"So do I. Never realized just how much I missed it."

"Back home to stay?" Chessie asked him, hanging up the windbreaker in a gilded wardrobe with a blossoming plum tree across both doors.

"Could be."

The appearance of the woman caught his eye, as she hesitated for just a moment at the other end of the long center hall, head turned to give herself a quick once-over in one of the antique mirrors that were everywhere in the house. Then she came to the foyer, someone accustomed to moving fast, decisively.

Right hand in the pocket of her pleated shorts. She held out her left hand.

"Mr. Tomlin, hello. I'm Anita Jeffords."

Long scar on the back of her right arm, a web of little scars radiating from one wristbone. He wondered if she had all of the hand she was concealing. She was quick to note his interest; she pulled her right hand somewhat awkwardly out of the pocket, needing to raise her shoulder to manage; her elbow didn't bend all that well. The hand hung limply. Intact, all fingers accounted for.

He was relieved. She was too young and good-looking to be maimed.

"Automobile accident," she explained. East Coast accent, he thought. The Big Apple, or even Brooklyn. But Brooklyn Heights. And a slight impediment, as if her tongue or palate had also been damaged, not a lisp exactly, a slurry whispering sound that was low-key, attractive. "I have some use of my hand." She made a small fist to prove it. "Although not much of a grip yet. Why don't we go into the parlor?"

"Fine," Tomlin said.

"Tea? Something stronger?"

Tomlin turned to Opal and said, "Chessie teach you her way of making lemonade, with that dash of cherry cordial?"

Opal beamed. "Surely did!"

"Lemonade," Anita said. "That sounds like just the thing." She smiled at Tomlin, but her bold brown eyes were more than necessarily watchful. The land-

lord had come to call. He liked looking into her eyes,
partly because there was a little yellow something
embedded near each dark pupil, like a grain of pol-
len, or a stinger. She wasn't a big woman, five-five
at best in flats, not an ounce of fat but still shapely,
with a good high bustline. He noticed a fleck of
something grayish on one cheek, like dirt, that she
had overlooked. Also traces of the same gray stuff on
her otherwise neat, short-sleeved shirt, as if she'd
been gardening, or whatever it was she did with her
spare time, just before he showed up. She wasn't
wearing makeup. She had naturally full sable brows
and lashes. Her heavy dark brown hair was bound up
in a horsetail to keep it off her shoulders and the back
of her neck, a cheerleader kind of thing to do, but
fetching. Her coloring was sallow, as if she stayed
indoors the year around. He saw a lot of her in his
casual appraisal, but realized there was much more
that he was missing, that he wanted to know about.
When their eyes met, Tomlin felt that agreeable little
buzz at the back of his neck. But it was *Mrs*. Jeffords.
Too bad.

He nodded toward the parlor, and followed her in.

"Just make yourself at home . . . that's stupid of
me, it is your home. Do you want to look around?
We haven't changed anything. I mean, it was perfect
the way it was. Such a beautiful setting, we've loved
living here."

She found a filter-tip cigarette in a box on the deal
table in front of one of the windows that flanked the
marble mantelpiece. "Do you smoke?" Tomlin shook
his head. "May I?"

"Sure." Opal, he observed, was a good housekeeper. No dust. The filmy cream curtains over the windows glowed in the diffused morning light.

When she had the cigarette going, Anita took up a station with folded arms beneath the twin portraits over the mantel. Tomlin came over, looking up at them. His mother, the sea wife, had a thirties bob and a rapt, dark eye, a lonesome way of leaning on her folded hands as if dwelling on an empty shore. His father seemed agreeable to be posed, but as always tight with smiles; Tomlin's childhood had been an anxious treasure hunt, looking for clues to the old man's moods.

"You favor your mother," Anita said.

"I know."

"Was your father an admiral?"

"Rear admiral, when he retired. He commanded battlewagons in the Pacific. Two of them were torpedoed out from under him. But he lived to a ripe old age."

"And you're a flier, I believe Mace said."

He looked at her. Something Italian, or Greek, about Anita. Her nose slightly hooked, but not obtrusive. Her eyes went out of focus easily, she seemed distracted by distances, unexpected black holes in her continuum.

"Not any more. I took early retirement."

"Oh, I see." She tried to think of something else to talk about. She couldn't. They just watched each other. Anita turned away politely to exhale, holding the cigarette in her right hand, giving support with her other hand propped under the elbow.

Tomlin wanted to touch her. Instead he patted one of a pair of toothy, grinning Ming dogs on either side of the hearth. The dogs were reproductions. The really valuable stuff his mother had collected—Edo period Japanese panel paintings, some Liao Dynasty glazed-pottery animals, an elegant but fragile lao hua li side table dating from the 1750s—was in storage.

When he took his eyes off Anita he noticed in a pier glass that the sliding doors to the library had been opened a couple of inches. A boy who could only have been Anita's—the same eyes, uncanny—was looking out at them.

"Hi," Tomlin said, smiling into the flawed glass.

Anita saw what he was looking at. They turned at the same time toward the library; she beckoned to her son.

"Tony, come here." The boy didn't move. She glanced at Tomlin with a slight helpless shrug. "He's shy."

"No school today?"

"Oh, he doesn't—I teach him myself. I'm fully qualified to teach at home. He's doing his math now." She took a couple of quick steps toward the library, raising her voice. "Tony this is, uh—" She needed help. She said to Tomlin, "I don't know your rank."

"Just call me Clay."

"Come on in, Tony," Anita said. "It's all right, you could use a break now."

After a few moments' deliberation, the boy shut the doors.

"How old is he?" Tomlin asked.

"Tony's seven. It's just that—well, he's not used to company. We really don't see many people out here."

Why not? Tomlin thought.

Anita had discovered her smudged cheek in the

brightness of the pier glass. "Oh . . ." Cigarette dead-center between her lips, she scrubbed at the spot with a tissue. "I do sculpture," she said. "You know the utility room behind the kitchen? There wasn't much in there, and it has such good light. I cleaned the room out and turned it into my studio."

"I'd like to see it sometime." He wouldn't mind just following her around for a couple of days, not having to say anything, observing her. "Where are you from, Mrs. Jeffords?"

"Anita, please. Oh, a little town in New Jersey. You probably never heard of it."

He found her response deliberately evasive. What difference did it make if he hadn't heard of the town she was from? "Quite a change of pace, down here on the bayou," Tomlin said, wanting to know why she was here, with a game arm and a kid who didn't go to school with other kids.

She addressed the inquiry behind his offhand statement. "I appreciate the solitude. And because I'm an artist, I—"

" 'Nita?"

"Carl, we're in the parlor."

He came in with a long stride (another fast-moving Yankee), bare-legged, very tan; spotted Tomlin and gave him a quick glib smile of welcome while obviously not knowing who the shit Tomlin was. A glance at Anita didn't give Carl any feedback. He stuck out his hand.

"Hi, Carl Jeffords."

Anita spoke up belatedly. "Carl, this is Clay— Tomlin."

"Of course!" Carl had a muscular handshake. He was shorter than Tomlin, thirty pounds heavier, chunky but not fat. He looked to be in excellent physical condition. Vivid blue eyes with an olive complexion, the nostrils of a baby bull, a day's growth of whiskers on an aggressive jaw. Quite a package. The kind of guy who seems to be so sure of himself, on top of things, that you've bought the policy or the extra doodads for the car or the quarter-acre homesite only a few minutes from the ocean before you really take the time to think it over. "What a pleasure, Captain Tomlin."

Tomlin had a chance to reply in kind, and didn't. After a moment's hesitation they let go of each other. Carl glanced at Anita again and shook his head slightly, chidingly (maybe he had tried to get her to stop smoking). Anita didn't say anything, just fidgeted with the cigarette. Carl looked back at Tomlin, expectantly.

Tomlin said, "How are you?"

Teeth flashed, white as talc. "Never better. A year ago, I sure thought I was going to have a nervous breakdown. Worked on the Street. Partner in my own commodities trading firm. Made a lot of money, but I wasn't happy. Down here, hell, I trade by computer, put together a little development deal here and there, plenty of time to fish."

"It's a good life," Tomlin acknowledged.

Opal walked in with a pitcher of lemonade and glasses on a tray.

"Lemonade!" Carl said enthusiastically. He seemed to have unlimited enthusiasm. He used his hands a lot when he talked.

"I'll bet you haven't had breakfast yet," Anita said to him.

"Uh-uh. Opal, would you do me up a mushroom omelette and half a dozen sausage patties?"

"Yes," Opal said. She poured two glasses of lemonade, handed one to Anita and one to Clay, smiling at him.

"Believe I'll have some lemonade too," Carl said.

"I'll have to get another glass from the kitchen," Opal replied, forbiddingly formal, and she left the parlor without looking at him. Carl stared after Opal with his smile just hanging on, scratched a whiskery cheek, turned back to Tomlin.

"This is one great old house, Clay. We have just enjoyed the hell out of being down here. Signed a new lease the day before yesterday, as a matter of fact."

"That's what I hear."

Having established his legal right to the Tomlin homestead for another year, Carl lifted his hands expansively, as if he now hoped to possess the house for eternity. He moved in closer to Tomlin, smile growing earnest. "No chance you'd be willing to sell, Clay?"

"I don't think so. Right now I only plan to be around for a week, maybe two."

Anita sipped her lemonade, looking at Carl over the rim of the glass.

Carl said genially, after a slightly too long pause, "Here?"

And Anita said quickly, "There's certainly more than enough room—"

"I don't want to put you folks out. I noticed Bob's RV out there. That'd do for me."

Carl coughed lightly into a fist and said to Anita, "Could I have a sip of your lemonade? Until Opal gets back with that glass, which I assume will be sometime today?"

Anita silently handed over her glass and picked up the cigarette she had put in an ashtray.

Carl had a drink and said thoughtfully to Tomlin, "So you're going to take the RV and—"

"No, I'll leave it where it is. I don't want to go anywhere. Just sit home by the bayou."

Carl said, nodding, "Oh, I get you. Well—sure. It's private, and I haven't been inside, but there must be all the comforts. All you need to do is hook up the electricity, lay in a few supplies—"

Tomlin said without emphasis, "I don't intend to be any bother."

"Hey, no! Glad to have some company for a change. You do any fishing, Clay?"

"Uh-huh."

"Maybe you noticed my boat on the way in."

Tomlin said, "Two boats."

Anita looked mildly at Carl and then away, smoking.

"Oh, yeah, that Chris outboard? Belongs to a friend. The Davis is mine. SatNav, all the electronics. Rupp riggers. I'll take you out anytime, say the word. Well—" Carl checked his Rolex watch, the professional scuba diver's model, waterproof to a hundred fathoms. "I put in a bid on some options at the close yesterday afternoon, better check to make sure I'm not getting wiped out. Honey, can you help Clay get settled?"

"All right."

Carl shook hands with Tomlin again. "Anything you need, ask." He went quickly to the library doors, slid them open. Opal, coming from the kitchen with

a glass in her hand, turned on her heel as Carl closed
the library doors behind him.

After about ten seconds of silence Anita said, "I
could show you my studio now, if you're interested."

"Sure," Tomlin said. He had nothing planned. He
had a lot of time.

In the library Carl stooped to rub the wiry head
of the Irish wolfhound lying on his piece of shag
carpet on the pegged, walnut-stained oak floor. The
boy, Tony, was seated in front of the computer
playing a game with wizards, monsters and dun-
geons. The monitor was a projection TV with a
forty-inch screen. It was dim in the library, the shut-
ters to the windows and doors facing the veranda
were closed. The ceiling fan squeaked. There were
old paintings of sailing ships, framed blueprints of
other ships, on the walls. Most of the volumes on the
shelves were devoted to naval history and architecture.

"Finish your schoolwork?" Carl said to the boy.

Tony nodded, absorbed in his game. Carl drifted
to the study desk and picked up the math sheet.
"Want me to check this for you, see if you did it
right?"

"Mom does that."

Carl looked over the page anyway. "Right here,
this next to the last problem, thirty-nine take away
sixteen plus four, the answer should be twenty-seven."

Tony didn't acknowledge the correction. He made
a wrong move in the game and said, under his breath,
"Shit."

"I need to use the computer now, Tony. Read a
book or something. Go outside and play."

The boy didn't say anything. The wolfhound began to pant, tongue lolling. Carl went over and stood behind Tony's chair. He watched the progress of the game. Carl had played a few times, out of boredom. Tony was better at solving the mazes than he was.

"Told you before," Carl said, placing a hand gently on the boy's shoulder to deemphasize the lecture, "these games give you bad dreams. We don't need you having fits, screaming and waking us up in the middle of the night." Tony didn't respond. Carl scratched his cheek where a mosquito had bitten him on his way from the boat to the house, leaving a welt. He tightened his grip a little on the boy's shoulder, reached around him and turned the computer off, then took the game out of the disk drive.

Tony's face was reflected in the now-blank screen of the big TV. He was looking at Carl.

"Who's he, Mom's talking to?"

"Nobody bad."

Tony sat there for a few moments longer, then reached up with his left hand and took Carl's hand from his shoulder. He slid out of the chair.

"Big Dog?" he said. "Outside."

The wolfhound lunged to his feet and followed Tony to the veranda doors. The boy stood only a little higher than the dog.

"Not everybody's bad, Tony," Carl said to him. "You know I wouldn't let anybody bad come walking in this house after you."

The boy hesitated on the threshold of the veranda, curtains beginning to billow around him from the breeze that was coming off the Gulf of Mexico. He looked a little grim. Maybe, Carl thought, it had been the wrong thing to say. But on the other hand, no matter what he said to Tony, it seemed to be the

wrong thing. Moody damned kid . . . Carl smiled,
going for the full effect, deep crinkles at the corners
of his eyes. Some days were better than others. He
could turn Tony around, anytime he really worked at
it.

"Going anywhere in particular?" Carl asked.

"Just outside."

"I have to go into town in a little while, Tony. Be
back late tonight. What if I brought you some new
Garbage Pail Kids, that'd be okay, wouldn't it?"

"Yes," Tony said, not having to think about the
offer. He was still nuts about his collection of Garbage Pail Kids, although he didn't like the shitty gum
that went with them. There weren't enough of the
grisly cards made to suit Tony, he'd taken to thinking
up some names of his own. Shrunken Hedda. Holey
Hannah. Cemetery Sal.

"Worth a hug?" Carl suggested. But Tony was
out the door already, perhaps having anticipated him.
"I'll get my hug later," Carl said, to his reflection
on the big blank TV screen. The truth was, he felt a
little let down.

On his way back from the Kroger supermarket in
Port Bayonne, Tomlin passed Carl at the wheel of a
black Mercedes-Benz 450SL sports coupe. Little windshield wipers for the headlights, that kind of car. Carl
was wearing a coat and tie. He honked and smiled,
hair streaming back from his temples. He looked like
a man who knew how to enjoy life.

Tomlin had left the windows of the RV open to air
it out. There was already a 220-volt line running
from the generator shed at the rear of the house, all
he needed to do was plug it in. The RV had good

carpeting, butcher block or marble cabinet tops, oak
cabinetry, too much velour for his taste, built-in
stereo and satellite TV, a ten-cubic-foot refrigerator.
There was enough room in the bathroom for a tub,
and the rack in the bedroom was queen-sized. An
electric baseboard heater was built into the bed structure. Nothing more he could ask for. A hell of a lot
more room than he'd had aboard the biggest carrier.
But he was edgy, dissatisfied about something, perhaps regretting his decision to be here in the first
place.

He stepped outside after carrying in the groceries
and saw young Tony watching him from thirty feet
away, idly swinging a stick at the grass. The enor-
mous wolfhound was off chasing a squirrel at the
edge of the woods.

"Hi, Tony," Tomlin said.

The boy didn't reply, continuing to look Tomlin
over, eyes in shadow with the sun behind his head;
he swung his stick with a little more vehemence.

"Want to have a look inside?"

Tony didn't trust the invitation. Or Tomlin himself. He shook his head curtly and walked away.
Tomlin went back inside, opened a can of beer that
had been cold when he left the store, settled into the
sheepskin-covered driver's seat of the RV and gazed
through the wraparound, aerodynamically styled windshield at the long bayou, almost a mile across at the
glitter of the horizon, where it joined the Sound.
There were a lot of birds in the air where the water
changed from fresh to salt, some of them ospreys
feeding. And he saw a couple of great blue herons.
Anita modeled birds in her studio, mostly with her
left hand, slowly getting strength back in her crippled

right hand. Her birds had a look about them, stark, elongated, that stayed in his mind. Along with the lady herself.

"Mist' Clay?"

Opal rapped on the open door, interrupting his reverie. She had a load of fresh linens for him.

"Make your bed up for you, Mist' Clay."

"Thanks, Opal."

She saw the sacks sitting on the dining table, and set the sheets aside. "Let me just put these groceries away first. By the way, Mrs. Jeffords say would you please join her and Tony for dinner tonight?"

"What time?"

"Oh, they eats early. Five-thirty, if that's all right."

"That's fine." Tomlin pivoted the seat around so he could see Opal as she sorted out his purchases, some things going into the fridge, others on a cabinet shelf.

"How long have you been working here, Opal?"

"Since the Jeffords come down, and hire me."

"About a year, then."

"Yes, sir."

"How long did it take old Carl to try to get you in the sack?"

"About the first time we was alone together. I told him, mains, you gone be pitiful if you do that again."

"You like her, though, don't you?"

"Mrs. Jeffords is a *fine* woman. What she put up with—Opal, bite your tongue."

"What's the matter with Tony?"

Opal was slow to answer. "Oh, you know, he awful shy."

"Shy is one thing. Looks to me like something is really bothering him."

"But he can be *so* sweet," Opal said, with a certain protective fierceness. "We gets along real famous on his good days." She glanced at Tomlin. "Mist' Clay, you know, I just don't like to gossip 'bout the folks I works for, Wolfdaddy say that is a shortcut to hell."

"Sorry, Opal. I can't help being curious about the people living in my house."

"That's all right, Mist' Clay. I understand. I know there ain't nothin' mean in your heart. Well—you be around for a few days, reckon anything you wants to know you'll see clear with your own eyes."

Tomlin finished off his beer. "What's for dinner, Opal?"

"Fried chicken."

"Bet that's something else you learned from Chessie."

"Chessie, huh. Come to fried chicken, I could give *her* lessons."

CHAPTER
FIVE

The five-acre estate in Alpine, New Jersey, had been commissioned by a mulatto pop singer under contract to a record company in which the Barzatti family had a substantial interest. The kid looked like an elfin woodland creature dreamed up by Disney animators, then dipped in creosote and blow-dried, but he had gone platinum five times before falling out of favor with the teenage public and into trouble with the IRS. The record label took over the house, passed the title through the labyrinth of Barzatti enterprises, and eventually, after some remodeling and extensive changes in the decor, Aldo Barzatti moved over to Jersey from his home in Long Beach, where the damp, cold Atlantic winters gave his old bones plenty of misery.

Don Aldo seldom left the estate any more to visit the neighborhood social clubs on Mulberry Street in Manhattan or in Ozone Park, out near the airport that was a major source of revenue for his thriving family. He liked the wooded seclusion of Alpine, and his heated indoor swimming pool. The family's underboss still came to him when there was business to be done that required his personal attention; for the most part he dealt with the heads of other families in the metropolitan area by messenger, seeing them only at Commission sit-downs or at important weddings and funerals.

The don was seventy-eight years old, his brother Johnny ("Rip-Dog") Barzatti a couple of years older, getting a little deaf and forgetful. John's son Frank, with a Wharton MBA, and Mark Greganti, a nephew who had ten years of experience with a top New York investment banking firm, were in their midforties, the whiz kids who managed most of the day-to-day family business. These four, plus family advisor Gabriel Solavarro, got together in Alpine twice a month for a briefing and then a home-cooked dinner. They met in the former pop idol's recording studio in the basement of the lavish mansion, a room so well soundproofed and difficult to penetrate the Feds never had figured out a way to bug it.

On the night of the 24th of October, they were all seated around an oval, cocobolowood table, an identical computer terminal in front of each man. The mainframe took up most of the room in what had been the recording booth, replacing the singer's twenty-four-track board. Frank Barzatti always tried to keep the briefings to half an hour, in deference to the older men with their shorter attention spans; but sometimes Rip-Dog got to clowning around, probably out of boredom, and unless Don Aldo called him down, which he was not often inclined to do, the meeting could stretch on and on.

"I don't understand all this fuckin' junk," Rip-

Dog complained of a four-color graphic concerning casino revenues that had flashed on their screens. "This the skim we're lookin' at?"

"This is the legitimate handle, Uncle John," Mark explained patiently, wishing the don would make up his mind to put him out to pasture, where he belonged. Though he had gallstones for eyes and scars like an Apache, Rip-Dog always looked so squalid, a flophouse glint of whiskers showing on his wrinkled chin. He dressed worse than any sidewalk loafer in Castelvetrano, his Sicilian birthplace.

"Down, or up, or what?"

Frank said, "Casino revenue was down two point six percent in September because of unseasonably bad weather in Atlantic City, but that's three tenths of a point above the average for the month since we started doing business in Jersey. The next graph here, you can see that our estimates for the year are right on target."

Rip-Dog took a cigar from his shirt pocket, looking in vain for an ashtray on the table. Every goddamned time, Mark thought. He smiled and said, "Uncle John, if you could just hold off smoking that, it's bad for the computers."

"Bad for the computers? I was smokin' these before anybody ever heard of computers and look at me, I'm still in the pink." He looked around proudly, and they all nodded respect for his longevity. "How the hell did we ever run a business without all these pictures? What is that, a pizza? I'll have mine with anchovies."

Laughter; either they rewarded the stale jokes, or he kept it up all night. But Don Aldo wasn't looking at anything, he seemed not to hear his brother. Don

Aldo had a big lump of forehead and a chin outthrust like a scheming god's. A scum of age dimmed his brackish eyes. He licked his lips, wool-gathering.

"Whose piece of the pie is that?" Rip-Dog demanded.

Frank said, *"Qual pezzo?"*

"The big one!"

"Ours," Mark said. Pie charts were a kindergarten device they employed to try to get across some of their sophisticated methodology for expanding the family's financial base. An attempt to explain the intricacies of LBOs, REIT security swaps and blind pool takeover bonds would border on the hopeless.

Rip-Dog settled back in his leather chair, seeming to be dissatisfied. "It ain't like lookin' at a suitcase full of hundred-dollar bills. It ain't got the same *visceral satisfaction,* you know?"

"Bank-to-bank transfers are a lot safer than suitcases," Frank told him. A favorite theme of his at the meetings, it was sort of like singing a lullaby to a cranky child. "The magic number is seven."

"Seven!" Rip-Dog repeated, now contentedly tearing the cellophane from his Davidoff cigar.

"Cash becomes untraceable once you've washed it through seven different corporate accounts in seven different offshore banks."

Mark looked at his cousin. "Anything on the takeover?"

Frank put some figures on the screens. "We've made a tender offer through our arbitrageur to acquire fifty-three percent of the common stock of Julep Time bottling company in Louisville. Two million and forty thousand shares at twelve and a half, which we'll finance entirely with high-yield paper."

"Why not pay cash?" Rip-Dog demanded. "We got plenty of cash, don't we?"

Frank said kindly, "Cash is old-fashioned, Pop."

Gabriel Solavarro looked up from his screen. "Who the hell is D. Foster Doyle?"

"Mr. Doyle is chairman of the board and CEO of Julep Time. That two-million-dollar item you're looking at is called a 'golden parachute'—Doyle's compensation for walking away after the hostile takeover which he helped us to engineer. Plus we give him another million-five in the form of a Swiss annuity."

Rip-Dog licked the tip of his expensive cigar and said, with a flash of the animosity that could still terrify young soldiers in the family, "Mr. Doyle is a *figlio di puttana!*"

Mark said, "These days they're known as Captains of Industry. It could be worse. Doyle promised not to go into politics. Okay, I've got one more item of business, it's not on the computer yet. Carlo hasn't been letting any grass grow under his behind down there in Mississippi. He's swung a nice parcel of beachfront property that can be rezoned hotel commercial with the right leverage, which of course means points to a local redneck. We finance through our new St. Maarten's holding company, with a secondary offering of preferred debentures. That is, if we're all agreeable."

Rip-Dog and Gabriel Solavarro nodded, trying to look sage about secondary offerings. The don appeared to nod also, but on the other hand he might have been falling asleep.

"That's it," Mark said, and Frank logged off on the mainframe. The two younger men gathered up a few papers and put them into nine-hundred-dollar attaché cases.

"Who's takin' me on at *zecchinetta*?" Rip-Dog wanted to know.

"Think I'll watch the football," Gabriel said. He had dropped close to four thousand the last time they played.

Rip-Dog gave his son a challenging look. Frank groaned. "Pop, you know I don't have any card sense."

Rip-Dog rubbed his hands together gleefully. "I know, I know."

The don, who hadn't moved in his seat, looked up, and with a slight sideways motion of his head indicated that the others were to go. He said to Mark, "You stay a minute."

"Yes, sir."

When they were alone the don fumbled for the cut-off button on his monitor. Mark had to help him find it.

"I don't say this isn't a wonderful thing. Our business is easier to take care of since Dominic installed the computers."

"Safer, too. Nobody unauthorized ever gets in."

The don looked at the rings on his large hands. Even when he had his fingers laced on the table, his hands shook slightly.

"So tell me. How did Dominic manage his escape so effectively?"

"Surprise. Brute force. He was naked when he ran out into the rain. He raided a parked car for a security guard's uniform, and made his way south. He picked up the old couple in a church. I guess they trusted him. Aren't you supposed to trust security guards?"

"The old couple—so that was Dominic's work?"

"Yes. They matched his blood type from the semen he left in the woman."

"That's an amazing thing, how they can do that."

"*Lo so che é.*"

"If Antonia has called me once today, she's called me ten times. 'Have you heard from Dominic?' She must be planning a coming-out party. A mother's love is a precious thing."

"He'll be here soon," Mark said.

The don shrugged. "That's to be expected."

"Well, we beefed up the neighborhood watch. The alarm system was recalibrated last week, and those new sensors are—"

The don got slowly to his feet. "Alarms. Sensors." He had to smile, though he was anguished. "Those things are toys to Dominic. After all, he wrote the programs for the computers, they will do what he tells them to do. What a brilliant boy. He has made us so much money. And caused me such heartache. I don't know why he is the way he is. I always thought Antonia was a little crazy. Too much religion, you know what I'm saying? Okay for women, but bad for men. Priests. I never trust a man who denies he has balls."

"Angel won't get in when he comes," Mark promised, feeling a little uneasy when the don's mind wandered.

"What is that, '*Angel*'? Never call him that in my presence."

"Okay, *Padrino*, I beg your pardon."

The old man made a conciliatory gesture, mouth

and chin in a mild convulsion; but he waved Mark off when Mark sought to take his arm and walked with him from the room. They heard Rip-Dog cackle outside, there was a smell of good food waiting: *bruschetta* and *luganega* to begin, then *bucatini algarganello*, pasta with a rich sauce made from the meat of the wild duck of Tuscany.

"Listen, he's my grandson. I understand, a little, how his mind works. For Dominic there is no good, no bad—only what he needs." Mark saw that the old man's eyes, rheumy in contemplation during their meeting, now were sharp and hard. The facial fidgets that sometimes afflicted the elderly had ceased. He lifted his pointed chin. "See that he enters my house peacefully," Don Aldo instructed, "but make sure he never leaves."

CHAPTER
SIX

Opal's fried chicken was worth the mild brag she'd put on it. She used nothing but salt, pepper, and flour to coat the pieces; the secret, she said, was to fry in pure fresh lard, not peanut oil or some other kind of grease. And you needed a well-seasoned iron pot. Fifty years' worth of seasoning was about right. Opal put a little piece of fatback in the butter beans for tang, pickled her beets in herbs she grew by the back porch steps in summer. Her biscuits were three inches high and so light you could blow on them and they would float. Tomlin, who had been riling his stomach with Navy chow for all of his adult life, made a pig of himself.

Tony ate part of a chicken thigh and a forkful of potatoes with cream gravy and drank half a glass of milk; his mother had to stare him into drinking that much milk. He didn't talk a lot, either. He had brought a muted antagonism to the table with him. In response to Tomlin's efforts to get a conversation going he said he didn't like sports; maybe fishing and hunting, fishing a little better. He had lost a couple of his baby teeth in the lower jaw and the new teeth were halfway in. He sat for most of the time wiggling a third loose tooth with the little finger of his left hand, and watching the ceiling fan. Tomlin didn't press him, or try to be a buddy.

Anita didn't eat much herself, but she had drunk almost three glasses of a good Dago red by the time Opal came in to clear the dinner plates. She smiled at Tomlin, who hadn't left enough crumbs to interest a fly. She held out the nearly empty serving platter to him.

"This chicken breast's tryin' to go to waste, Mist' Clay."

"Opal, you've just about done me in already."

"I could wrap it up for you, little snack while you're watchin' the football on TV tonight. Now you *are* gonna have a piece of my blackbottom pie?"

Tomlin groaned good-naturedly, holding up both hands to defend himself. He couldn't see Opal too well where she was standing; the red flare of the sun low over the west bayou was in his face. He hadn't paid enough attention to the time; and darkness came swiftly at this season of the year.

"I'll sneak back to the kitchen later on, Opal."

"Don't think I won't hear you. I'll be mighty put out if you don't come for some of my pie."

Anita reached for her cigarettes, smiling absently, studying Tomlin's sun-reddened face.

Tony said softly, "Mom, can I *go*?"

"Not yet. Clay—"

"Uh-huh." Tomlin looked at Anita and almost couldn't make her out. Just like that, he was losing them. Jesus, he thought, was he ever going to get used to this?

"I was wondering. Did you always want to be a pilot?"

"No. I was afraid I didn't have what it takes. I was one of those kids who throw up on carnival rides. But my roommates at the Academy, they were so gung-ho I finally had to say, yeah, I'm going down to Pensacola too. Sometimes you do things you're afraid of because you're more afraid of how you'll turn out if you don't."

"I think I know that feeling."

"The first time I took the stick of a T-2, it was my life from then on."

"How did your roommates do?"

"Ted washed out, some problem with his inner ear. Jeff went down on a night raid, and the NVA never gave him back. Anita, I don't mean to be rude, it was a great dinner, just some things I need to take care of, a couple of letters I want to answer."

"You don't need to apologize. We enjoyed having you. Tony, if I see that look one more time, you can take it up to your room and sit on the bed with it."

Tomlin, moving a foot beneath the chair, bumped the package he had stashed. "Oh-oh, I almost forgot." He reached down and set the package on the table. Wrapped in white paper, with a blue ribbon bow stuck on it. Not too neat, but the best he could do. "Present for you, Tony."

Tony looked at the present, and at his mother, puzzled. "It's not my birthday," he said in a low voice.

Tomlin smiled in his direction. "I was afraid of that. But I'll bet you one thing, *somebody's* having a birthday today, right now there's a party going on. I just missed it, that's all. We can't let a perfectly good birthday present sit around unopened, can we?''

Tomlin saw the bright spot of a match as Anita lit her cigarette.

"Well—" she said, sounding amused. The match went out. He smelled cigarette smoke. There was nothing where her face should have been. He quietly took a deep breath.

"Go ahead, Tony," Anita said.

The boy got out of his chair and came around to where Tomlin was sitting.

"What is it?"

"I know, but I'm not telling," Tomlin countered.

Tony unwrapped a box, which he opened. He lifted out a model Corsair airplane, accurate to the minor detailing of the Sidewinder missiles mounted under the wings.

"Hey!" Tony said, holding the gray airplane with the old-style high-visibility insignia a little above his head, turning it in his hands. "What kind of plane is this, a fighter?"

"No. The A-7's not a Mach one plane, it bleeds off speed too fast to be an effective fighter. It's an attack plane. Carries more than fifteen thousand pounds of armament—two-thousand-pound bombs, a twenty-millimeter cannon and a couple of AAMs—missiles.''

"These things?"

Tomlin reached out and Tony touched the airplane against his hand. "Yeah, those are the Sidewinders."

"Anthony, what do you say?"

"Thanks, I like it," Tony said to Tomlin. "You're sure you want me to keep it?"

"It's yours."

"I've got a GI Joe aircraft carrier in my room, but I don't have a plane like this. Did you ever land on an aircraft carrier?"

"Lots of times."

"How? Is it hard?"

"Not any harder than balancing on one foot on a cake of soap in the shower," Tomlin said. Then he wished he hadn't used that analogy, you had to be careful talking to kids. Tony might try the balancing act, and hurt himself. "I'll show you exactly how we did it sometime."

"Tony, Clay has to go now."

"Oh. Okay. What kind of plane did you say this was?"

"An A-7 Corsair, Tony." Tomlin pushed his chair back and got to his feet, the disappearing light a red haze in his field of vision, the fan blades creating dim shadows on the white tablecloth. He wasn't sure how he was going to make it now. The thought of being helpless made him clumsy. He bumped against the boy, reached for the table to steady himself and upset the glass in front of him, spilling the wine that was left in it.

"Hell, I'm sorry! That was dumb of me."

"Don't worry about it," Anita said. And, raising her voice, "Opal, would you bring some club soda, we've had a spill."

Tony withdrew, the airplane in one hand, to a corner of the dining room, stood there looking at Tomlin, his enthusiasm failing.

"Thanks for having me," Tomlin said. "I'd better be on my way."

The veranda doors were closest to him. No use trying to make it through the house to the front door.

He'd waited too long, that's all; but he'd been enjoying himself.

Tomlin left the dining room hesitantly, but once he was outside he walked away with more assurance. Opal had come out of the kitchen with a bottle of seltzer and a cloth. She watched Tomlin go, and looked at Anita.

Tony put the model airplane down on the sideboy as if he was no longer interested in it. "Kind of drunk, isn't he?"

"Not on half a glass of Dolcetto d'Alba," Anita said, with a glance at the stain on the table. "Maybe he's not feeling well."

"He's drunk," Tony said, challenging her. "Just like you-know-who."

"I don't want to hear you talking like that," Anita said, her tone too sharp for the offense.

Tony raised his voice. "I didn't say anything *bad*! All I said—"

Anita took a step toward him. Tony backed off.

"Don't yell at me, Tony."

"I'm sorry," Tony said. At least he had her full attention now, even if she was a little mad. But Anita changed direction and went outside on the veranda with her own wineglass. Tony sulked for a few moments, caught Opal looking back at him as she was sponging wine out of the damask cloth, and tore out of the dining room.

"Bite your tongue," Opal said sadly to herself.

On the veranda Anita sipped her wine and, astonished, saw Tomlin lose his balance near the slab by the carriage house, then fumble to find the door of the RV. It was disturbing to watch, but she watched him anyway. The sky was cobwebs, the evening indigo, the surface of the bayou a moody orange. Insects died crisply in the pale blue light hanging from the roof of the veranda. She heard Tony at the computer in the library and drifted that way. The doors were closed but she could see him through a space between lace curtains, trying to find a way through the terrors of a maze to get to an evil sorcerer. The sorcerer had fireballs at his fingertips, and commanded winged monsters that flew out of caves. The boy had only a sword to defend himself with. The game ended soon, and badly.

Tony heard his mother come in. He turned, with an expression bland beyond terror, his lips white, and said, "I'm dead. He killed me."

She held him, cheek against the top of his head. "It's just a game."

His hand, half the size of a man's, fastened on the scarred arm. "You got hurt!" he howled.

It scared her every time, when he seemed unable to differentiate between the fantasies he pursued, the reality still haunting him. She coaxed him away from the computer, and upstairs to take a bath. Big Dog got up from his rug and followed them, as he did every night. It had been more than a year since Tony had allowed his mother to see him naked, he bathed with the door shut now. But he wanted Big Dog in there with him. Big Dog and Tony played with the wind-up boats, the wolfhound getting both front paws and his muzzle wet, leaving hairs in the tub which Opal complained about. Anita sat on the edge of Tony's bed with a dull headache from the wine, paging listlessly through the new *Time* magazine, hearing, half a mile away, Wolfdaddy on the upright piano, at least three other good musicians accompanying him on trumpet, bass and trombone: an old-time spiritual, done up Dixieland: "Lord, Lord, You Sure Been Good to Me." She'd always meant to go down the road to one of the services, which Opal attended frequently. She knew she would be welcome, she'd probably enjoy the singing, even if she didn't know the songs. A long way from her Catholic girlhood, she thought. But her own religion meant nothing to Anita any more; it only nagged her occasionally, when she was giving in to guilt and woe from all directions. These days she was just a little to the right of agnostic. And what might that be called? she wondered, then came up with the appropriate word from her considerable vocabulary. *Nullifidian*. The sound of it exactly suited her present mood. I am a nullifidian.

Anita went down to her own room, the former master bedroom, and chose one of her books from crowded shelves: *Oliver Twist*. She carried it back to Tony's room. He was out of the tub and putting on pajamas. The night had cooled off; she closed both windows.

"Hey, hold it," she said as Tony was climbing into bed. His hair was still wet. She rubbed his head briskly with a towel. He struggled and groaned and laughed. This was the part of the bedtime routine she most enjoyed. The part she hated sometimes wasn't necessary if he fell asleep while she was reading to him.

Tony was fond of Dickens, partly because she had many different voices, and could mimic English dialects. She had the ear of an actress, although she'd never done much on stage. *My Fair Lady* and a couple of Wilde plays in college. Tony was still absorbed and wide awake when Anita finished the chapter. She didn't want to read any more. She was restless tonight, despairing.

"Please?"

"Tony, that's enough for now, time to hush."

"And goodnight to the old lady whispering hush!" Tony said, quoting from another of his favorite books.

Anita bent to kiss him. "I'm *not* an old lady." But she felt obscurely frightened. As if she was now fated to wither, between midnight and dawn. Good God, but she'd had a mixed-up day, just because a man had come around whom she found interesting. She needed to go and soak in the tub, do her hair and especially her nails, which she'd been neglecting for too long.

"Where's Big Dog?" Tony asked, beginning the part of the ritual that distressed her.

"Right at the foot of the bed, where he always is."

"The Magic Ring?"

Anita looked through her pockets and took out an heirloom dinner ring with a paste sapphire nearly the size of a robin's egg. She placed it on the two-drawer nightstand beside Tony's bed.

"I never forget the Magic Ring."

"Is it powerful tonight?"

She nodded.

"But you have to say it!"

Anita said, "The Magic Ring is always powerful."

"What if he tries to touch me while I'm sleeping?"

"The Magic Ring will protect you." Her head was throbbing. She looked away from Tony, at his chalkboard and overflowing toy shelves and the Lego machinery piled up on his dresser.

"Well, what will it do to him? Say it!"

"It will—the Ring will make him—blow up—"

"How many pieces?"

"A million billion pieces," Anita replied, wondering if she was going to get out of the room without letting him see her cry.

"A million billion pieces, smaller than see-nots?"

"Smaller than see-nots," Anita assured him. She smiled calmly.

Tony, satisfied, snuggled deeper in the bed. Anita turned the overhead light off, left the lamp on his desk burning. She began to cry then, dreading the muck of tears and the blue aftermath, but unable to help herself. Tony's eyes were closed. Only Big Dog watched her leave the room. His tail thumped the floor once, then he put his head down between his long forelegs.

CHAPTER
SEVEN

Carl made it into the lounge of Murray's Driftwood at a quarter past eight; he saw Wink Evergood in a padded corner booth, alone, and joined him, pushing his big attaché case across the seat ahead of him.

"Almost gave up on you," Wink said pleasantly. He wore three gold chains with his nearly unbuttoned shirt, of a material so thin a scar on his upper right bicep showed through. Carl nodded wearily. Wink looked at the attaché case. "What've you got there?"

"A hell of a lot of paperwork. Options on land purchases."

"I'm beginning to think you're some kind of workaholic. Mace Lefevre fix you up?"

"He knows the wheels that need the most grease," Carl said, looking around for a waitress. He wanted a drink, and right now. The room was nearly full. There was a cocktail piano elevated behind the bar; the woman playing it wore a full-length black gown and had a remarkable neon-pink mouth. It was about

all you saw of her, in the little overhead spot. The
mouth, and eyelashes like flytraps. She kept both the
piano and the vocals on the quiet side. One reason
why he liked Murray's.

"Spent a lot of time on that deal, haven't you?"
Wink said.

Carl grinned sourly. "I've had a lot of time on my
hands, down heah in the Deep South."

Wink, always full of himself, said with a show of in-
genuity, "Sure must be an easier way to make money."

"The company I work for appreciates low-risk,
high-yield investments." Carl twisted another way in
his seat, trying to get the attention of a waitress with
skin the color of peanut butter and eyes like a heat
wave; she was waiting for an old gentleman to count
out a heap of one-dollar bills at a nearby table. She
glanced Carl's way and smiled. He relaxed and turned
to face Wink again. "Real estate will always be
solid, if you know where to buy."

"Yes, sir?" the waitress said. Carl looked up at
her, feigning surprise.

"You didn't believe me," he said.

"Oh, I believed you."

"Well, I mean, you're still here. You're not in
Atlantic City."

She had great dimples. Her skin was a little coarse,
but the smile made you overlook that. "Atlantic
City, I just need to think about it."

"It's a tough choice? Six hundred a week at least,
compared to, what did you say you were making
here?"

"Oh, two fifty. Three hundred, but that was during

the summer. I don't know, I got to thinking, maybe I wouldn't be able to do it.''

"Deal blackjack? Honey, anybody can learn to handle a deck of cards! They put you through a school. You still got that business card I gave you?''

"Uh-huh,'' the girl said.

"I want you to take another look at it. Because I wrote a name on the back of that card. I wrote a phone number. Maybe that doesn't sound like much to you, but there's ten people, maximum, in the whole world, who have that very private number. All you need to do is get off the bus, go to a phone. All you say is, 'Eddie, Carl said that I should give you a call.' That's it. You'll be shown every professional courtesy at one of our great resort hotels. Eddie will personally look after you.''

"What does he get out of it?'' she said, still smiling but skeptical.

"The pleasure of doing me a favor,'' Carl said.

"I'm really thinking about it,'' she assured him.

"Good. So while you're thinking, why don't you bring me a seven-and-seven. And listen, uh—''

"Rochelle.''

"Rochelle, if there's anything else you want to know, you want to talk to me some more about this, I'll be happy to give you the time. I mean, I've done a lot more already than I'd do for most people, but I don't want you to have any doubts about my intentions. I sincerely want to help you out.''

"I appreciate that.''

"Carl.''

"Carl.'' She went off to the bar, and Carl groaned softly. "God, all that raw material, and what she's doing with it.''

"She's banging this airman first class over at Keesler, that's what she's doing with it. And that's why she won't leave Biloxi."

"Shit, love," Carl said despondently.

"She's in a fog. She didn't even know what you were talking about, when you said you'd give her the time."

Carl looked at his chronometer with all the push buttons and made an effort to cheer up. "When are we meeting the girls?"

"Nine o'clock, figured you'd be running late. We've got reservations at the Swashbuckler."

"Good, I'm starved. Who did you get me tonight?"

"Cindalou."

"Jesus, the biter," Carl said, but he didn't look too unhappy about Wink's choice.

Wink finished his draft beer, looking around the room. He said, "Looks like we get a break for Thursday night. That tropical storm hit the Florida keys and turned inland. Some rain and a little wind, probably, but the Gulf won't be running too heavy."

Carl rubbed his midnight-blue jawline and said with a hint of pique, "I'm having a problem with Thursday night."

Wink stared at him for several seconds before speaking. "What kind of problem?"

"Guy who owns the house we leased, he showed up unexpectedly. He wants to hang around for a few days, there's nothing I could do."

"What's his name?"

"Clay Tomlin."

"Tomlin, hey. Saw him yesterday, think it was, over the Bluebelle marina. What the hell. You know, we got into it one time, him and me, basketball game. He took all the shit I could get away with, then he caught me under the jaw with an elbow, man, I was wired together for three months. Probably cost us the championship, I was hitting seven of thirteen from the floor when I went out. Clay Tomlin.'' Wink settled into an easy kind of silence, thinking back, smiling. Then he thought ahead, not liking the potential complications. ''Well, we got delivery schedules, that's all, our man in Atlanta wants it very punctual, and I sure hate to see two million six worth of world-class blow float back down to May-he-co.''

Wink moved his shoulders and popped his fingers, giving the last lines a jive rhythm. Rochelle showed up with Carl's seven-and-seven.

''I'm thinking,'' she said.

''Thatta girl,'' Carl said.

Wink asked her for another draft Miller's, and tossed a few Spanish peanuts into his mouth.

''What do you want to do?'' he asked Carl.

''Get him off the place.''

''Yeah,'' Wink said, chewing.

''Nothing severe, nothing to attract attention.''

''Okay.''

Carl took a long sip of his seven-and-seven, looking at Wink.

Wink said, ''Well, he just got out of the Navy, didn't he?'' Carl shrugged. ''I think that's what he told me. Maybe he's due for a checkup, over at the VA hospital.''

Carl nodded. ''Could be. Three or four days in the hospital, but nothing severe.''

''What's he driving?''

''White Corvette.''

Wink chuckled. ''Damn, those hotshot Navy pilots! They get their wings, next thing they got to have is a Corvette.''

"Oh, yeah, and he's bunking outside, in that RV used to belong to his brother.''

"Okay,'' Wink said, "don't worry about it. I'll talk to my Cajun *cousin*. Me and Tom Paul will come up with something.''

Rochelle put Wink's draft beer in front of him and bent low to catch Carl's ear.

"What you were saying, I really would like to talk to you some more. When you're free.''

"I'm free when you're free,'' Carl said instantly. "What time are you off?''

"Twelve-thirty.''

"I'll be here,'' Carl said.

When Rochelle was out of earshot Wink said, "You ought to tell her about some of the sports I've seen in casinos, they don't like the cards they're getting, they throw loaded ashtrays at the dealers, or spit on them. Well, do I give your regrets to Cindalou?''

"What're you talking about? It's eight thirty-five now. I'll feed us and fuck her and be back here at midnight.''

"Oh, boy,'' Wink said, grinning. "Tell me something, did you like dark meat before you came down here?''

"You know what, I've never had any. But I'm an equal-opportunity ass-chaser.''

Wink looked again at the cocktail waitress with the dimples, and the hairstyle like Tina Turner's. "Well, maybe you're in for a treat, if it's as good lying down as it looks standing up.''

CHAPTER
EIGHT

The temperature around eleven o'clock dropped to the low sixties, but Anita didn't close her bedroom windows; she liked it cool. There was no more music from the Next-Thing-to-Heaven Church of the Right-Way Gospel, only the music of God's lowly creatures, tree toads and peepers. And apparently Clay Tomlin had left a window of the RV open; she heard his television. There was a basketball game on.

In Carl's room next to a common bath, which he didn't use, were six security TV monitors behind the doors of an armoire. She had one small monitor on a bookshelf in her room and could change the picture, going to any side of the house and as far as the boat dock, with a hand-held control. The images on the monitor were good because the floodlights stayed on through the night. She wondered if the lights bothered Tomlin. She also wondered when he was going to say something about them, and the cameras, and what she would tell him when he did.

At a quarter past the hour she walked down the hall to look in on Tony, who was sleeping at the edge of the bed, one foot almost touching the floor. She moved him and pulled the covers up without disturbing him. Big Dog was on his feet, stretching; he wanted to go outside. She went downstairs with the wolfhound, and out onto the front veranda. Her eyes on the RV. Trying to think of a reason for going over there, the attraction was irresistible, and a little nerve-racking. Anita shuddered in the night wind, hugging herself. She had put on a cardigan sweater but she was bare-legged.

The door to the RV was unlocked and loose, banging a little when the wind caught it. Enough of an excuse, she thought. Just to look in on him, see that he was all right. His behavior after dinner was still a puzzle to her.

Anita crossed the lawn and the drive and stopped a couple of feet from the side of the RV. Only one light showing, and the television. She had been inside a couple of times, to look around. Opal's brother Roland did the yard work and maintenance around the house; he would wash the RV, drive it slowly for a few miles to make sure everything was working properly. Even so the tires needed replacing, they had begun to rot from the climate.

"Clay?"

"Yeah." He answered promptly, but she was sure he had been asleep. Instant wakefulness and response would have been a requirement in his profession.

She was going to tell him about the door, close it for him, go back to the house. She said, "Could I come in?"

"Sure."

Anita opened the narrow door and stepped up into the RV. There was a night-light on under the cabinet above the dinette. Tomlin was stretched out, shoes off, a round pillow behind his head, on the sofa bed behind the driver's seat. He was facing away from the television mounted over the windshield. His eyes were open, his expression pleasant, but he didn't look at her.

"The door wasn't shut," Anita explained. "If it wasn't for the wind, the mosquitoes would be eating you alive."

"I must have dozed off." He didn't move. "How about a drink?"

"That's all right, I don't think—it's late, I can't stay. I just let Big Dog out to run."

"What time is it getting to be?" His watch was on his wrist, a few inches from his head, but he didn't look at it. He listened to the play-by-play of the basketball game, the Hawks at Golden State. "Two minutes left," he murmured. "What happened to that seventeen-point lead?" To Anita he said, "Do you like basketball?"

"No. Baseball. When I was little my father used to take me to see the Yankees." There was a copy of *Navy Times* and a scuffed flying helmet on the dinette table; the helmet had a checkerboard band running front to back and the name *Rattler* stenciled on one side. "Rattler. Is that you?"

"Uh-huh. Everybody in the Navy has a nickname." He sat up then, stretching. Still not looking at her, though she didn't feel ignored, or unwelcome. "Sure you won't have a drink?"

"Well—if there's any beer—"

"Refrigerator," Tomlin said. "Opposite the microwave. I'll have one too."

Cans of Miller's took up one shelf of the compact fridge. Anita popped two of them open, carried them to the sofa where Tomlin was sitting and looking rather vaguely at the closed blinds of the window opposite him. Anita stared at him and shuddered unexpectedly, she didn't know why. She held out one of the cans of beer. He paid no attention to it. After a few seconds she turned and put her beer on the lamp table, turned back to Tomlin, shuddered again but less violently, reached down, picked up his right hand and carefully placed the Miller's in his hand. He touched the top with the forefinger of his other hand to see where the opening was, and, not lowering the level of his steady gaze, drank.

"Thanks," he said.

Anita sat down beside him.

"I—don't understand what—"

"It's an extreme form of night blindness. It isn't hereditary and, thank God, it isn't degenerative. As far as anyone knows, the problem is a shortage of certain enzymes responsible for the production of visual purple and the general health of the retinal cell machinery. Or, the enzymes are there, they just don't do the job in artificial light."

"Lazy enzymes?"

Tomlin grinned ruefully and had another sip of beer.

"You can't see anything now?" she asked him.

"No. It's the same as if I were sitting in a closet lined with tar paper. My vision stops, or I start to see again, at about 2,500 lux—that's a little less light than the sun gives out when it's just over the horizon on a clear day. I can make out shapes and distinguish colors. The light outdoors on a sunny day at noon in high summer is about 113,000 lux. They figured, at the Jules Stein clinic at UCLA, that I recover twenty-twenty acuity around 45,000 lux.''

"Doesn't someone make fluorescent lights that duplicate the spectrum found in natural daylight? Nurseries grow plants with them.''

"Plants are more easily stimulated than my photoreceptors. I can get Vita-Lites that produce 2,500 lux, but they take up about six square feet of space. And I'd need fifteen or twenty of those in one room just to read a newspaper.''

"The game's over," Anita said, glancing up at the television.

"Yeah, I know. The Hawks lost by one point. What a way to start the season.''

"Well, thank God," Anita said.

"Why, you don't like the Hawks?''

"I wasn't talking about the game. When you left the dining room tonight—''

"Oh, yeah, that must have made a terrific impression. Did the stain come out?''

"Sure, don't worry about *that*. But I thought—I was thinking of all kinds of terrible things. Like—it might be a brain tumor.''

"Nothing so tragic. The—the problem cost me a career, and it's been hard on my social life. I'll get used to it. I'd better.'' He had emptied his beer can and was methodically folding it. She'd seen Carl do that and thought it was childish, showing off; now she admired the strength in Tomlin's hands and wrists.

"Could I get you another one? You could have mine, I just took a couple of swallows.''

"Thanks," he said, and she passed him her can.

"There's nothing—an operation, or—"

"No. The specialists at Johns Hopkins and at Wills Eye Institute in Philadelphia didn't have a clue. At Wills they tried a couple of things, injecting calmodulin and PDE into the vitreous humors. That was supposed to help the retinal cells adapt to low light levels. It did, but then the cyclic GMP levels rose, and that could have permanently impaired my daytime vision. So I decided to yield to Nature and stop being a damned guinea pig."

"I don't blame you. If there's any way I can be of help—"

"Thanks, well, as long as I have a place to hole up at night, I'm okay. Winters are short on the coast, and we have a lot of daylight from March to November. The TV control is on the table there, if you want to switch to the news. See if we went to war with anybody today."

"You must really miss flying."

"Yeah, all the time. Then I have to think, well, I had better than twenty good years, survived two tours in Vietnam and a couple of Qaddafi's lousy fighter pilots over the Gulf of Sidra, nothing to complain about."

Big Dog was barking on the veranda. Anita said, "He's finished his business and now he wants in. I'd better be going too, it's late."

"Not that late," Tomlin said, and then, after waiting for her to come back with something, "I didn't hear your husband come home yet."

Anita got up from the sofa. He turned his head and looked right at her and she wondered, for a moment, if he'd been telling the truth about the condition of his eyes. But she realized they weren't focused on her, or anything, and he didn't blink. He was just waiting again.

She didn't have to say anything, but she said, "That isn't unusual." A little dryness, nothing bitter.

"You have to go?"

"Yes," she said, suddenly angry, but not because he'd asked.

Anita was at the step, a hand on the door, when Tomlin stopped her.

"What you found out about me, I'd just as soon not have it get around."

"Okay, I understand." She opened the door but didn't step down into the night. She felt a rush to her head, her heart gave a sudden kick, she was at the edge of something exhilarating and, probably, foolish. "Carl's not my husband," she said. That was it. She didn't look at Tomlin or wait for any kind of reaction. But she was two thirds of the way to the veranda with Big Dog racing out to meet her before her heart steadied.

Upstairs she looked in on Tony again. Force of habit, there were times she went up and down the hall all night long, finally crawling in next to him to try to snatch a couple of hours' sleep, her mind raw from obsession. Tonight he had kicked off the covers again. She went near the bed and saw something that hadn't been there a little while ago: the model Corsair airplane Tomlin had given him at dinner. It was on the pillow. Tony had left it downstairs in the dining room earlier, she was certain of that.

Pulling up the light blanket, looking at the boy's

face, she had the suspicion that, although his eyes were closed, he wasn't asleep.

"He can't see at night, that's all," Anita said softly, breaking her word to Tomlin already, but badly wanting the boy to know; what harm could that do?

CHAPTER
NINE

In Alpine, New Jersey, at three-thirty in the morning on October 26, one of the two telephones beside Aldo Barzatti's bed rang.

The don was awake; he had not slept, nor, in fact, had he been able to close his eyes. Despite new medication his prostate was giving him fits.

He could tell by the sound of the ring that it was the in-house line. He turned his head and looked at the telephone, thinking, with mild contempt but no fear, *alarms. Sensors. Child's play. The boy is a genius, didn't I tell them?*

He had heard no disturbance outside the big split-level stone house. The Ethiopian hunting dogs were quiet in their kennel.

Don Aldo let the phone ring, but didn't take his eyes off it. He was thinking ahead, what he ought to do. Calm, but not peaceful. The ring was soft, nothing to get on the nerves, just a persistent demand for attention. Of course, there could be only one satisfactory way to go, although he had a houseful of *picciotti*. Why risk needless bloodshed in his own home? Stamina was not required of him; the key was desire, his willingness to have it over with. But he had never shied from difficult choices, decisive action.

Don Aldo moved to the left side of his bed, where he could comfortably reach the telephone. It had rung twelve times. On the sixteenth ring, completing a second group of eight, he picked up the receiver and held it to his ear, saying nothing.

"Do you love me, Grandfather?" the Angel of Death asked him.

"Yes," the don answered, the speed of his pulse sickening him, bringing on a wave of blackness. He sank back into a pile of pillows. The connection was broken.

When Don Aldo was fully sensible again, a matter of half a minute, he discovered that he had wet his pajamas a little. He refused to wear the undergarment designed to prevent potential embarrassment from more frequent incidents of incontinence. What the hell, they could call it anything they liked, it was still a diaper.

Don Aldo sat up on the edge of his bed, feeling for his carpet slippers. When he had them on he went into the bathroom, which had a large round window through which the stars of a clear night shone brightly. The bathroom was equipped with everything he might need for comfort or hygiene. A marble tub, with a railing, that he walked down into, a palatial barber's chair from a shop he had patronized in Little Italy in the twenties and thirties. He liked his daily shave the old-fashioned way, burning hot cloths, inch-deep lather, the slip-slap music of a straight razor on a long piece of leather. Bay rum after, always bay rum. But he had never allowed himself to become a slave to habit, except in his own home. One reason why he had outlived nearly all of his peers.

The don dropped his pajama pants and stood at the toilet, holding his joint. "You wanted to piss, now piss," he said crossly. But it took a long time. He counted each drop. Eight, finally. Eight was a fated number, about which he was very superstitious. He had been born in the eighth month of a year that ended in eight, the eighth child to survive in his family, in a village in Sicily that was exactly eight kilometers from the sea. His last name contained eight letters. In his lifetime he had personally killed eight men. He had served a total of eight years in prison. He had once won more than $300,000 in Vegas playing roulette when the number 8 had come up four times in a row. As it was not a juiced wheel, the odds against this happening were just about incalculable. Fate. And today was the 26th of October. Two plus six made eight. The neatness of it was reassuring.

There was a knock on the outside door to his bathroom.

"Is everything okay, Mr. Barzatti?"

His male nurse, who was called Curly. "Yeah, yeah, just trying to piss," the don muttered.

"Anything you want, let me know."

"Can't get to sleep," the don said. "Maybe I'll take some steam, have a massage. Give me ten minutes."

"Yes, sir," Curly said, and he went downstairs to turn the sauna on.

The don took off his pajamas and flushed the

toilet, went slowly back to his room, half expecting to see Dominic sitting on the end of his bed, waiting for him. But he was still alone. Dominic would choose the time and place, when he was ready, when he felt secure. In the meantime the *picciotti* could turn the house inside out, they wouldn't find him. Nineteen thousand square feet on three levels, plenty of places to hide, although he was unfamiliar with the layout. Dominic's genius nowadays was his ability to adapt to circumstances while concentrating like a hungry predator on his immediate needs. His strength was his ruthlessness, which was a family trait magnified to terrifying proportions.

Don Aldo put on a heavy terry-cloth dressing robe and took a pistol from the drawer of his nightstand, a .38 revolver with a shrouded hammer. The pistol didn't make much of a lump in the right-side pocket of the robe, particularly with his hand there too, disguising the telltale outlines.

Curly, wearing white twill pants and a muscle shirt under an unbuttoned white smock, came upstairs to get him. They rode in a small elevator to the recreation wing of the house, which contained, along with a game and party room and a small gym, the pool complex: there was a big sauna with a cold plunge next to it, then a shower and a massage room with lockers against one wall.

The sauna temperature was up to 112 degrees when Don Aldo walked in and hung up his robe. There was enough bench room, on two levels, for a dozen naked bodies. Curly went whistling off to the massage room to warm some towels and lay out his unguents. The don poured a big dipperful of water on the hot gray rocks and took a seat.

Twenty minutes of the heat was all he could tolerate. When he came out of the sauna with the robe over one arm and his hand on the revolver he looked around carefully, but Dominic wasn't there. Curly was still whistling in the massage room beyond the showers; Don Aldo caught a glimpse of his knee-length white smock before he spread the robe on the low tile wall around the plunge. The chalky green water was six and a half feet deep, almost a full foot over the don's head; the plunge was eight feet in diameter. The water temperature, 57 degrees, felt shockingly cold when he jumped in, holding his nose.

He stayed under only long enough for his bare toes to find the body on the bottom.

Glancing down through the mineral-cloudy water, Don Aldo saw Curly bare to the waist and with a still-bleeding knife wound just beside the right shoulder blade. A twenty-pound platter from a barbell set had been thrust into the waistband of his white twill pants for ballast.

Don Aldo broke the surface of the plunge choking and trying to yell and reach the robe he had left lying on the tile perimeter, but it wasn't there any more. The Angel of Death was hunkered down in its place, reaching out to push his head underwater again. *Anyone could whistle*, the don thought, trying to adjust to what had happened and not go flailing at the water, wasting his limited energy, this couldn't be what Dominic had in mind for him, to drown him in the plunge.

He was right; after a few moments his grandson let go of his skull and the don got his nose high enough to breathe. But he couldn't get a grip on the slippery tiles and the ladder was out of reach.

"Dominic—you—what—you—trying—"

"No, not Dominic. I'm Angel."

"Angel—that was—foolish name your mother—called you—"

"I like Angel."

"All right—all right—why—do you want to—scare me like this?"

"I only want to talk to you, where nobody can try anything."

"We'll talk. But—help me out first."

Angel shook his head, relaxed, intent, one knee down, a forearm across his other knee.

"Dom—" the don started to say, and took in water; he was doing a toe dance on the back of the dead Curly, trying to use the muscular masseur's flesh as a springboard. But weakening, struggling. "Angel, okay. We are—your family. Huh? No one wants—to hurt you. Only help."

"Yes, that's what I need. Help me, Grandfather."

"Angel—I'm drowning."

Angel shook his head again, he didn't think so.

"I won't let you drown. Just tell me what I have to know."

"How can I? I—must protect you, Angel. Protect you—from yourself." Don Aldo's feet slipped off Curly's back and his head went under again, bumped hard against the side of the plunge. He almost swallowed a lungful, and broke the surface gasping horridly, seeing no change of expression on the face of the Angel of Death.

"I want my wife. I want my son. Tell me where they are, Grandfather."

"Listen—to me. You know what you did—to her, she almost died—"

"But I'm sorry I did that. I wouldn't hurt her again."

"You have—no control," the don said, stepping on Curly's head. His lips trembled squeamishly. "It is a beast inside of you. I—I have killed—men, but—never for pleasure."

"Do you love me, Grandfather?"

"I will not—betray them. I will not—feed the beast in you."

The Angel of Death studied him solemnly, with just a hint of a frown. At last the don was able to get a finger grip on the rim of tiles. He stayed as still as he could in the water, head thrown back, looking up into amber eyes. Men should not have eyes like that, he thought. He shuddered from the effort he was making to stay afloat. He knew that if he went under again, he would die.

Finally Angel said, "I'll find them anyway. Good-bye, Grandfather."

He reached out with both hands. The don closed his eyes, resigned, believing that he had done his best.

Angel's strong hands grasped him at the armpits; he was lifted from the plunge. His knees wouldn't hold him. Angel kept him on his feet with one hand, placed his lips against the don's cold and fibrillating cheek.

Don Aldo felt a sudden jerk and flare of pain in the genitals, saw something out of the corner of his eye, a splash, a familiar shape vaguely like a fish dwindling in the six and a half feet of water, a wispy thread of blood rising to the surface. There was a shocking flood of warmth on the inside of one of his thighs. He stared into the eyes of the Angel of Death.

"You—kill me—?" He hadn't even seen the knife. Angel was just too quick for him.

But Angel shook his head, as if his grandfather had spoken a sacrilege.

"You are don of dons," he said. "I have too much respect to kill you. I just cut your dick off."

CHAPTER
TEN

Carl's night out hadn't gone as well as he had bragged it would, when he was sitting with Wink Evergood in the lounge of Murray's Driftwood. They had met the girls for dinner and Cindalou was pleased to see him, cuddling right up on the banquette under the low lights, giving him little loaded glances and squeezes and laughing throatily at his jokes, letting him order for her from the poster-size menus with the imitation-leather covers. She was, possibly, twenty-one, and worked at First Federal where Carl kept his local money. She had a semi-punk hairdo, a sulky mouth and extravagantly sinful eyes. Junk jewelry, patterned black stockings, a tight skirt, a vest over a filmy lavender shirt. He had bought her some good perfume, forty-nine dollars for an ounce of the stuff and she really stunk out loud, she must have been wearing all of it.

But the evening went to hell between the Newburg crepes and the bacon-wrapped filets. Cindalou was called away to the phone and came back holding her stomach, mouth agape, hysteria flashing in her eyes. Kent, her estranged husband, under court order not to go near Cindalou or four-year-old Shanda, had showed up at the trailer park where Cindalou lived with the baby and a maiden aunt, packed up the kid and fled in his van. Before Carl and Wink and Wink's girlfriend could get her out of the restaurant and calm her down a little, Cindalou was screaming. Carl took over. They called the cops and they called Cindalou's lawyer, who met them at the hospital emergency room where Cindalou was given a tranquilizer. Next stop was the police station, to prefer charges, with Cindalou dulled and mumbling and sweating.

About then they brought Kent in, handcuffed, and little Shanda in her flannel nightgown, clutching a doll and alertly checking out everything that was going on. A state cop had routinely investigated Kent's ramshackle VW van, parked to the side of Interstate 10 about twelve miles west of Gulfport, and found Kent underneath with a flashlight trying to do something about a broken steering coupling. Once the cop had an affirmative on wants and warrants he requested backup, and Kent took off through the roadside scrub, not getting too far. Kent was about five-nine, underweight, with a bad attitude, the kind who will never be able to get out of his own way. When Cindalou saw him she came alive and tried to ream out his eyes with her half-inch fingernails. There was a lot of scuffling and yelling and Shanda, competing for attention, screamed loudly in a policewoman's arms. Kent broke down then, blubbering, saying that he knew his rights, by God, maybe nobody wanted to give him a decent break in life but they couldn't keep him away from his li'l baby girl, because Shanda was all he had in this rotten stinking world. What a great evening. It was already a quarter past twelve and Carl left the police station, only to find out his luck hadn't improved. When he got to Murray's Driftwood he was told that Rochelle, the black girl he'd been hitting on, had gone home early from work with a migraine. Where was home? Nobody knew for sure.

So Carl drove back to the bayou, arriving at the house at one-fifteen. The RV was dark. Lights on in Anita's room and he thought, what the hell, they could at least nibble on some *ragusano* and wild boar salami from Sardinia, share a bottle of Etna red, and maybe . . . maybe . . . But when he knocked Anita said firmly, "I'm just going to bed, Carl," so that was that. In a sour mood Carl hit the sack himself, without any loving, only about the third night since the Fourth of July he'd been unable to accommodate his often ferocious need for pussy.

He awoke about seven o'clock after a not particularly good night's sleep and felt instantly out of sorts, shivering because the electric heater in his bedroom wasn't on. He heard a motor on the bayou and went to the window in his Countess Mara pajamas to have a look. He saw Clay Tomlin leaving the dock in a johnboat with a snoring smoky old Evinrude mounted on the transom. The sun was just up, but it was already late to be doing much fishing for specks around the snags and stumps and in the deep holes at the edge of the marsh grass. Maybe he was just out to have a look around his property.

Carl wondered if the man was fully aware of what he had down here. With the idea of making an offer

to his absentee landlord, Carl had researched the title
and found it unencumbered, a direct line of family
ownership from Tomlin's maternal great-grandfather,
Tobias Park. Originally the property had been even
more impressive, 1,128 acres of wooded hummock,
wetland and shoreline; all but approximately 247 of
these acres had been deeded or sold to the federal
government for the national seashore and wildlife
refuge immediately adjacent to the east. Land forever
protected in its natural state. Carl was all for that,
understanding the ecological significance, and who
wanted a coast that was nearly solid concrete with the
Gulf smelling like a backed-up toilet for fifty miles
out to sea? Look at what had happened to the Medi-
terranean after less than a century of careless pollut-
ing, you went for a dip below some of the world's
loveliest villages, you were odds-on to develop a skin
disease. But there was still room for development
here, properly handled. Much of Tomlin's acreage
was buildable, and part of the bayou could easily be
filled in. Port Bayonne was a fast-growing place.
People were attracted to the area because of the
short, mild winters, and because Florida was getting
so crowded and dangerous. Many of them wanted
and could pay for luxury homes, but there was a hell
of a shortage of sites with good views and easy
access to the still-clean waters of Mississippi Sound.
The area was subject to knockout punches from frequent Gulf hurricanes, but the Barrier Islands immediately offshore afforded some protection. Carl
envisioned a jewel-box development, pricey, a Jack
Nicklaus golf course. He had made a couple of over-
tures to Mace Lefevre, not getting anywhere. Mace
had said flatly that Tomlin wouldn't sell. But Carl

was naturally suspicious of Mace's strategic place in the scheme of things. Childhood friend of Tomlin's; a wheeler-dealer himself despite his unpretentious style. Tight with the local power brokers, the redneck *La Cosa Nostra*. Probably he'd had his eye on the property long before Carl showed up. He could afford to bide his time, slowly persuade Tomlin to unload. Jesus, the guy was in his early forties, he'd been a fly-boy for years, you didn't just flush that drug out of your system overnight. In Carl's opinion, Tomlin would want the kind of action and life-style four or five million cash money would support very well. Give him a few weeks of fishing and nostalgia, he'd be on his way.

In the meantime he was *in* the way, which brought Carl back to immediate business—which made him a touch jittery. They were running another load in tomorrow night. The first trip had been all cream and honey, two million five cut up half a dozen ways: Wink, his *cousin,* Tom Paul, who Wink had said could do a good job of keeping his mouth shut, the helicopter pilot they'd recruited, and Carl's contacts in New Orleans, who set up the buy. The second trip was going to be the last one. The combined U.S. Navy–Coast Guard drug interdiction effort in Gulf waters was proving to be too effective. You could slip a boat like Wink's through a hell of a lot easier than a small plane flying at night, but forward-looking infrared radar was like a noose around the throat of the Yucatán Channel. Count on luck once too often, get a little greedy, it was a straight shot to the slams.

Anyway, Wink was going to look after the fly-boy, which might hurry up his decision to leave town again, and it wouldn't hurt if Carl worked up a proposal he could pitch in the meantime. It was basically a matter of knowing what Tomlin wanted, arriving at the offer he would take. Thinking about cutting a deal the family was bound to approve of, which would enhance his stature and jump his name to the head of the list of guys deserving to be made, lifted Carl's spirits. His stomach was burbling and he remembered the steak he'd missed out on last night. He put on his polka-dot sulka robe and went down the back stairs to the kitchen to see what Opal had to offer this morning, besides a cold shoulder.

Tomlin had left the RV before he should have, just able to make it down to the dock without falling, and he still wasn't seeing all that well as he guided the johnboat, the outboard throttled way down but still uncomfortably loud, along the gradually narrowing bayou that curled back into the long grass, dividing on the way into numerous bronze-green channels, some only two feet deep, that were separated by woodsy hummocks. Home to coon and possum and armadillo, the shy, stoic gator, and so many different kinds of birds that he couldn't remember half their names any more, even if he had seen them clearly flitting through the marsh shallows, perched in low treetops. The sun over his right shoulder was a full but fuzzy orange, as if he were looking at it through a heavy mist. The blunt bow of the johnboat, twelve feet from where he sat, was indistinct to his eyes; but his vision was coming back, slowly, with the broadening of the light. Peace of mind, on the chilly stillness of the bayou. Purging himself of the fear he woke up with every morning, always awakening too early and in blackness, that today would be the day

sight did not return. In spite of everything the oph-
thalmologists had told him, he still hadn't learned to
deal with this fear; it was wearing out his gut. All of
the other times he had been afraid in his life—plenty
of times, pick one: the first carrier landing at night,
the first time under enemy fire in Vietnam, each
having a guaranteed pucker factor of ten—fear had
diminished with the end of the ordeal. But there was
no foreseeable end to living without his vision from
sundown to dawn, the exquisite uncertainty that made
toughing it out so punishing and ultimately destructive. Psychologically he was nearing burnout, of no
use to himself or anyone else. There was an insidious
strain of self-pity and morbid despair which he often
didn't recognize in time to reject it.

But today is a good day, he thought. It will be
clear and warm and during the long light-hours I will
very nearly forget what darkness is.

He came around a bend to a thirty-foot breadth of
the channel and saw that he had company, a man in a
boat smaller than his. And he caught the flash of
sunlight from mirrored discs as the fisherman made a
smooth whispering cast into shadowy water.

"Hello, Mist' Clay."

Tomlin cut his engine and drifted. "What are the
specs biting today, Wolfdaddy?"

"What they most likes to smell. Live bait. A little
fresh shrimp is all I ever uses." Wolfdaddy, the
contended backlander, for whom fish in the water
was a solid comfort, better than coins in his pocket.

"Mind if I hang around and try my luck?"

"No, sir! 'Nother twenty minutes, maybe, 'fore
they stops bitin'. But if you don't get no trout in the
mornin', well, there's redfish in the evenin', reckon

so. What your daddy used to say. If we don't want too much, or ask for too much, well, then, there'll always be enough.''

"Yeah, I guess he did say that," Tomlin answered, thinking about his old man then, wishing he was around to talk to. The old man could give names to all the familiar-sounding birds. He could tell you that next Tuesday at five thirty-seven in the afternoon when the tide began to change, getting exactly five inches higher, there was a notch at the east end of the big grassy bar two hundred feet west of Petit Bois where the snapper were going to run, in astonishing quantities. Fish were creatures of habit so it was more a matter of observation and knowledge of tide tables than clairvoyance, but that had been the old man's strong point: observation, then action. The biggest lift he could get as a kid was to have the old man look him in the eye and say, not unsympathetically, *So it's hard. But you're harder.* Maybe his father had known something about him he still wasn't sure of. It was a comfort to think so.

Tony was sitting at the kitchen eating Frosted Flakes and going over a list of spelling words he was being tested on later; he barely acknowledged Carl's presence, and, when Carl smiled and asked him if he could spell "umptillion," Tony said it wasn't on his list, and he didn't have to. Carl stopped smiling. He ordered breakfast from Opal, going into great detail about how he wanted his eggs, which he knew would annoy her; but who the fuck paid her wages anyway? He said to Tony's back, "I didn't forget about your Garbage Pail Kids, got 'em upstairs, and maybe when you're a little nicer to me I'll give them to you.'' Tony ignored him, moving his lips as he sounded out one of his spelling words. Carl poured himself a mug of coffee and grabbed a fresh cinnamon bun, carried them with him to the parlor to check the bulletin board on the computer, his only link, other than an occasional call from a pay phone, to the family.

CHAPTER
ELEVEN

Anita was in the shower and thinking about Tony's schoolwork, as she did first thing every morning. He was far ahead of his grade level in reading and math, scoring in the 98th percentile on the California Achievevmnt Test he had taken in April. His progress with some of the fourth-grade material she was now giving him surprised her, despite his IQ. But he was industrious and a perfectionist, perhaps too impatient with himself when he couldn't immediately get the hang of something new, like the simple prealgebra equations he had begun to work on, or French grammar. Anita felt good about Tony's progress, and unhappy sometimes because she knew something important was missing from his education: interaction with other bright kids his age, a positive, competitive classroom atmosphere. His temper flare-ups, his episodes of the sulks, were a consequence in part of a lack of playmates and his isolation on the bayou. She had taken a good look at the Port Bayonne school

system and thought it was mediocre. He would not
get the intellectual stimulation he required in one of
the city's second grades. That was one thing. But her
decision to keep him home was largely emotional.
She knew she could not stand the tension of having
Tony away from her for seven hours a day.

She had dreamed last night of homecoming, a big
family reunion. Her father, her brothers and sisters,
all the nephews and nieces, quite a few of whom she
had never seen, not even photographs. They were all
there, in the big house on Sheepshead Bay. Then the
dream had turned ugly; smoke filled the house, but
no one could locate the fire. Only Anita knew where
the fire had started, where it was burning out of
control. In her bedroom. The fire consumed all of her
precious things, destroyed every trace of her as a
child: her Madame Alexander doll collection, her
First Communion dress, her teenage diaries, the pho-
tos and posters personally autographed to her by TV,
movie and rock stars, which an uncle who was a
William Morris agent obtained for her—she sobbed
heartbrokenly in the smoke-dimmed foyer of the house
from which everyone else had fled, forever.

A sad rather than a scary dream, the sadness lin-
gering long after she was awake and delaying the lift
in spirits she usually got from her morning shower.
But better than some of the other dreams, like the
one where she called and gave the code and the voice
at the other end, familiar and terrifying, said Sorry,
no messages this time: they were all dead, every last
member of her family. Or the one that took place on
the subway to Brooklyn, and the train stalled under
the East River; suddenly she was alone in her graffiti-

fouled car, with nobody else on the entire train except for—

Anita turned off the water and pulled the double shower curtain open and there was Carl, in his spiffy robe and pajamas, standing in the doorway to her room getting an eyeful, a kind of guilty, hang-dog expression on his face as if he was up to no good and contemplating being kicked for it. She yanked the curtains back to conceal her nakedness and said, trembling, "My bathroom is off limits to you, Carl. Now and forever, and you better remember that, goddammit!"

"I need to talk to you, Anita," Carl said.

"It can wait!"

"Here's your towel, get dried off, huh?" He picked up the folded towel she had left on the commode seat and handed it to her; Anita snatched it angrily.

"I'll see you downstairs after I'm dressed."

"Angel's out," Carl said.

She stood in the tub with the towel pressed against her forehead, holding it there with one hand, and tried to take a deep breath. She couldn't. Her reaction was not fear, at first, but deep bitterness: *why couldn't they keep him there?* Then the shock wave came, her head jerked, she groped with her free hand, trying to brace herself against the shower curtains as if they formed a solid wall. Off balance, she tore the curtains from some of the plastic rings holding them on the rod and tumbled out of the tub into Carl's arms.

"Hey, hey."

"I'm all right," she gasped. He had an arm around her waist, the towel between them, but barely. "Where

is he?'' Her tongue felt thick and awkward, para-
lyzed at the root.

Carl attempted to get a better grip on her, but she
was slippery from the bath gel she used to keep her
skin soft. Hair knotted on top of her head so it would
stay dry in the shower. Anita trying to push off with
her weak right hand, stand up by herself.

"Who knows? He flew the coop, killed some
people."

"Oh—oh, God."

"Last night he got to *El Padrino*."

He knew the scream was coming, and clamped a
hand over her mouth. Fingers smelling of cinnamon
bun. Anita writhed, her eyes above his hand huge
and dark and flashing terror. His arm around her
waist, he had raised her up so that her feet were off
the floor, toes scraping his instep, a shin. His dick
coming up hard, never able to get her like this before
but thinking often how it could be managed, her
terror a stimulant driving away what little inhibition
remained, respect for the don's wishes regarding his
grandson's wife.

"No, listen, the old man's still alive. He didn't tell
Angel a goddamn thing. You're safe. You and Tony.
Non hai paura, 'Nita."

She was struggling now, aware of his heat, his
intention, even as he began kissing her breasts. The
towel slipping lower, it was draped over his hard-on.
He tried to snatch the towel away, press more closely
to her.

"Come on, come on," Carl said, lips against her
throat. "We got to, I'm dying, you need it too—"

He pushed her down on the fluffy bath mat, Anita
kicking but her legs too wide apart and the towel was

gone, he was *there*. Carl didn't think she had the strength in the hand he was ignoring, her right hand, to stand him off, but he felt her nails ripping through the skin just below his eyes and, grimacing, he fell back enough to allow her to slip out from under him and scramble, sobbing, on all fours into her bedroom.

"I told you, never! Never! *Vattene!*"

Carl got to his feet grinding his teeth, a habit that had cost him plenty, replacing crowns, and looked first in the mirror to see what the damage was. Some torn skin, a little trickle of blood. He wiped it away with toilet paper and followed Anita into the bedroom, tucking his robe closely around him, his lust controllable now, although he was shaking. He felt chagrined, he really liked her, it didn't have to be this way if she was just willing to be reasonable . . . act like a normal woman.

Anita had pulled on a robe of her own and was standing sideways to the windows, jaw thrust out, giving him a look at the pewter candlestick in her left hand, all Dago now and ready to kill him.

"Christ, Anita," Carl complained, dabbing at the blood under his eye, "I didn't deserve that."

Anita wiped her nose with the back of her right hand. Her breast was still heaving under the robe. "It's called rape, Carl. You fucking lowlife. I could get you killed for what you tried to do."

Carl waved off the threat tiredly and sat down on her bed.

"Oh, shit, listen, the don and I had a talk before I ever came down here, I said to him, you know, what if, and he said, Just don't hurt her. That's all, he didn't want it to be bad for you, otherwise let nature take its—"

"Shut up, Carl. He's coming here, isn't he?"

Carl said blankly. "The don?"

"*Angel, lu sciocco!*"

"Why don't you lay off that kind of language, Anita? We still have to get along, don't we? Now calm down. Because there's no way that Angel can—"

"Don't lie to me! Oh, God, just don't lie to me, Carl!"

She started to walk around the room, looking for her cigarettes. Found them. Backed away from him to put the candlestick down and get one of the filter tips lighted.

Carl said, "Let me apologize for the way I got carried away in there."

Anita nodded, almost indifferently, beads of water still glistening on her face, breath coming harshly with clouds of smoke. A fast pulse in her throat.

"Anita. Honey. Even if Angel had a way of finding out where you are—and believe me, he doesn't—I'd never let him get close to you."

Anita's lips scrunched and her eyes teared. "You don't have any idea—of what Angel is like."

"He's just a man," Carl said, indignant because some assholes in Jersey who were supposed to be good had let Angel get past them for ten minutes alone with the don, who was not in the best of health. "I never met a man I couldn't handle, one way or another. In my neighborhood, in the Army, in the rest of the goddamn world which I have seen plenty of. That's why Don Aldo picked me to take care of you and Tony. And for a whole fucking year I've been sitting down here in this fucking swamp. But—it's not just a job to me any more." He got up slowly from the bed, made a fist, hit the mahogany bedpost lightly and repeatedly, brow knitted, he was trying to be as sincere as he'd been in his life. "But you're not just some broad to me. You gotta know how I feel about you, and the boy. So why can't you—" Carl bit his lip, the bedpost shook. "—loosen up? Anita, you must get a little turned on sometimes, I mean a *year*—"

"Did you see my back?"

Carl looked up, touched by surprise, what was this leading to? "Yeah. Yeah, I saw it." She didn't say anything right away, continuing to stare at him. "Sorry," Carl muttered, humbled by the realization of just what he had seen. "It must have been really rough—"

"Try to get this straight, Carl. No man is ever going to have the use of my body again. The doctors put it back together, I made it work, and now nobody, *nobody* touches me."

The absolute-zero tone of her voice finally turned Carl off, from moderate tumescence he went to slack weight between his legs. He shrugged helplessly.

"I don't understand how the guy could've been such a lousy lover," he said, coming up with his own rationale for her frigidity.

"Angel? It had nothing to do with—*love*. And after a while he just couldn't tell the difference between sex and torture. Would you mind letting me get dressed? Tony's waiting for me."

"You better now? I just hit you with it, guess I shouldn't have, but I—believe me, the guy's loose but they'll pick him up pretty soon. Doesn't he have some kind of fit where he can't move?"

"Once I saw him do that," Anita said, tensing as if something had come into her throat she couldn't force back down. She stubbed her cigarette out and leaned against a wall, blank and exhausted.

"Let me bring you some coffee," Carl suggested, really wanting to be helpful. "Maybe a shot of grappa, *caffè corretto*."

"Coffee would be fine," Anita said, with no change of expression, a full charge of dread impacted in her forehead between her haunted eyes.

CHAPTER TWELVE

Tony was riding his bike on the driveway, Big Dog trailing after him, when Tomlin came up from the dock with his fishing tackle but no fish. He paused near the RV to look out toward the Sound as a trio of Navy fighters in fingertip formation went by at two thousand feet. Probably en route to Pensacola. He watched them until they were nearly out of sight.

"What kind of planes are those?" Tony said behind him.

Tomlin turned. The boy had parked his bike; he had the gray Corsair model with him.

"F-14s. Tomcats."

"Are they fast?" Tony asked, making a pass through the air with his own plane.

"Real fast, when they turn on the afterburners."

"What are those?"

"Extra power. It's like, you're in your swing over there pumping away, doing the best you can to go higher, and I come along and give you a big push from behind." The boy nodded. "School's out early today," Tomlin observed.

"Mom said I could have the day off, I'll make it up Saturday. She's not feeling so good."

"Sorry to hear it," Tomlin said, glancing at the house.

"Don't you fly any more?" Tony said.

"No, I can't."

Tony examined the statement carefully, as if it contained a secret. He let Tomlin keep his secret. "Do you want to?"

"More than anything, Tony."

The boy swooped his model plane down low, wheels touching the concrete slab. "Is that a good landing?"

"You need to keep the nose of your plane cocked up, because you're hanging a big hook and coming in fast."

"What's the hook for?" Tony said, turning his model over to look for one.

"Okay, there are four cables on the landing deck of a carrier. You want to grab the third cable with your hook because that's the sweet spot on the deck and you're coming in at 150 miles an hour; that cable has to stop the aircraft in one hundred feet or less, even though you go to full power the instant you touch down."

"You stop and go at the same time?" Tony said, trying to understand the contradiction.

"Full power, in case something happens to the cable, or the hook bounces off; otherwise you have no chance of getting airborne again. It's over the side or over the bow, or maybe a bad deck accident. Because there are always planes sitting around, just behind the foul line, loaded with high explosives."

"What's—" Tony started to say, but Tomlin cut him off with a gesture of inadequacy.

"I really can't describe what it's like, Tony, you have to see a carrier catching planes to appreciate how the system works. Maybe I can arrange that."

"How?"

"I said maybe. I need to go over to Pensacola today on business. Getting someone your age aboard the *Lexington* might be tough, but—hey, where're you going?"

Tony was already halfway to the house, at a dead run. "Tell Mom!"

Anita, wearing corduroys and an old green sweater, her feet bare, sat in the middle of her bed. She dialed the long-distance number on a cordless phone. It was a double-shuffle relay by way of Wichita, Kansas, that only took a few seconds, but could never be traced by professionals or the most dedicated phone phreak.

The woman at the end of the relay, who answered after four rings, said pleasantly, "Seven six eight two. Go ahead, please." Her voice was upper-class British; whenever Anita heard her speak she thought of tranquil English gardens, heavy on the mums, tea with a lot of milk, rich marmalades.

Anita said, "Orphan."

"Just a moment." After ten seconds she came back on the line. "Roseanne delivered a boy on 21 October. The baby has been named Michael Joseph. He weighed eight pounds two ounces at birth. Roseanne is doing fine, and she took the baby home the day before yesterday. Louis has been promoted to vice-president, marketing, at Waring-Sloane. The re-

sults of your father's three-day physical indicate that
he is in generally good health, with a five-point
improvement in his blood pressure—''

"Shit," Anita said, sniffing, one eye and a nostril
leaking. She reached for a tissue.

"Sorry?" the pleasant-sounding English lady said.

"Don't read me any more of that. I don't want to
hear it, not today. What I want—I have to get in
touch with somebody."

"I am not authorized to—"

"Just listen. I need to talk to Don Aldo. Or, or,
his brother John, or one of John's—"

"That isn't my jurisdiction," the woman replied,
voice still beautifully modulated, with no hint of
emotion.

"I don't care about your—can't you understand,
everything's changed, I'm—I must know what's going
on, somebody has to tell me what they're going to
do, because—"

"Shall I continue with the rest of the message?"

"*Stuff* the bloody message, can't you comprehend
what I'm telling you, I'm scared, he's going to *find*
me. Somehow. I . . . need . . . help."

"Good day," the anonymous woman said, not
miffed, not cheerful, just doing her job. And she
broke the connection.

Anita was still holding the cordless phone in both
hands, staring out the windows with her shoulders
hunched, when Tony burst into the room, talking
fast, really excited and happy about something; she
tried to focus on him, smiling automatically, but she
didn't have a clue as to what he was talking about
until she related "aircraft carrier" and "Pensacola"
and saw, behind Tony, Clay Tomlin standing reti-

cently just outside the door to what had been his parents' bedroom.

"Oh, Tony—today—I just don't think so—"

"Mom! Why *not*?"

She looked at the clock on the tall Regency dresser. "It's almost nine already, and it's a hundred miles to Pensacola—"

"Clay says we'll be back before dark!"

Anita let go of the phone and briefly put her head in her hands. "Tony, don't *yell*."

"I'm not yelling. I want to go. We never go anywhere."

She looked up at Tomlin, in the doorway. "I wish you'd come to me before you invited him to go along."

"I know I should have," he said. "And I know what you're thinking. Why don't you come too? You can drive."

"Drive?" Lately she hadn't even been going out to the supermarket, preferring to let Opal shop, using their second car, an Olds Firenza wagon. She couldn't remember the last time she had left the house. But her head was pounding with black blood, she didn't want to think about that right now, or anything else.

"We'll have lunch at the Officer's Club," Tomlin said, "and if the *Lex* isn't around I'll give Tony a tour of the flight line at Sherman Field." When Anita didn't react he glanced at the phone on her lap. "You look as if you've had bad news. If that's it I apologize, I didn't mean to intrude."

Tony looked around at him swiftly, dismay in his face. Anita, despite herself, shook her head. "Oh, no." She wondered how she could be lying, but even more remarkable was her feeling of relief because

Tomlin was there. The last thing she wanted was for him to leave. Or if he did, she damn sure wanted to go with him. The alternative for her today was Carl, so ballsy now that he had a reason to be on the alert. Carl would hang around and maybe, if she got to feeling low enough, bleak and vulnerable, he'd make another play, his answer to everything: blue, lonely, frightened out of your wits? Get fucked.

"Well—I woke up with quite a headache, but—Pensacola doesn't sound like such a bad idea."

"All right!" Tony shouted, and then, reacting to his mother's pained expression, he backed off a step. "I'm sorry."

"That's okay. Tony, you can't go anywhere in those ragged shorts, go and change now. Your good sneakers and khakis and a flannel shirt, it's not that warm out." Anita glanced down at her own ratty sweater. "And I can't go like this, can I?" She caught Tomlin's eye, seeing that he didn't at all mind her barefoot, hair in a tangle. "Give us twenty minutes, Clay? We'll meet you downstairs."

"Sounds like a winner," Tomlin said, standing aside as Tony hustled past him out the door, on the way to his room.

Carl was aboard his Davis sportfisherman, named the *Lollapalooza*, attending to minor chores in the engine room—checking the halon level in the automatic fire extinguishers and all of the many gauges, filters and dipsticks—when Tony's voice carried to him against a southeast wind that had been gaining strength for the past hour. Carl couldn't be sure, but maybe Tony was calling him. He squeezed up through the narrow opening beneath an upraised cockpit step in time to see Anita getting behind the wheel of the white Corvette. Clay Tomlin was sitting in the passenger seat with the kid on his lap, and away they all went before Carl could hop over the *Lolly*'s gunwale and find out where they were headed.

Well, what was this shit: not a word to him, or maybe Anita had left a note. Carl was most annoyed because she was with Tomlin. That fly-boy. He wasn't hyper like so many of them, just had that enviable kind of cool that grows on a man after he's hauled his ass through so many jams he can't remember them all. Carl didn't have the impression that Anita was running away, though; he'd worked on her for better than half an hour while she sipped her coffee and said not a word, looking wan and tragic: foredoomed. Getting a little of her spirit back once he convinced her that Angel, although deadly, was a fugitive without many resources to count on, no friends, shut out of the family. If that wasn't enough, he was subject to catatonic seizures, only a matter of time until he slowed down to the speed of a courthouse monument, and became easy pickings for the cops. In the meantime Anita and Tony were in a seamless deep-cover situation, her own father didn't know where she was. Carl doubted that even the FBI, with their expertise, could have found her. Angel didn't stand much of a chance. But he'd proved how good he was at getting out of lockups. After his first escape he'd come very close, almost getting to Anita while she was still helpless in the hospital. So the don had decided on stringent precautions. Simpler and easier for Anita and Tony if the don had just ticketed Angel for a clipping; but Angel was flesh of his flesh. Maybe now he had cause to regret his decision.

A little later in the morning Carl took his boat out, but not to fish. He encountered a chop on the shallow Sound, cutting across it without much of a roll. The forty-seven-foot family-owned boat, around half a million with all amenities, power and electronic options, was designed not only for the demands of tournament fishing. The *Lolly* could also handle some big, rough, multidirectional seas with her sixteen-foot beam and the fiberglass hull that was reinforced with Divinycell and Kevlar. He had sailed her as far west as Padre Island, and was considering a much longer cruise in the spring to some prime fishing grounds in the Pacific off Costa Rica. But of course he had to stick very close to home now, at least until Angel was dead or back in the deep freeze somewhere.

The day was still sunny, but thick stratocumulus had begun to build up in the southern sky. The Biloxi marine weather station was calling for winds gusting to twenty-five knots by midafternoon, rain in the evening. Carl heard no performance flaws in the twin diesel 625s. He kept his speed moderate following the channel markers between Horn and Petit Bois islands, then turned to starboard and away from the wind, making thirty knots in deeper water down to the Chandeleurs.

He chose a leeward anchorage, his horizon clear of ships or small craft. He went down to the saloon and opened a rod stowage compartment beneath the L-shaped couch. His guns were under a false bottom in one of the compartments, packed in flat foam-lined aluminum cases. He carried them, along with a pair of Wolf Ears and a shotgun shell courier tailored from parachute material, out to the cockpit. There he rounded up the empty Clorox bottles he'd been saving for target practice and assembled two of the weapons, a futuristic 12-gauge automatic shotgun called the Jackhammer, and a more conventional, eight-shot Benelli assault gun equipped with a recoil pad. He loaded the Jackhammer's disposable plastic cylinder magazine with double-O buck, threw a couple of the red, white and blue-labeled bottles over the side, and, when they had drifted thirty feet astern, he obliterated them with two quick bursts from the eighteen-inch barrel, the big pellets throwing up a lot of spray. The gulls that always hovered around small craft in these waters disappeared instantly. One hell of a big noise echoed across the water, he was a little stunned by the power he held. It gave him a rush to the roots of his hair. Double-O had too much energy for in-house fighting, though, the pellets would carry through paneled walls at close range. Number 4 or 6 standard shot would be about right, given the rapid-fire capability of the Jackhammer. Keep the Benelli aboard and the 'Hammer underneath his bed in the house, he thought, along with the backup Detonics 9mm auto. The old Mac, one of the good reliable ones, concealed in the hit-kit in his car. Then come on, Angel. You crazy son of a bitch. Ready when you are, if you've got what it takes to get this far.

CHAPTER
THIRTEEN

He walked a block and a half east from Bergenline, cold gritty wind in his face, the skyline of Manhattan across the river giving back the autumn sunset in a display of heavenly fire that reminded him of Isaiah (30:27, 30). Also—while he was thinking about it—Revelation 9 and Zephaniah. He was wearing a cheap new black windbreaker he had taken off a rack in front of a store on the Upper West Side a couple of hours ago, when the temperature began dropping, paying nine dollars in cash, most of the bills he had left from the fifty-one dollars and change stolen from the purse of the woman he'd killed in upstate New York. He still had three or four dollars in his pocket, but he wasn't worried about money, or anything else. He felt a little tired, having spent his day on the streets trying to locate the man whom he had finally traced here, to Union City, but once he got to work the tiredness, the lassitude that might become a problem if he wasn't careful, would probably vanish.

Two-sixteen 47th Street. Not the worst street in town, or the worst building on the block. From what he'd seen of it, largely an ethnic neighborhood, bodegas and charcuteries, golden-haired women with ruby lips, pale men with little gold earrings and small mustaches, quick sensitive eyes.

He went up the steps past an old woman airing a fretful baby in a stroller, found the name on the mailbox, saw that the latch on the inner door was broken and heard a loud radio, louder voices. He opened the door and went in. Four kids sprawled on the steps in front of him. Two boys and two girls. The ghetto blaster like a big roadblock squarely on the second step. He paused, hands in the pockets of his windbreaker. Faded flannel shirt underneath, unpressed blue twill workpants, workman's scuffed hightops. Not a tall man, but husky. They had glanced at him coming in and, since they didn't know him, had never seen him before, he was going to have to plead the fact of his existence if he wanted to get by.

Angel waited, listening to incomprehensible rap music, to a language he didn't understand. The girls not more than fourteen or fifteen, one very slim and pretty, the other already fattening in the hips, both with coarse wavy hair and headbands and dark pouting looks, the guys sleek, hairy upper lips, liquid, cynical eyes. Their pretended ignorance of him gradually became more elaborate, their enjoyment of his predicament wearing thin as he just stood there, looking at them, not pissed off or servile, not much of

anything except his stare was unwavering and he
didn't blink, and his eyes in the weak light of the
stairwell and downstairs hall had a low amber shine,
unusual and not all that pleasant to see in a human
face.

One of the girls put out her cigarette and requested
another, and, while she was getting a light, gave
Angel four separate glances. And the bigger of the
two guys, who wore a snappy Borsalino and a draped
leather jacket, shifted his position on the stairs a
couple of times, maybe getting ready for something,
glowering but not looking directly at Angel, who was
standing all of two feet away. Their conversation fell
off, but they got the tempo going again, both girls
uneasy now and laughing too much, the hippy one
wrapping her arms loosely around her boyfriend's
neck, using him as a kind of shield as she dared to
try staring Angel down. They were offended. He
hadn't done a thing, hadn't opened his mouth, wasn't
trying to be tough with them: but the tension in the
crowded area at the foot of the stairs was now beyond
their sufferance. They couldn't think of any more
insults, which Angel obviously didn't understand any-
how, and he wasn't going to go meekly away; the
only thing left was to get rid of him through the sheer
force of their ill-will.

Four pairs of eyes against one. A slight sneer building up on the lip of the big Cuban kid.

When the Angel of Death said to them, "Do you
love me?"

The radio rap went on, interminably. The other
boy tried to laugh, but he couldn't make much of it.
Nor were they able to turn to one another again,

gabbing, dismissive. His dead-level, screwy question had cut through their obligatory defiance, their contempt for anything or anyone that wasn't a part of the tight little group.

The younger, prettier girl, not taking her eyes off Angel, got up slowly and stood against the stair railing. The boy in the Borsalino slid his radio toward him. Not worried or intimidated, possibly just tired of the pointless game. But his dark eyes were a little wider, watching Angel carefully . . . his hands hidden in his pockets that way.

The girl with the hips gave her boyfriend a nudge and with a faint petulant sigh he got up too, stepping down and to one side in the hall, cigarette hanging from a corner of his mouth.

Angel walked past them up the steps, not hurrying. Although he missed her by several inches the girl against the railing felt his passing as something electric, hell-raising. She prickled all over. There were no smart remarks behind his back. And they stared at him until he was out of sight.

(A week later, after the unholy stench from apartment 4B had brought the cops around, the pretty Cuban girl did her best to describe Angel, and the impact of the only words he'd spoken to them. *Do you love me?* "You had to hear *him* saying that, otherwise it don't mean nothing. But him saying it, man, you knew you were going to get out of his way. You didn't even want to be in the same building with somebody like that. He kill that dude in 4B? Wasn't the way he looked, just a feeling I got with him going by me, that he could do the number on somebody, sure didn't want it to be me.")

On the fourth floor Angel stopped in front of apartment B and rang the bell. After a minute or so he was aware of being scrutinized through the peephole, then a lot of locks were undone and the door was opened to him.

"Thought you got lost. Come on in. Long time, where you been keeping yourself?"

He was a sad slouching man with thick and dirty eyeglasses. His name was Paul Baldric. Angel walked past him into the hallway and said, "I was kept." Baldric chuckled as if he felt he ought to, but he didn't see the humor of the remark. He closed the steel-clad door and went through his locking-up routine before taking Angel into the living room, which was a shambles: terrible furniture, dirty dishes on a table, a TV with a picture that had roll-over problems. Baldric hastened to shut the television off.

"Been meaning to get that thing fixed. You know anything about TVs?"

"No."

Baldric turned to Angel, rubbing his palms together like a man with circulation shortcomings, although he wasn't more than thirty-five. And it wasn't particularly cold in his apartment. He had bad nasal congestion, a shut-in's pallor.

"So, uh, you mentioned a problem on the phone. How can I help you?" A slight emphasis on the *you*, a hint of obsequiousness.

Angel said, "There's a computer I need to locate. It's in North Jersey."

"That certainly narrows down the field," Baldric said, nodding eagerly.

"They must have changed the security, but I designed the system. I can superzap it once I bypass the log-on.''

Baldric backed up a step, the hand-rubbing becoming a hand-wringing. "Sounds difficult. Like, uh, AT&T, maybe? This something might get me into trouble? The FBI already come down on me pretty hard for hacking, even though I didn't profit from it; hell, you know those missile systems analysts at JPL don't have any sense of humor.''

"You won't get into trouble.''

Baldric sniffed and dripped, going into a pocket of the cardigan sweater he wore over an undershirt for a wad of Kleenex. "Well—okay, then. This way.''

He showed Angel to a room, also excessively locked, next to the bedroom, in which there was nothing but a dirty bedroll on the floor. He opened the door of his hack shop, turning on overhead fluorescents. In contrast to the rest of the apartment the room was orderly, filled with gleaming computer equipment; printouts and manuals were stacked on steel shelves.

"Got all the peripherals you'll need," Baldric said. "Teletype, high-speed digital analyst.''

"Good-looking," Angel said approvingly. "Expensive.''

"Well, you know, I put in a few months at Disney in the digital-intensive areas of their new park, socked some good bread away. Nobody writes code better than me, present company excepted, but I don't get along so good in a controlled environment, that's the problem with us old hackers, right? Maybe I could give you a hand, I've heard you're the best at hiding programs.''

"Sure," Angel said, and, after another look around, "use your bathroom?"

"Across the hall here." Baldric went over to the windowless bathroom and reached for the chain-pull on the overhead light. While he was up on his toes Angel took two quick steps, throwing down and locking the blade of his knife, and came up behind Baldric. No more emotion in him than if he were there to lay some tile. Angel slashed Baldric deep across the back of the neck, and, when Baldric fell gasping across the high rim of the bathtub, trying to reach the wound with a hand that just flopped uncontrollably, he stepped in and planted the knife blade to the hilt an inch to the inside of the right shoulder blade, angled to slice through a ventricle of the heart. He pulled the knife and put it down on the sink, grasped Baldric by the ankles and dumped him into the tub.

While Angel was running water in the filthy basin, cleaning the knife blade, Baldric sat up, his head wobbling like an infant's. With his pierced heart beginning to fibrillate Baldric had a convulsion and died speechless as Angel took a long leak. After flushing the toilet Angel drew the shower curtain around the tub and turned on the water to get rid of the blood. Then he went across the hall to Baldric's hack shop and sat down in front of the computer, a 4-meg IBM clone. He booted up the machine and just sat there for a while with his hands on it, looking at the ready light, listening to it run, the monitor still blank and unable to tell him secrets. But, given enough time, he could find out everything that other men had confided to their machines. He had now come to the source, the godhead, of his true affection. His hunger. But there was something in his nostrils, a perfume scent, girlflesh, accompanied by an image of the Cuban with dark eyes and young tits on the stairs; in passing, his own flesh had acquired an indelible stain, a portion of her appealing flux. He was nauseated then by the force of his erection, at a time when all he yearned to do was free his mind to wander in the vastness of the electronic field, the universal machine that began at his fingertips. He had known for years that it was possible, with his intellect, his knowledge of circuits, algorithms and cross-assemblies, to meld his mind timelessly with the silicon universe, discover secrets a single human brain could not conceive. He had important work to do, but here (again) was this unwanted distraction, desire of the flesh. Flesh, which he knew to be cheap, cheap as mud, frequently pestilential and always, in the end, disappointing. The mystery he had not been able to solve, in spite of multiple debauches, was how and why flesh should also be so mysteriously, agonizingly attractive. So many flaunters in the world. He always asked his question of them, but he did not have to hear their answer: their flesh answered for them. They all loved him. Both men and women wanted him. But no man had the time to purge so many flaunters, like the little Cuban, although it was gratifying when the stains they had left on him faded with their dying breaths.

His dilemma, he had come to realize, lay in the genesis of the primal stain, the one placed on him before all others, the most difficult to eradicate. Some called her Sin. But he knew her by another name.

The answer to his dilemma, like all the answers to questions which he did not yet know how to ask, lay in the ever-expanding core of the machine.

Now he turned on the monitor and typed a single word, the name of her by whose death he would be forever cleansed of lust:

ANITA

CHAPTER
FOURTEEN

The *Lexington* had been in port for a couple of days for repairs, so Clay Tomlin and his guests were given permission to go aboard for a tour. He seemed to be on friendly terms with nearly everybody who counted at the Pensacola Naval Air Station, where Navy and Marine pilots were trained. There had been a Tomlin in the United States Navy for more than one hundred years. Three of them were graduates of Annapolis. But it seemed to be his fate to be the last of the line. Forty-three already, with no chick and no child.

The carrier's landing deck was much smaller than Anita had thought it would be, and she'd already seen one of the planes he'd flown, an A-7, up close on the flight line. Sixty thousand pounds of airplane. All of it coming to a dead stop after dropping down out of the sky at 10 feet per second. He'd done this over and over again, day and night, sometimes under terrible conditions: rain, no horizon, forty-five-foot seas that caused even the largest carriers to wallow and roll. All the night landings had a high pucker factor (he didn't explain the term but she had an accurate idea of what it conveyed, sucking up the seat through your asshole until it was close to clogging your throat). A few red lights to home in on, a mirrored cross of light they called "the meatball" to tell him if he was on course or about to fly into the bridge of the darkened carrier.

Scary? There was no such thing as a routine landing on a carrier, even on a fair day, a case-one recovery where the pilot had full visual contact with the deck. "Because we'd come in from cyclical ops near bingo fuel, just enough pounds to squeeze out a flyby if something wasn't right aboard. And the flight deck crew always had problems with the cables or the tugs or the plane that landed just ahead of you. I usually had a hundred and ten planes in my wing, Toms, Corsairs, all of which had to be recovered and moved off the landing deck with extreme precision."

They were on the fantail of the *Lexington*. Tony had his model Corsair with him. Tomlin pointed off to port.

"Out there at three quarters of a mile is where you come into your break, Tony. Carrier Control Approach hands you off to the landing signal officer, who is standing right about here. He's in touch with the air boss on the bridge, and with your plane. He's also a pilot, so he knows everything that can go wrong on an approach. The LOS has the option of letting you land or waving you off. He knows if you're left or right of course or on glide path, and he can tell how fast you're going from the lights mounted under the nose of your plane. The same three approach lights you have in the cockpit."

"You showed me those."

"Right. The red light means you're coming in too fast, green is too slow. Amber, you're on speed. So you're closing on the carrier, which is always steaming away from you, and most of the time it's a visual approach. You lock into your groove, drop the hook, you're down, it's so quick you're too busy to think. But you never get casual about it. I've known good pilots who have made a hundred takeoffs and landings, and the day comes when they just can't do it any more. There was a kid in my squadron in Vietnam, came up one morning for his preflight, walked all around the plane, then walked off the deck with his helmet in his hand. Looking sort of puzzled and lost. He just shook his head and said, 'That's it.' "

"Was he scared?"

"I don't think that's the right word. Nowadays they call it burnout. He'd lost his confidence, or his air sense. But I was glad he didn't try to push it, get himself in a jam and kill his back seat and maybe his wingman along with himself. Getting into one of these planes and flying it, day after day on a six-to-nine-month cruise, has to be the greatest, the *only* thing in your life. You have to need it, I mean the rush you get catapulting off the bow of a carrier going five hundred knots and flat-out across the sea."

Anita looked at his face, and his ecstatic eyes, and tried to imagine him in another ten years, would he still be carrying on like this? She didn't think so. There was more man than boy to him, he'd find another groove that would satisfy him. She thought, *Maybe for everything bad that happens in life, there is an equal reaction of good*. For the last three years her philosophy had been exactly the opposite. Call it

Anita's First (revised) Law. She looked at her watch. It was twenty-one minutes and seventeen seconds past three o'clock in the afternoon, a kind of dreary-looking day with too much snap in the wind to be standing out here for so long. Kind of interesting to be aware of the moment when you knew without any trace of doubt that you were in love with a man. The sad thing was, she couldn't do a thing about it. Anita's Second Law: *All things good come to she who waits, too late*. Pilots weren't alone in suffering from burnout.

She said reluctantly, realizing that Tony was tired and couldn't absorb much more today, "We've had a wonderful time, Clay, but I think we should be getting back now."

Tony protested; they still hadn't been belowdecks where the hangars were. But Tomlin promised to bring him back. He carried Tony off the ship, and the boy had fallen asleep in his arms by the time they reached the car.

They didn't talk much on the way home, listened to some tapes while Tony slept and Tomlin held him close. The music he liked was country (but nothing much after 1970, when they started wearing polyester leisure suits on Music Row in Nashville, and thinking Top Forty), Cajun and gospel. Most of all he loved the blues—down-home blues that originated in the levee camps, gambling dives and prison farms of the Delta South. She listened to Robert Johnson, Blind Lemon Jefferson, Sid Hemphill, Sonny Terry. To homemade one-string instruments that twanged and resonated eerily, sitarlike. To funky breakdown harmonicas and caterwauling acoustic guitars, the sound produced by stroking the strings with the cut-off necks of whiskey bottles. *Your daddy was a preacher, your mama was an alley cat.* The sentiments mournfully humorous and to the bone. *Leave so early next mornin', your real man never know.*

Anita enjoyed driving, and the Corvette was a super car. At the end of the road she felt almost at peace. Carl's boat was missing from the dock; good. Big Dog was on the veranda. Opal was cleaning windows. *I'd like to stay here forever,* she thought. She looked at Tomlin, a little startled. He smiled at her as if he'd been eavesdropping, then got out of the car with Tony on his shoulder. The boy trying to wake up. Big Dog came down to them and licked Anita's weak hand.

"I don't know when we've had this much fun," she said. "Now maybe he'll be interested in something besides those computer games."

Tomlin leaned Tony against the side of the car and reached in for the Corsair model and the dark blue officer's bridge cap he'd bought for the boy.

"Why don't you come in?" Anita said, wishing he'd say something and not just smile—which, come to think of it, was unusual for him, he just didn't smile all that often.

Tomlin put Tony's hat on his head and looked at the gray sky; there would be no sunset. And there was a sprinkling of rain in the wind.

"Too close to the witching hour," he said apologetically.

Anita nudged her son, who was yawning. "*Cosa dici,* Anthony?"

Tony looked up at Tomlin. "Thanks. What's the witching hour?"

"Just after dark."

Tony interpreted this as best he could. "Are you afraid of the dark?"

"Not exactly. I'm just not all that used to it. See you tomorrow, Tony."

He was crossing the drive to the RV when Tony called after him, "Could we go fishing? Tomorrow afternoon?"

"You got it," Tomlin said, and started to whistle something as he let himself into the unlocked RV "When the Saints Go Marching In."

Tony tried whistling too, going up the steps to the veranda with his mother. He carried a tune pretty well.

Wink Evergood's *cousin* Tom Paul had come over from Morgan City eighteen months ago when the oil business in Louisiana started to go to hell. Three dollars in his pocket. Since then, thanks to Wink's stewardship, he had acquired a one-bedroom professionally decorated apartment in the Stella Maris condominium tower, a $21,000 Nissan 300 ZX sports car, and a bass boat. He was happy to do anything Wink asked of him.

What Wink wanted to do tonight was go hunting, but they didn't load the coon hounds into the dog box in the back of Wink's Silverado pickup. In wind and intermittent rain they took a rutted road south of the Interstate to the marshes of the Tchoutacabouffa, parked, put on waders and hardhats with lights on them.

Tom Paul said, "Tell you about this little girl I been busy with, she's from up north. Indiana, I think. She was entertain her mama and papa for a

few days and they say to me, where we can get us
some authentic Cajun food, and I say, nowhere around
here, this is the Magnolia State, not Louisiane. But
what I'll do is, I'll cook for you. Because to tell the
truth, I was missing home cooking myself. So you
got to start the *roux* early, you know, simmer it all
day long. I was in Dolly's kitchen soon in the morning. The mama and the papa, now they drink too
much the night before, they don't wake up until past
eleven. Mama she come into the kitchen with bags
under her eyes; man, she smell my cooking, the
shrimp and the crawfish going strong. She pull up
short and give a twitch and I can tell she want to
leave in the worst way, but that wouldn't be polite,
no? Put on a smile and say to me, Tom Paul, can I
give you a hand? Well, you know I can't resist a
little joke, so I open up the ice chest I brought and
pull out the three-foot gator tail I had in my freezer
since the last time I was gone home to Breux Bridge.
I slap it down on the butcher block and say to her,
'Why don't you just filet that 'un for me, haw?' She
and Dolly both like to be down on their knees for
half hour, scrubbing the puke out of Dolly's living
room carpet.''

Wink chuckled, and they went off looking for a
snake.

Cottonmouths tended to be a clannish bunch, particularly in cool weather. They hung around in clumps
of palmetto, and the low branches of cypress trees;
they could hang from the branches by their tails to
scavenge whatever came by on the slow-moving water. They were known to be heavy eaters, sometimes
gorging themselves until they died of massive belly-
aches. They were not particularly aggressive, for

venomous snakes, but if they decided to go after a man, they would strike faster than a rattlesnake.

Wink found a specimen he liked backed up in the decaying roots of a fallen cypress, kind of a mud-colored snake without well-defined markings. Only the inside of its mouth was distinctive, a flash of white, and the vertical pupils of the eyes also distinguished it from similar-looking but harmless water snakes.

"Big sucker," Tom Paul said. "Go five feet, six-seven pounds maybe."

"Don't let him slide out into the water there."

"Just woke him from his nap; man, he's too cold to make any sudden moves."

Wink held the croker sack open while Tom Paul maneuvered the snake hook into the tangle of branches, and pulled the cottonmouth into the bag. The snake thrashed around in the bottom of the sack before settling down to await whatever they had in mind for him.

"No need to stir this 'un up," Tom Paul said. "He's plenty mad already."

"Good," Wink said.

In Wolfdaddy's snug quarters on the tree-house platform of the Next-Thing-to-Heaven Church of the Right-Way Gospel, he had a narrow folding cot with an old Army blanket on it, a couple of shelves, a kerosene lamp, a footlocker under the cot, and a charcoal brazier on which he cooked the fish he caught in the bayou, throwing the heads to his tabbies. He made hush puppies from his sack of cornmeal, and also could whip up a pretty good cattail salad. There was just enough room in the shack for him to turn in a complete circle with his arms extended, fingertips brushing the drafty walls of packing crate boards. It was enough shelter; it suited him fine. On the mostly mild evenings of Lostman's Bayou he stayed outdoors all night under the stars, high enough not to be visited by mosquitoes when there was any kind of wind blowing. He smoked an old Dr. Grabow pipe and enjoyed his own company, mulling selected passages from the Bible that he planned to include in his next sermon.

Because of the light rain he was indoors when he heard Wink Evergood's Silverado truck go by on the road, where there was seldom any traffic, particularly after ten o'clock at night. He knew the sound of this truck. He knew something was up.

He opened the door of his shack and saw the truck going down toward the house with only its parking lights on. Oh-oh. He said, to a cat that had walked across one foot, "There they go again. Pick up more of their wicked dope to sell to little children."

Wolfdaddy turned and took down a battered pair of pawnshop binoculars from a hook screwed into the front wall. He went outside to the edge of the platform and raised the binoculars. The night was dark and wet, but he could see enough of the back end of Wink's truck to certify his conclusion. Then, except for a smudge of taillight, he couldn't keep the pickup in view any more. But Wink appeared to have stopped, pulled off the road short of the gate to the house. The smudge of red stayed a constant size on the lenses of the binoculars.

After rubbing his eyes he looked in another direction, to a floodlight at one corner of the roofed dock on the bayou. He saw Carl Jeffords' boat tied up and

someone—might have been the man himself—standing
on the foredeck, leaning against a grab rail. But
everything dim, hard to make out, a strain on
Wolfdaddy's old eyes. He lowered the binoculars,
mouth working, forehead deeply wrinkled. A cat
yowled irritably, wanting to be left alone. Wolfdaddy
quieted his trembling lips with the back of one hand
and had another look with his glasses, sighting the
house itself this time, the surrounding shimmer of
floodlights.

"Just ain't right, what they do," he said to himself, dismayed. Dope trafficking going on right in his
own backyard, so to speak. There was a time when
the nose candy had him down to 120 pounds, with
barely the strength to hold his horn to his lips. He
knew what evil blow caused. Praise Jesus, he was
saved now. But there were all those others, in mortal
danger because they were ignorant of what could
happen to them, unwashed in the Blood as well.

Wolfdaddy went back into his shack and emerged
again with his thinking cap, the mirror-studded top
hat. He got down on both sore knees and looked up,
seeing nothing but blackness, no trace of the heavenly light that would lead him, some rain in his face.

"What is it *I* ought to do, Lord?" he asked,
humble in his need for guidance.

Wink and Tom Paul got out of the pickup and Tom
Paul lifted the croker sack with the cottonmouth wa-
ter moccasin in it from the truck bed. They walked
down the road toward the house on Lostman's Bayou,
Tom Paul holding the sack nearly at arm's length.
The snake was quiet.

A flashlight aimed at the road went on and off a

couple of times, shining through the slow rain. They came up on Carl, who was wearing foul-weather gear from his boat.

"What have you got in the sack?"

Tom Paul obligingly gave him a look.

"Jesus," Carl said, backing away, "won't that thing kill him?"

"Nobody hardly ever dies from a cottonmouth bite," Tom Paul said. "Diamondback rattler, that's different. They got beaucoup poison. But this one bite him, guarantee he'll be low sick for a while."

Wink said, looking at the lit-up grounds, "He's in the RV? What about those damn floodlights?"

Carl took a remote control handset from inside his slicker and shut the lights off.

"That'll take care of the alarms too?"

Carl nodded. "Everything. I'm going back to the house. You don't need me. Tomlin's taking a shower, at least he was a minute ago."

"That's perfect," Wink said. The men separated, Wink and his *cousin* continuing on in the dark toward the RV parked by the carriage house.

In Tony's room Big Dog lifted his head suddenly, and after listening for a few moments got up, showing surprising agility for his size. Tony was snoozing peacefully in the bed, on his side, not having budged an inch since his mother had tucked him in. The Magic Ring and his blue Navy cap with *Lexington* on it in block white letters were on the night table. Big Dog looked at him, but there was no use whining at Tony. He went to the door and began scratching anxiously, although it wasn't his bladder that had aroused him. Usually Anita heard him and came to let him out for a run. But tonight she wasn't in her room. She'd had a creative inspiration and had gone to the studio to work.

Wink Evergood went around to the other side of the RV to check if Tomlin was still in the shower. He was. Singing. Doing a pretty good job of sounding like Waylon. "Mamas don't let your babies grow up to be cowboys." Wink hurried back to join Tom Paul, who had tried the door and found it to be unlocked.

"Okay," he whispered.

Tom Paul picked up the croker sack he had left on the slab, opened the door, stepped up softly into the RV so as not to rock it and give his presence away. He dumped the water moccasin out of the sack. The snake just lay there, not much darker than the carpeting, lumpish and disoriented; from a few feet away it would look like a big cow flop. Tom Paul didn't worry about the sluggishness. Snake, he'd warm up and get moving, look for a shadowy place to hide in. Tom Paul put the sack over one shoulder, hearing Tomlin more clearly as the shower was turned off. Then he stepped out of the RV and quietly closed the door.

For about half an hour Anita had been working, from photographs, on the figure of an egret, not getting the head right and sore at herself because of it. She had stopped glancing at the monitor so frequently as she became absorbed and then frustrated. When she backed off from the framework she had constructed for the clay bird she saw that the TV screen was dark; but the monitor still seemed to be working. While she was staring at it, getting a little worried, the lights came on again around the veranda and the picture, in spite of the rain and some mist, improved. Anita sighed. She looked from the monitor to her egret, decided not to try to do any more tonight, and began cleaning her hands. Her right hand ached. All of the unaccustomed driving had been a strain. She still had only about 60 percent of the full function of her hand. The little finger would be forever weak, nearly useless. She had a total of fourteen steel pins and screws of varying size in her bones, most of them up and down the right side. On damp, chill days she sometimes felt like she was 104 years old, not 34. There was a plate two inches square near the hairline where the slight indentation didn't show unless she pulled her hair severely back. The activity of the part of her brain that was destroyed had been duplicated by another part of the brain, all those extra cells pitching in like little soldiers. She still had permanently numb spots on the cheekbone below her right eye, on the inside of her right forearm. There were two toes she couldn't feel any more; when she was extremely tired she often limped. One heavy blow from a speeding car driven by a maniac. If he had hit her head-on, well.

Looking in a full-length mirror in favorable light, she could see that she still had a very nice body. But her emotions demanded that she feel deformed, an untouchable. She didn't look that often into mirrors any more.

Anita lit a cigarette and turned off the studio lights. She didn't know what to do with herself then, but it was a cinch she wouldn't get to sleep tonight unless she bombed her remaining brain cells with a tranquilizer. No, thanks. Carl was home; he'd looked in on her while she was working, his face ruddy with good cheer, a satisfaction he didn't attempt to explain. He asked her how the day had gone and she said, Fine, Carl, Tony had a real good time. He told Anita he was going to stick around, for a change, how about a drink later? In the meantime he would just check the computer, see if there was anything new..

Anything new. That was one way to put it.

After his shower Tomlin pulled on a long-sleeved chamois shirt, a pair of Levi's and his docksiders. He made his way slowly and by touch to the midcabin area of the RV, opened the refrigerator and took out a Miller's. He had left the TV controller on the dinette table, but had to feel around for it. When the TV was on he sat down on the sofa, opened his beer and took a swig. He thought about the day they'd had, his own feelings about being aboard a carrier again after a year away. Not as hard to take as he'd anticipated, because Anita and Tony were there with him.

Watching Tony all day, he'd come to understand why so many pilots had to get out after a few years, unable to take the long separations from their wives and kids.

He tuned into a pro basketball game on the SuperStation, the Celtics going against the Rockets. He listened to the game, but in the dark his mind was on Anita. She had one of those shaggy haircuts that, windblown, was all the more becoming. How long would it take to count all the flecks of gold in her dark brown eyes? He wondered why, after laughter, she pulled back so quickly, into reticence, a sad introspection. He wondered everything about Anita, and knew very little. But he wasn't going to let much more time go by without making a sincere effort to find out what she was all about.

Meanwhile, how about another beer?

Anita had come out onto the veranda and was standing by the glider that hung from the roof near the right angle which the veranda made with the front and the side of the house. Finishing her cigarette slowly, a little bit of breezy moisture in her face and hair. Not enough rain to hear it falling. She was looking at the RV, at the light the television screen cast on the swept-back windshield, a jumpy light like a ghost in a bottle. Two more puffs, she would go in and talk to Carl, probably open the verdicchio di Villa Bucci, the last bottle she'd hoarded for so long.

That's when she heard the piercing cry from Tomlin in the recreation vehicle, a cry that drove a spear of ice from the nape of her neck to her bowels, and caused her to singe the back of one hand with the cigarette she was holding in the other.

CHAPTER
FIFTEEN

"Clay? Clay!"

Anita snatched open the door of the RV and went in wet, having slipped on the slick grass of the lawn getting over there. She didn't see Tomlin inside.

"Clay, what happened?"

The toilet flushed; he came out of the bathroom to her left with a hand up so he wouldn't bump his nose against something. He looked surprised.

"Anita, what's the matter?"

"What do you mean what—" She choked, she couldn't breathe. She turned to a club chair and slumped in it, staring at him, wiping at her rain-slicked face. "I heard you yell."

"Did I?" he said, puzzled. "Yeah, I must have. That rookie guard on the Rockets hit a three-pointer to hang the Celtics out to dry."

"Is *that* all? You scared the, the—"

"Shit out of you?" He paused in the kitchen, leaning against a cabinet. A slight grin on his face.

Furious, Anita sat up straight, then began to see how ridiculous it was and choked again, this time with laughter. "Not . . . quite. I don't think."

Tomlin felt for the refrigerator door, and opened it. "Long as you dropped by, how about a beer?"

"Okay." She couldn't sit still so she got up, and went toward him. "I'd like to use the bathroom."

"So I did—"

"No, you *didn't*, and don't be funny, I got a little wet—from the rain—and I want to borrow a towel."

"Sure, help yourself." He straightened, beer in hand, and closed the refrigerator door. She had to go sideways in the narrow kitchen space to squeeze by him, but they still made considerable contact. "Still raining, huh?" he said, humid hair brushing under his chin.

"Yeah."

In the bathroom she took a hand towel from a rack to blot her face and hair. Mirrors everywhere on the nice-looking oak cabinets, she saw herself from several demanding angles at once. Good thing *he* couldn't see what she looked like right now. When she returned up front Tomlin was sitting on the couch next to the lamp table, on which he had placed her beer in a cork holder. She took it and sat opposite him in one of the leather club chairs, feeling cozy, no light except for the flickering TV screen, very tall men in short pants flinging themselves at each other. He had turned the sound off.

"So basketball is your favorite sport," she said, inept as usual at getting a conversation going. Particularly when she was absolutely certain they both knew they didn't want to talk, and she still had this good buzz on from fright or, no, it wasn't fright any more. She had a swallow of beer, staring at him in the meager light.

"Yeah, basketball. And I like Australian rules football."

"You do? I guess I don't know what that is."

He didn't explain. He didn't say anything at all, for the time it took him to drink at least half a can of beer. Anita slipped her flats off and tucked her feet under her in the chair, which had a tendency to swivel. She didn't take her eyes off him.

"Hi, Anita," he said, after quite a while.

"Hi," she said timidly.

"Is your name really Anita?"

That startled her; a little of the beer she was drinking went down the wrong way, but she managed not to cough.

"Of course. Why?"

"So you're Anita," Tomlin said in a mild tone of voice, "and the boy is Tony and the guy's name is Carl. But Carl's not your husband, and he's not Tony's father. So what is he, exactly?"

Santa Maria, she thought, here it comes. And knew she was grateful, it had begun to be a burden whenever she was around him.

"You might say—he's somebody who looks after us."

"Federal witness protection program?"

"No. It's nothing like that."

"Then why are you hiding down here in Lostman's Bayou?"

Anita sighed, trying to think just where to begin. And while she was mulling it over she saw something odd happening, although the light wasn't very good so maybe—

Anita got up slowly, beer in hand, the chair squeaking a little.

"Where're you going?"

She was still looking at the seat cushion next to him on the sofa. Damn it, was it moving? How could it be? She said, "Clay, don't say anything for a second, please?"

He lifted his head at a questioning angle.

"And don't move," she added.

"Why?"

"Shh." She was standing in front of him now, looking down at the sofa, at the cushion rising, was he doing it? No, he had a beer in one hand, the other on his knee.

Anita put her beer on the lamp table, reached down and picked up the sofa cushion in one neat jerk. She almost fainted.

"Dear . . . God!"

"What's the matter?" Tomlin asked her.

"Snake. Huge. It's next to you."

"How close?" he asked, as if she'd been talking about a housefly, not a reptile.

"It's—real close."

"Okay, okay, I'm not moving. Don't do anything to upset the snake."

"Upset *it*—"

"Anita," Tomlin said, "there's a bolo knife in the cabinet drawer next to the stove. Just back off slowly, open the drawer, and take the knife out."

There was a lot of tension in his face, but he was maintaining his poise, keeping very still. His attitude gave her the courage to do what he'd asked of her. On the way to the knife, which was a lot like a machete, she discarded the sofa cushion.

He heard the cabinet drawer open. "Do you see it?"

"Y-yes."

"What does the snake look like?"

"Sort of—a muddy brown color, the light's not so—" In her fear her speech was slurring badly.

"What's it doing?"

"Lying next to you."

"Head up or down?"

"Up." Anita was holding the bolo in both hands, which were shaking. She moved cautiously back toward Tomlin. Knowing the snake was aware of her. Knees trying to lock. Snake eyes like Angeleyes, she felt toxically cold.

"About forty-five degrees?"

"Uh-huh."

"Probably a cottonmouth," he said. "How much room do I have?"

"Its head is—a foot from your side. Maybe a little more."

"Move down here to my left. Don't stand in front of me."

"Okay."

"As soon as I'm out of the way, cut the snake in half with that bolo."

"Clay, you can't possibly move fast enough—"

"I've got moves even this snake hasn't seen. Just be ready."

"I—can't," she said. But she didn't back off. Her mended bones were electrified by eyelight, edgy beneath her skin; she felt a gritty change in her blood even before Tomlin encouraged her.

"Yes, you can. What's it doing now?"

"It's—quiet—"

"I think you're still a little too close, from the sound of your voice. Take another step out of the way, all right?"

"Yes." And she moved with an ease that surprised her.

"Here we go," Tomlin said, looking relaxed, his tone of voice casual. He smiled slightly, as if he might be enjoying himself. Then, as quick as she could blink, he wasn't sitting there any more, the RV rocked on its wheels as he lunged into the club chair and hit the wall with a protective forearm. The cottonmouth had struck, its head was under the lamp on the table, it was starting to coil rapidly when she stepped in with a strong downstroke and beheaded it, the sharp blade of the bolo sticking in the tabletop. She let go of it and turned away, hands over her mouth.

"Anita?"

She took a sobbing breath and grabbed him with both hands to keep her balance. "Chopped its head off. But it's still moving." She looked in fascination at the thrashing of the headless body on the sofa, blood spotting everything.

"Don't go near it," he warned her. "Don't touch the head, it could still bite you." She had no intention of leaving him. She had torn two buttons off his shirt. He had her face in his hands, which were cold from perspiration.

"It didn't strike you?"

"Missed by a whisker. Less."

"I killed it," she said, still amazed. Tears made seams down her cheeks. Thrilled and frantic, she kept trying for better handholds, bumping him around. "I didn't think I could, but I did, I killed it."

"Stop shaking," he said. "I've got you."

"I know," Anita said. "What are you going to do about it?"

Fifteen minutes later, on the queen-sized bed in the back of the RV, Anita, half in ecstasy and half in doubt, said, "I can't."

"Yes, you can," Tomlin said, and went on with what he was doing, a perfectionist when it came to removing any and all doubts forever.

CHAPTER
SIXTEEN

After several hours in Baldric's hack shop, the computer, dialing those numbers which Angel considered most promising, had contacted seventy-five other computers and was now dialing number 76 for him. A North Bergen exchange. Angel sat back in the spartan swivel chair and sipped some tea he had made in the kitchen, the only thing Baldric stocked, other than an unopened box of Ritz crackers, that Angel had considered touching. He wasn't that hungry anyway. His stomach had shrunk considerably while he was being drip-fed at Silver Birches.

It was a characteristic of his mental processes that he was not easily distracted by memory; he had almost no capacity for daydreaming. And it was difficult for him to recall anything that had no bearing on his immediate needs. He had been confined to Silver Birches for eighteen months, but now that he was out it was as if the institution had ceased to exist. He would remember it only if he saw it again.

He was without guilt or remorse. He knew caution but rarely experienced fear. He killed in frenzies that were more like seizures than expressions of rage; he killed to enhance the possibilities of survival. He killed because it was time to kill. The impulses that prompted a murderous outburst were like two frayed, highly charged wires wavering back and forth in a dark space of his limited, primitive emotions. When the naked ends of the wires came together, he was galvanized. Bump into him on the subway, and Angel might look blankly at you, not give it a thought. Or the wires might touch and flash.

A message was appearing on the high-resolution monitor in front of him. Angel paid strict attention.

> *WARNING!*
> *THIS SYSTEM IS PROTECTED*
> *BY DETECTION AND*
> *TRACER EQUIPMENT.*
> *FAILURE TO ENTER*
> *THE PROPER USER ID*
> *WITHIN THIRTY SECONDS*
> *MAY RESULT*
> *IN YOUR ARREST*
> *AND PROSECUTION.*

Angel hitched forward in his chair and tapped out on the keyboard, SORRY. GOOD DAY. The monitor went blank. He waited while the automatic dialer contacted computer number 77, from a list of 229 which Angel had compiled from a printout of every computer telephone number in three counties. The shower was dripping in the bathroom across the hall, but he had forgotten about the body in the tub. As long as it stayed wet, the body wouldn't be an affront to him for at least two more days. Angel watched the monitor and ate a Ritz cracker. He drank some tea.

CHAPTER
SEVENTEEN

Twilight.

A hell of a lot of birds seemed to be having a good time out there.

Tomlin didn't feel so bad himself, with Anita close to him and breathing deeply in sleep.

He hadn't turned the heater on last night, but they shared a big down-filled comforter and each other's skin. When his fingertips lightly traced the tributary scar on her right forearm she moved closer to him, face at his throat. Enthralled by anatomy, he went on tracing: an ear, the line of her jaw, the bridge of her nose. All the planes of her face—nothing indefinite, softening, or weak there. Nothing he wanted to change. Not the thickness of her brows, nor a provocative overbite, nor the little bunching of muscle at each corner of her mouth. He hadn't seen the scars on her back and one hip yet, but he had felt them in the night, hard to the touch like sap leaked from a smooth, young tree. That he would like to change, he thought, for her sake.

"What are you doing?" Anita said softly, pleased that he was doing it. And she nipped at a finger, the bite changing almost instantly to a full-lipped caress.

"Can't wait to see you," Tomlin confessed.

"Not enough light yet?"

"About another half hour."

"Then you'll be able to see me." She had a fit of shudders. Under the comforter Tomlin put an arm around her waist and she slid a leg luxuriously over his, snuggling to his elevated penis, slick as bait. "Did you wake up like that?"

"I did," he said, pleased with his potency. Loverman.

She stroked him; chummy, not ready yet to prompt another round. "It really did happen."

"Three times."

"I hope," she said, a certain severity in her tone, "that you're not going to turn out to be one of those men who keep score."

"Not even when I play golf. Especially when I play golf."

Anita kissed each of his eyes, ravishingly. "That's for not paying attention when I wanted to jump and run. I must have had you a little crazy."

"Once I got you on your back it went okay."

She tweaked his earlobe. "I guess you know we've opened a can of worms, don't you?"

"I wouldn't put it exactly that way. What's it all about, Anita? Where's Tony's father?"

She tensed; he babied her until she was all smiles, but still furtively worried.

"I don't want to explain that now. I just want to

go on feeling—really great about waking up, for a change. The trouble is, I'm almost afraid to try again with you, because how could it be as good as it was last time?"

"Never complain in advance," he said, kissing her, his hands on her breasts.

"Clay? I'm afraid I'm a little sore. Until last night it had been a very long time. So would you just hold me, not get me going again?"

"Sure."

"Feel my heart beating? That's what you do to me. I want to tell you something. Last night—well, I—I came right away, soon as you put it in me. I was so shocked, I didn't want you to know. Something else. I never wanted to talk about sex with a man before. I was always too embarrassed. I never said 'fuck me' before. But I can say anything to you, can't I? That's how good I feel, how much I trust you. God, I'm babbling. How long have I known you? A couple of days?"

"I knew you as soon as you walked in the other day. And shook hands. Left-handed. I felt—"

"Sorry?"

"Needed. *Was* it an automobile accident?"

"Sort of." Tomlin felt her shying from him again, although not physically. "I promise we'll talk about—everything. Later. But what can we do today? Could we go somewhere?"

"Mace Lefevre offered me the use of his boat, anytime."

"Perfect."

"The light's getting a little better in here."

"See me now?"

"Not quite. Not as well as I want to."

"Thank God for the sun," she said. "It's—like an evil spell, isn't it? Nightfall, the witching hour. 'When Churchyards yawne, and hell it selfe breathes out contagion to this world.'"

"You did some acting? What's that from?"

"*Hamlet*. I wasn't an actress. I taught Shakespeare at Rutgers before I was married."

"You're full of surprises."

"Lovely, lovely surprises." She kissed him, once, twice, the third time with a lot of action behind it. By then she was on top of him.

"Thought you were sore."

"I am," she groaned. "So—you know—would you—with your tongue—"

"Delighted." But first he held her very tight. "Do you love me?" he asked her.

Anita hit him in the ribs and under the chin with a knee and then an elbow as she fought to get out of the bed.

"Don't, don't, don't *ever* say that to me!"

Tomlin sat up, stunned, seeing her dimly, crouched against the door of the bedroom, breathing harshly.

"Anita?" She didn't answer him. He heard her sob. He got out of bed carefully. She didn't run away. "Should I say it first? Okay—I love you, Anita."

Shuddering, crying, she came back into his arms like a lost child.

"It was what *he* used to say. Just before he would do s-something terrible to me."

"Not just another bad marriage."

"Bad, no, Lord: it was the whole nine yards. I am so *scared*. I need to use the bathroom. And I'd better take a shower."

"We'll take a shower."

"All right. That would be nice, bathing with you.
Clay. Oh, Clay. What am I going to do?"

Her sobs were like explosive hiccups. He did his
best to soothe her, but she just had to wring out the
fear alone. One last convulsion and she was calmer,
slack in his arms.

"What kind of guy *is* he?"

Now barely breathing, Anita said, "Angel is—hell
itself."

Tomlin anchored the *Shady Lady IV* in nine feet of
water on Mississippi Sound, near one of the buoys
that marked the inshore limit of Dog Keys Pass. A
nice grassy bottom there, and plenty of shade to
attract tripletails, also called blackfish. He'd seen his
father pull twenty-pounders from the water in this
location, too much fish for Tony to handle by himself. They shared an eight-foot casting rod, using a
jig sweetened with fresh shrimp. Blackfish were a
tough catch, but if one hit, it was bound to be plenty
exciting.

They did their casting on the shadow side of the
big buoy, floating the jig in upcurrent so it would
drift slowly toward the shade, which was a likely
place for blackfish to be hanging around waiting for
smaller fish to come struggling their way in the
strong eddy.

After twenty minutes of casting, with Tony getting
bored but not complaining yet, they hooked one.

From the way the Ambassadeur reel was singing,
and the fact that the fish headed straight for the
underside of the buoy, Tomlin knew they had at least
a ten-pound tripletail on the line, and he might go a

couple of pounds more. The fish was using his weight to try to drag and break the line over the rough surface of a mooring cable. But Tomlin had loaded fifty-pound test on the reel, and he hauled the blackfish away from the buoy, explaining exactly what they were doing, and what the fish was trying to do to get away, to the excited boy.

"We have to keep him out from under the buoy and play him around until he gets tired. Let's take up a little more line now, get him moving southwest in the current. Can't snatch him in all at once, even line this strong will break. Are your arms tired?"

"I'm okay!"

"We'll see him in a minute. He won't do much jumping, he'll just bear down and try to use his power like an arm-wrestler. Take up line and set the drag. Thatta boy, you know something, we're gonna land this one!"

"Yeah!"

"Anything I can do?" Anita said, enjoying the moment, a hand lightly on Tony's shoulder.

"Get the net," Tomlin said, now working the big fish carefully toward the port side of the transom.

"Hey, there he is!"

Tomlin also caught a glimpse of the blackfish shimmering a couple of feet below the surface of the pass, using all the power of his slab-sided body to throw the hook. After fifteen minutes of gradually maneuvering the fish to the boat, Tomlin got the net on him.

Anita took their picture with the blackfish, using a Polaroid camera Mace Lefevre kept on board. Tomlin moved the *Shady Lady IV* closer to Ship Island, dropped anchor over a flat that was likely to be harboring small fish and gave Tony, now a confirmed angler, a smaller pole for fishing over the side while he and Anita had a couple of cold beers in the saloon.

"You're good with Tony."

"I just try to remember what it was like when I was about his age."

"Most people can't do that. Or they don't want to remember."

She was trying to get around to the subject that was bothering both of them; she'd move up to it like a blackfish sniffing bait, then veer quickly away and run, turn and study the bait from a distance. Finally, after failing to find a chair that was comfortable, then getting up and walking around and looking out to see how her son was, Anita spoke.

"I suppose Angel is a genius. You wonder where it comes from. A hundred years ago everyone in our families kept goats and had a few olive trees or a wineshop in town, and tried to survive the blood feuds. There's a cruel streak in our people, of course. And a kind of fatalism that goes with being on a small rock in a big sea. The cruelty gets passed on. I haven't seen any sign of it in Tony yet, but who knows?"

"You're Sicilian?" Tomlin said.

"We all are. Angel was born Dominic Barzatti. My family name is Morecante, and Carl's is Buffano. Jeffords is just a cover name."

Tomlin nodded. After a long silence Anita came and sat down next to him. He held her hand.

"Where did you meet your husband?"

"I've known Angel almost all of my life. We're related other than by marriage. Third cousins. We'd

run into each other when we were kids, at the really
big family weddings. And funerals. Just hello, how
are you, what've you been up to? We never dated. I
seldom went out with boys in high school, my father
was very strict. He didn't think I needed to go to
college. He wanted his daughters around the house to
wait on him and make him happy. My other sisters
married young. I promised to shave my head if Papa
didn't let me accept my scholarship to St. John's. My
father barely spoke to me for two years because I'd
threatened to dishonor him. When I did well at school
I think he was proud, although he never let on to me.
Sicilians are clever, but they aren't deep thinkers and
they don't have a high regard for scholars, which
they assume is a waste of brainpower. Also there
isn't much money in teaching school. Now Angel—he
was smart in a way that proved to be useful to his
family. Computers. I suppose Angel is a genius. He
has to be one of the top programmers in the world.''

''How did you two get together?''

''I was working on my Ph.D. at Princeton. Angel
was living there too, in the town. He was employed
by one of those small but prestigious companies,
funded with government money, that are doing re-
search on the far edge of super-computer technology.
I never even pretended to understand what he was up
to. We ran into each other one night, at Houlihan's
or Ruby Tuesday or one of those places. I had a date,
he was with a couple of colleagues. We hadn't seen
each other, maybe it was six or seven years. Something seemed to happen; he'd matured, filled out, I
don't know. I was attracted and I guess he was too,
he called me up a couple of nights later. Six months

after that we got married. My mistake was, I didn't go to bed with him first.''

"Why was that a mistake?" Tomlin said, more or less to keep her talking, because he knew what the answer had to be.

"Because—after the first flush of the honeymoon, which followed one of those ostentatious Catholic weddings, which my father was thrilled to pay for, I—I just didn't like doing it with Angel. I wasn't a virgin by a long shot, I'd had it good and I'd had it bad, but I never had it before where I just couldn't seem to *care*. Am I making sense?"

"You didn't love him."

"Yeah," she said forlornly. "My first rational thought after that extravagant wedding was, 'Oh, shit, what have you done?' I suppressed it as long as I could. Until after Tony was born."

"Why get married in the first place?"

"I had been madly in love with a bright guy who was a total flake. He made a lot of demands on me, in a charming way, but he was absolutely irresponsible. I cried a lot over good old Bill until I finally had the guts to cut him loose, and I guess at least a pound of my flesh went with him. So painful, that kind of love affair. Then Angel happened, at the opportune moment. Another bright guy, which is a must with me, but solid, dependable, serious—and family. Somebody I could really talk to. That was the trouble. He was a fantastic listener, or so I thought, but he just didn't have anything to talk about himself, except computers. He wasn't at all interested in what was going on in the world, or even a mile down the road. He never watched TV. He read nothing but technical stuff. He played a lot of handball to stay in shape, and worked forty-eight-, sixty-hour shifts at a time. When we were together I talked and talked; I thought the relationship was wonderful but I was just entertaining myself.''

"Did he love you?''

"What was love to Angel? The sex act bothered him. He'd wash and wash afterward, like it was a kind of penance. But he kept coming back for more, and getting more and more out of control, like a car racing 120 miles an hour but with no driver. Does that make sense? He worked at sex like he worked at his computer, as if he was faced with a problem he needed to codify so he could program it. Until I had to tell him, no, no way, I'm pregnant, we can't do it again until after the baby comes.''

"He listened to you?''

"The prostitutes started then. Pickups, night after night, or on his lunch break; ten minutes here, an hour there. I'm certain now that Angel never had any sex before we were married. I don't think he ever— that he knew how to—jack off. It was that bad. But once he'd had me the urge, the drive, just went out of control. Then Tony was born. I think Angel was really frightened, somehow, to have Tony in the house. What do babies do? They cry for food and spit up and fill their diapers. The—the absolute uncontrollable messiness of it drove Angel wild. There was a stretch where he didn't come home very often. That was all right with me. By then I was scared of him. I'd seen Angel in the bathroom looking at a sore on his penis. And the expression in his eyes, such horror and disgust—man, did I handle it badly. I blew up at him. How could he do such a thing to us, he was never going to touch me again, and so forth,

a real wop wingding. He broke down and cried, the
tears were gushing. I think something broke in him that
night, that he couldn't fix. He wasn't the same man
afterward. I'd always been able to get in touch with
Angel before, find at least a hint of feelings. But the
wild crying sterilized him. All human feeling stopped.
And the killings began.''

"Good God," Tomlin said. Her grip on his hand
was so fierce it hurt. And she wasn't naturally
left-handed.

"My fault, my fault," Anita moaned. "If I'd just
let him alone, if we hadn't met—he had his life
straight up, he was doing okay, and I—"

"Anita, cut it. Who did Angel kill?"

"A kid prostitute. Maybe the same one who dosed
him, he never told me."

"But he told you what he'd done?"

"In detail. I didn't believe him. I thought he was
having some kind of breakdown, hallucinating. I was
scared, of course. But it was nothing compared to the
scare I got when he went out and did it again, and
brought me a videotape of himself, mounted on some
whore like a dog while he broke her neck.''

Tomlin didn't say anything this time. The *Shady
Lady IV* rocked in the swell from another boat passing through the channel nearby. Tony continued to
fish patiently from the cockpit. Anita picked at polish
flaking from a thumbnail, her lips white.

"So you called the police?"

"This is the part you're not going to understand
too well.''

"Tell me anyway."

"He was—horribly, horribly sick, that's obvious,
isn't it? And—in Angel's family, nobody ever called

the cops, unless a favor was needed, or there was a payoff to arrange."

"Mafia?"

"It's the word everyone uses, but not in the *Fratellanza*."

"I don't know anything about gangsters."

"The generic name is wise guys. Never mind, I'll educate you later. If there is a later."

Tomlin just looked at her. "I don't think you're any part of it."

"No, I'm not and I never was. Anyway, when I started to get over the shock I got in touch with Angel's grandfather. His father is dead, and his mother—well, she's a woman, that's all, and only the don could deal with Angel now. Don Aldo Barzatti. He's the head of the most powerful of the families in this country, *capo di tutti capi*, known and respected everywhere in the world. The Barzatti family owns fifty-four percent of my father's import business, which is something I found out only after I was married to Angel; he punched it up on the computer one night. I suppose the don was the only one who would loan Papa any money when he was struggling to support a large family with a little grocery store."

"So you called the don, and—"

"He said he would be delighted to see me, at this little cafe on Mulberry Street where he used to hang out. Angel and I were living near New Brunswick then, in New Jersey, I was teaching at the University. I drove into the city for my appointment with the don, and we sat at a table in the back where the flies weren't so bad and drank bitter coffee and I told him everything."

"You had the tape with you?"

"Angel erased it right after he showed it to me."

"So you couldn't prove he'd murdered those women. Did the don believe you?"

"I don't think so, but he was shocked. I guess he had ways of finding out about the prostitute on the tape. He patted my hand and wiped my cheeks. He said he would have a talk with Dominic, and not to worry. Don't *worry*! Like hell, I packed up Tony and went home to Brooklyn. Which is where Angel caught up with us four nights later, I suppose right after he and the don had their chat."

"Caught up with you?"

"My sister Roseanne and I took the kids to King's Plaza to shop. There was Tony and me and her two girls. Roseanne drove. It was July. A Thursday night, the mall was crowded. After we shopped we decided to walk a couple of blocks to her father-in-law's restaurant on Avenue R to say hello and get the kids a Coke. It wasn't dark yet. A lot of traffic on Flatbush Avenue, a lot of people on the sidewalk. Angel must have been double-parked outside the exit to the parking garage, or maybe he was on his way to the mall and saw us walking. He was driving our other car, a gray Subaru. I was on the outside of the sidewalk, holding Tony's hand, talking to Roseanne. She stopped for a few seconds to look at something in a store window. Maternity wear, I think, Roseanne's always pregnant. Angel gunned the Subaru, cut off another car in the inside lane and jumped the curb. It was the squealing of brakes that saved us. I turned around, recognized our car—maybe I had a glimpse of his face behind the windshield, I don't know. What I'm telling you is still fuzzy in my mind, and it was seven

months after the fact before I began to remember any
of it.

"My first thought must have been Tony. I had him
by the hand and I just yanked him with all my
strength toward Roseanne, it's a miracle I didn't pull
his arm out of the socket. Angel scraped the Subaru
against the side of a lamp pole, which deflected his
aim a little bit, and I took one or two steps out of the
way before the Subaru hit me. I remember seeing
Roseanne's face a split second before the impact. She
was just starting to scream. Then I went flying.
Everything I'm telling you now I was told later. They
were winding up the awning at the fruit stand next to
the maternity shop. It was sort of folded, like an
accordion, seven feet above the sidewalk. I hit that,
bounced off, plowed through all the peaches and
pears and zucchini piled up in baskets outside the
store and rolled into the gutter. If I'd hit anything
else except the awning—plate glass, a brickfront—
that would have been the end. Bad enough as it was.
About a third of my scalp was torn away. I had a
hole in my palate. I was doing some serious bleeding
and my brains were on the curb. Tony thought I was
dead; he went into shock, the kind you die from.
Angel must have figured I was dead too. He drove
off. Nobody wrote down the license number. Roseanne saw who it was, but she kept her mouth shut."

"What happened to Angel?"

"The don had him picked up. Angel had no explanation. He pretended it hadn't happened. Maybe he
didn't remember. While he was talking to Don Aldo
again he had a catatonic seizure. I'd seen him a
couple of times just sitting for hours, staring into
space, not moving much or talking. I didn't know

what it was then, and he wouldn't see a doctor. This time they put him in a place out on Long Island. You can imagine the prognosis wasn't very optimistic.''

"What about you?"

"I had operations. Physiotherapy. Speech therapy. Psychological counseling. It was a slow recovery. I'm never going to be a hundred percent. Well, Angel broke out of the sanitarium, which wasn't all that security-conscious, found out where I was and came to visit. Don Aldo had a couple of men waiting for Angel. He should have sent ten. It took both *soldati*, three hospital guards and two squad cars full of cops the best part of half an hour to subdue him in the parking lot. Angel's not that big, but then again he isn't really human. Just what he is, I don't know. I'm not even sure why he's determined to kill me. Because I ratted on him to the don? Because I didn't share his pleasure in strangling prostitutes?''

"Do you still feel responsible for whatever Angel is?"

"Not any more. I just want a life of my own! I want something back, for what I've been through.''

"This is what you wanted? Lostman's Bayou? A full-time bodyguard, an assumed name?"

"The don thought it would be a good idea. For a while. Just in case the worst happened—again.''

They looked at each other wordlessly for a few moments.

"Did it?" Tomlin said.

Anita nodded.

"When?"

"Three nights ago."

"What are you going to do?"

"Yesterday I wanted to run."

"What do you want today?"

"I want you," she said, looking at him a little cautiously, not pleading, but not all that optimistic.

"Clay!" Tony yelled. "I've got a bite! Another big one!"

"Hang on to that pole!" Tomlin bolted from his seat, stopped, turned back to Anita. For a moment she was bleak and frozen, meeting his eyes. He wasn't smiling. But he looked okay. He looked happy. He bent to kiss her, a quick one, but warm.

"I'll bet we can work something out," he said.

CHAPTER EIGHTEEN

Wolfdaddy was having a late lunch in the kitchen of the house on Lostman's Bayou when Tony and Tomlin came in, lugging a Styrofoam cooler with the fish they'd caught on ice. Tomlin had already cleaned and filleted the big one, which wouldn't have fitted inside the cooler otherwise.

"Opal, I caught these myself! Clay helped me hold the rod. Can we have some for dinner?"

Opal said skeptically, "You always turn up your nose at fish before. Say, 'Give me peanut butter and jelly.' "

"I know, but I *caught* these! Clay says he'll cook them on the grill, he knows how." He was holding himself between the legs and doing a little dance.

"Better go to the bathroom," Tomlin said.

"Yeah, okay. I'll see you later? Mom says I have to do some schoolwork, or else."

"See you later, Tony."

Opal was sorting through the fish filets. Wolfdaddy

got up from his lunch to have a look. "I'll freezer-
wrap most of these," Opal said. "What is this big
fish here?"

"Tripletail." Tomlin poured himself iced tea from
a pitcher. "How are you keeping, Wolfdaddy?"

"Just a joyful in the bosom of Jesus." He'd eaten
two big bowls of vegetable soup, and was working
on a corned beef sandwich.

"That's good news."

Wolfdaddy trimmed off a crust of the Italian bread,
which he had trouble chewing. "Reckon all the news
ain't good. Opal tells me how a cottonmouth got
loose in your trailer last night."

"No harm done," Tomlin said.

Wolfdaddy nodded. "Could've bit you bad, though."

"That's for sure."

"Reckon how a snake that big could've got inside,
'out you knowin'."

"Beats me. Cottonmouths don't like hanging around
the house anyway."

"I knows that." Wolfdaddy put down his sandwich, frowning. He belched, sighed, drank some tea.
"How about if it was somebody put it there on
purpose?"

Opal suddenly stopped wrapping fish, glanced at
Wolfdaddy, and headed for the laundry room.

"I don't need to hear this."

Tomlin waited until Opal was out of earshot; then
he sat down opposite Wolfdaddy, who reached for
his mirrored top hat and put it on, confirming seri-
ousness, probity.

"Who have you got in mind, Wolfdaddy?" Tomlin
asked him.

"Tell you what I seen last night, and some other

nights 'fore you come home to the bayou. Then you can draw your own conclusions.''

Carl was feeling surly when he sat down at a corner table with Wink Evergood at the Landlubber, partly because Wink was having a nice lunch and didn't look perturbed that their scheme to get Clay Tomlin off Lostman's Bayou had gone awry. And Carl had spent a restless night knowing Anita was getting it on with Tomlin. Carl had gone out in the rain when he began to wonder what was happening, and he'd come across two bloody pieces of snake outside the door of the RV. Walked around to the back then and heard them, Tomlin fucking her and Anita sounding like it was heaven. The bitch had done everything but kick him in the balls, swearing that she was never going to let another man touch her, and all the time she'd known what she really wanted. Carl kept rubbing his forehead as if he needed to make sure there weren't any horns nubbing out there. He wanted to kill Clay Tomlin, shove an anchor up his ass and drop him ten miles out in the Gulf.

"Hey," Carl said, "have a beer." He wiped clam sauce from his lower lip with a napkin.

"Pauli Girl," Carl said to the matronly waitress who had come over to the table. "Make sure it's ice cold." Nearly three o'clock, they all but had the place to themselves. It was warm out, a little hazy. A big standing fan was operating near their table, which made it easier to talk without their voices carrying to the help.

"Now what?" Carl growled at Wink.

Wink shrugged. "We've still got plenty of time.

But we'll have to get a little severe with him, since the snake idea didn't work out.''

"Don't tell me about it, just do it.''

Wink had another slice of garlic bread. The waitress brought Carl a frosted bottle of beer and a glass that didn't look too clean. He drank his beer from the bottle.

"Like the old saying," Wink told him, "If you're lucky, it's okay to have sawdust for brains.''

"There's nothing dumb about Tomlin. That's what has me worried.''

Outside a car came to a hard sliding stop in the parking lot. Wink tilted back a little in his chair and glanced through the front window but didn't see anything. He turned his full attention to the linguini that was left on his plate. Carl brooded. His back was to the Landlubber's front door. He couldn't see Clay Tomlin when he came in and looked around. They weren't hard to find. Tomlin headed straight for their table, carrying a brown paper sack in one hand.

When he was a few steps away Wink looked up, chewing; he swallowed hard in surprise before he was able to smile.

"Hey, what'ya say, man?''

Tomlin didn't say anything. Carl looked around and scooted his chair back a few inches. The breeze from the standing fan flicked his necktie across his chest. He stared at Tomlin, who didn't look at him.

Tomlin pulled a quart bottle of Jack Daniel's from the sack, set it down beside Wink's plate. Wink's mouth twitched; he didn't understand.

"What's that for?''

Tomlin said, "For breaking your jaw again, asshole.''

Wink didn't need a handwritten invitation. He was quick coming up out of his chair but Tomlin had anticipated this, and before Wink could move on him Tomlin diverted him by kicking him hard in the ankle. Then he kicked him in the knee. When Wink started to buckle and his hands dropped, Tomlin jabbed and then crossed, hitting Wink on the jaw where he knew the bone was glass; sure enough the jawbone snapped audibly and Wink sat down stunned, almost knocking over the big fan. He wasn't going to fight with a lame knee and a busted jaw. He just sat there breathing hard while Carl wrestled Tomlin away from the table, pinning his arms behind his back; they crashed into another table, upsetting it.

"The next thing I break is your lease, Carl," Tomlin told him, struggling to get free; but Carl had him just right, with a punishing grip on one wrist.

"Take it easy; you gone crazy?"

At the front of the restaurant the proprietress grabbed the receiver of the wall telephone, yelling over her shoulder, "You all quit that damn scufflin'! I'm callin' the po-lice!"

Carl let Tomlin go immediately, shook his cuffs out of his coat sleeves, straightened his tie, and walked over to the woman with a friendly smile.

"No need to do that. Just a little disagreement, it's all settled now. I'll get them out of here." He had his wallet in his hands. "Hundred dollars take care of this for you?"

Wink got up slowly, hands on the back of a chair for support, his right foot not touching the floor. He grimaced. He looked at Tomlin, still a little surprised, then hobbled painfully away, grunting. He bumped into a table and nearly fell. His jaw was beginning to swell. He went past Carl with his head down, the leg that Tomlin had kicked still not bearing his weight very well.

"Hospital," he muttered.

Carl gave the proprietress two fifty-dollar bills and went outside. Tomlin put the bottle of whiskey back in the sack and followed them.

"And don't none of you come back!" the proprietress called after him.

Carl was putting Wink into his Mercedes. "I want to talk to you," Tomlin said.

Carl hesitated, then came over to him.

"You figure this out?" Tomlin asked.

Carl gestured indifferently, keeping both hands up in case Tomlin wanted to start something with him. Tomlin's face was flushed.

"So, you got something against Wink. That have anything to do with me?"

"It has to do with running shipments of dope to my dock at night."

Carl cocked his head to one side and smiled in disbelief.

"You want to deny it?"

"Deny what? I didn't hear anything I need to deny."

"Try it this way. How about that don you work for? What would he do if he got the idea you've been smuggling coke in from Mexico and banking the profits for yourself?"

He hadn't known if it was true or not, that part about Carl being in business on the side and cutting out his employer, but when Carl tried blandly to stare him down, something gave in his face; his shoulders dropped.

"Anita has a runny mouth," he said sulkily. "That doesn't mean I know anything about any goddamned dope."

Tomlin said heatedly, "Leave her out of this. I hope like hell you've left her out of this."

Carl shrugged. "So that's where it is with you two."

"That's where it is."

"I guess I should have seen it coming. Look at it this way, maybe you're just taking advantage of her situation, the way she is right now. But I'm the one who really matters to Anita, whether she wants to admit it or not." Carl was breathing a little hard, getting angry. "For what it's worth to you, Anita's squeaky clean."

"Yeah, thanks. I want you off my place. By tonight."

"Shit," Carl said disgustedly. But he didn't like the look on Tomlin's face, and he needed to be cautious about a man who had tuned up Wink Evergood so efficiently. "Okay, I could move down to the boat for a while if you insist—"

"What I said was, *off* the place. Get far away from Lostman's Bayou."

"You don't understand something. I can't just go away and leave Anita and Tony. Didn't she tell you—"

"About her wacko husband? She did. So what? Take your boat and go somewhere I don't need to look at you."

"I've got a very solid lease, pal."

"Signed with a phony name."

"Guess again. Let me tell you something, Tomlin.

You're getting into trouble here that could get you killed.''

Behind them Wink Evergood opened the door of the Mercedes, leaned out and puked his lunch on the asphalt.

Tomlin said, "Outstanding, Carl. Why don't you get off the muscle? This is my hometown, the high school was named for my grandfather. You really want to find out who can fix who?''

"I didn't mean me. I meant him. Angel. Look at Anita in bed sometime. Take a look at all the scars. Angel did it to her. And that was just for practice. Don't even think about what he'll do to you, if he finds you with her.''

Wink said crossly, "Carl? Need to get this jaw wired up, man.''

Tomlin thrust the bottle of Jack Daniel's into Carl's hands and walked away to his Corvette.

"By tonight,'' he said, not looking back.

Mace Lefevre's girl Elizabeth pulled the office copy of the leases on the house at Lostman's Bayou and brought them to Mace, along with a slim file of correspondence. Mace put on reading glasses with half lenses to look them over, then handed the leases, turned to the last page, to Clay Tomlin.

"Nothing illegitimate about these, Clay. You can see right there, both the old and the new lease are in the name of the Stan-Dak Corporation of Mamaroneck, New York, and signed by legal counsel for the corporation, Franklin E. Bookhultz. The yearly rent was paid in advance, on signature.''

"This Bookhultz is a bona fide attorney?''

Mace took off his glasses and folded them, frowning. "Naturally I looked him up in the guide to the New York State bar. Old family firm. Bookhultz, Rediger, and Seaborn. Larchmont, New York. What's this all about?"

"Carl has connections with the mob. The Barzatti family, whoever they are. He's been using my property as a cover for dealing in drugs. And his name isn't really Jeffords, or did you know that?"

Mace sat down behind his desk. "Sure, I knew it. A.k.a. Carl Jeffords. Real name, Carlo Buffano."

"Well, what the hell, Mace?"

"Clay, all kinds of people use more than one name, and there's nothing wrong with that if it's done without intent to defraud. It is news to me about this family tie of his. I certainly didn't know anything about his possible involvement in drug trafficking. You have proof of that allegation, by the way?"

"Jesus Christ, Mace, who do you represent here?"

"I represent the estates of your late father and brother. I represent you, and I don't want to see you get into trouble because you're not real damn sure of what you're talking about. And, yes, I've done some fee work for Carl, lining up a real estate parcel west of town that we've just about finished drawing up the papers for."

"Let me tell you about dope, Mace. The Navy's had a real problem with it. I saw a nineteen-year-old kid working flight deck on the *Kennedy* lose both arms above the elbow when a catapult malfunctioned. I saw another kid with his head up his ass get steamed alive. Both had been sniffing coke. I lost three good pilots from my squadron in Vietnam because they were hooked. I hate dope, Mace. I want Carl the hell out of my house."

Mace just shook his head. "Not without cause. So if you have proof of what you say he's been doing—"

"Wolfdaddy had a clear view one night of the boat that came in from Mexico. Wink Evergood's boat, we saw it the other day at the marina. Wink, Carl and the boat driver off-loaded the coke into the bed of Wink's pickup truck, and covered it with a tarp. Wink drove the truck to a rendezvous near Red Creek up in the DeSoto boondocks, where a helo picked the stuff up and flew it somewhere else."

"How the hell could Wolfdaddy know all *that*?"

"By putting together what he saw with other bits and pieces. Coming back from Red Creek, Wink ran into a hard rain, and got stuck on one of those gumbo roads. He had to walk out and call for a tow the next morning. The tow truck driver is Mr. Dawlie Simms, brother-in-law of a member of Wolfdaddy's flock at the Next-Thing-to-Heaven Church. So that's how Wolfdaddy knew where the truck had been after it left Lostman's Bayou."

"So what?"

"While they were cleaning up Wink's truck at the garage where Simms works, somebody else noticed coke dust on that tarp. He knew just what it was, because he'd been a user before coming to Jesus. He took a little sample of the powder to Wolfdaddy. Then Wolfdaddy asked Dawlie Simms to go up to Red Creek, where he ran trotlines on weekends, and see what he could find out. There's no place up there to land a light plane, but room for a helo. Simms found spent flares around a patch of trampled grass, and skid marks the rain hadn't erased. End of story. Can I get Carl arrested?"

"Hell, no. Maybe the DEA would be interested in keeping an eye on him from here on, but you can't break his lease on testimony from somebody who lives in a goddamned tree and a bunch of other niggers, who probably wouldn't want to testify to begin with.''

"That's great. You still plan on doing business with Carl?''

Mace said without reluctance, "Not after what you've been telling me.''

"You haven't heard it all yet,'' Tomlin said, then filled Mace in on the snake and his encounter with Wink Evergood at the Landlubber.

"Jesus,'' Mace said, agitated. "They're probably swearing out a warrant on you this minute.''

"He and Carl have too much to hide. But the fact that they went to the trouble of dropping off that cottonmouth where they hoped I'd step on it means Carl wants to get rid of me. It might just be sexual jealousy''—Mace shot him a look but Tomlin didn't elaborate—"only I don't think that's it. They've got another shipment coming in before long, and Carl's afraid I'll be trouble for him.''

Mace thought this over. "You've been trouble, all right, really stuck your neck out. And I'm telling you, there's nothing we can go to the sheriff about.''

"You mean I have Carl whether I want him or not.''

"That's it exactly. I got to know a bit about Carl this past year, but what I know is all surface: he's affable, fits right in with all kinds of people, drives a fancy boat and a Mercedes-Benz, shoots a good game of golf. Taste in women runs to trash, that sort of thing. But he never lets you enjoy the feeling that he's somebody you can lean on. Maybe when he runs out of tricks, can't get what he has to have with smiles and gentle persuasion, he'll go big-time mean on you in a hurry.''

"That's the Carl I know," Tomlin agreed.

"Be careful," Mace Lefevre said.

CHAPTER
NINETEEN

Since leaving Don Aldo's house Angel had gone without sleep, without closing his eyes, for thirty-eight hours, when the system he'd been searching for finally announced itself on the computer monitor in Baldric's hack shop, in crypto that he was familiar with because he'd invented it.

He had another swallow of the tea that had gone cold in his cup before hitching himself closer to the keyboard to tap out a response, hesitating for a few moments, letting the code come up from wherever it was stored in the billion-odd back ways of his mind. For Angel there was pleasure in this renewal, this act of memory, the pleasure another man might feel on seeing a beautiful sunrise, or a work of art.

Then he typed his instructions in the code they hadn't bothered to change.

The scroll on the monitor disappeared, and was replaced by a single blinking word:

SHUTDOWN

Now he could take control of the system he had designed, by activating an alternative entry he had built into the basic program years ago, a command so deeply hidden not even the sharpest computer professionals could hope to find it, even if they suspected that it existed.

He waited; seven seconds.

Another word appeared.

JACKPOT

Angel typed a greeting.

ANGEL IS HOME

And the Barzatti family computer responded:

HELLO, ANGEL. WHAT CAN I DO FOR YOU?

One minute and forty seconds later Angel pushed his chair away from the keyboard and the monitor, which he left on. He got up then, stretching carefully, knee joints and backbone popping, and went into the bathroom. Water was dripping slowly onto the head of the corpse he'd left in the tub. There was a vaguely unpleasant odor in the air. Angel took a leisurely pee, relieving himself of much of the tea he'd been drinking. Then he took off his clothes and hung them on a hook on the back of the door. He stepped into the tub between the feet and spread knees of Paul Baldric and turned the shower on full.

Soaped himself with a somber air of contentment, never looking down.

When he had dried off and put his clothes back on he returned to the hack shop across the hall. He had lost track of time, and from the light filtering into the apartment it could have been either daybreak or dusk. The information he'd retrieved from the family computer was still on the monitor:

> *BARZATTI, ANITA*
> *(MORECANTE)*
> *AKA JEFFORDS*
> *LOSTMANS BAYOU, MISSISSIPPI*
> *(601) 939-6757*

The telephone number had referred him to the computer in the house on the bayou.

Angel had decided, while bathing, to send a message, and had conceived an appropriate format, although to pull it off would require a lot of work. But he wasn't in a hurry. He sat down again in the only chair in the room, legs outthrust, staring at the monitor. Soon his eyes closed and his head sagged forward. He fell deeply asleep, looking as if he'd been hypnotized.

CHAPTER
TWENTY

Carl was on the bridge of the *Lollapalooza* backing it away from the boat dock when Tomlin drove up to the house in his Corvette. Carl sounded his siren and waved, friendly and casual. Tomlin didn't wave back, just stood beside his car until Carl was on his way south to the Sound.

Tony had come out of the house when he heard the siren.

"Where's he going?"

"On a trip," Tomlin said, wondering if it was true. "You probably won't see much of Carl any more."

Tony put his hands on his hips, unconsciously emulating Tomlin, and stared at Carl's boat. "That's okay," he said. Then he looked up. "What about you?"

"This will always be home for me, Tony. Where's your mother?"

"She's working." Tony relaxed his stance. He

went down on one knee in the grass at the edge of the drive to tie a loose shoelace. "You said you might have time to teach me how to use a casting rod."

Tomlin looked at a cloud bank out on the Gulf against which the *Lolly* looked toy-sized. But the sun was still shining. "Sure, I've got time."

He put a trolling motor on one of the johnboats and they went slowly up the bayou with Tony steering; fish might be biting, Tomlin reasoned, there was no sense in wasting a practice session. His mind still half on Carl, leaving like that; no real good-bye, just a fuck-you honk of the siren, he'd be back. Maybe after he took care of business at another, prearranged point along the coast. Then, it might come down to a simple confrontation, with Anita in the middle; and maybe, Tomlin thought, Anita wouldn't want to buck Angel's family. The godfather, or whatever he was, might decide that she and Tony ought to move again. For Tony's sake, what else could she do? Tomlin's counteroffer would be weak on security. Once the sun went down she'd have to take care of *him*. But the thought of losing either one of them depressed him badly.

"Carl wasn't my dad," Tony said unexpectedly. Tomlin was behind him and couldn't see his face beneath the bill of the Navy cap.

"Yeah, I know."

"Can I try it now with a jig?"

"Okay."

"What're we fishing for?"

"Specs. Speckled trout."

"How big are those?"

"Big enough to give you a fight."

They didn't catch anything. Tony got torn up a

couple of times casting in too close to snags, but he
didn't lose his temper or act bored, he'd just turn
around to see how Tomlin was taking it. And it
occurred to Tomlin that what the boy liked most this
afternoon was sitting close to him, and being taught
something that was always going to give him pleasure. Before either of them realized how much time
had passed, it was getting dark, and Tomlin couldn't
follow the flight of the jig so well.

"I had another father once," Tony said, after forty
minutes of silence on the subject of fathers.

"I heard. Do you remember him?" Then he wished
he hadn't asked.

"No," Tony said. He opened the cooler they had
brought along and took out a can of Mountain Dew.
Tomlin helped him open the can because Tony's
hands were tired from holding the rod for so long.
They each had a drink. Tony lay back between
Tomlin's knees and rested his head against Tomlin's
breastbone. "Sometimes I do," he said, looking at
the sky. Then he said, in the same bland tone of
voice, "I'm tired."

"Me too. Lot of fishing today. And I need to be
heading in."

"Because it's the witching hour?"

"That's something I said because I didn't want to
tell you that I have a—kind of a problem."

"You can't see in the dark."

"Right. How did you figure that out?"

"Mom said so. She was talking to herself. She
thought I was asleep and couldn't hear. You can't see
anything?"

"No, not after the sun goes down. Until the next
morning."

"That must be weird. Do you get scared?"

"I've been scared, Tony," Tomlin admitted.

"I sleep with the light on. I won't let anybody turn off the light. Uh-uh." He turned up his face, which was tacky around the mouth from soda. He showed a good smile with some teeth missing. "Big Dog could be your Seeing Eye dog. I bet we could train him. Would you like that?"

"The question is, would Big Dog like it?"

"Well—you sleep most of the night anyway, don't you? So it could be worse."

"That's the way I look at it. Do you want the rest of this here Mountain Dew?"

"No, thanks. I like Sprite better. Are you going to cook the fish on the gas grill like you said?"

"I'd better leave the cooking to Opal tonight. Want to take us home now?"

Carl sat under the Bimini awning of his boat, moored away from the intercoastal waterway and the incoming traffic off the Gulf—charter boats, commercial fishermen—on the north side of Ship Island. He enjoyed a gorgeous sunset and another seven-and-seven while he continued to think about his problems.

The shipment of coke from Cancún, due about two A.M.—he and Tom Paul could handle it okay, without Wink, although the alternate rendezvous, a boatyard that was in receivership seven miles east of Port Bayonne, lacked the privacy of Lostman's Bayou that he was accustomed to. Floating debris was always a hazard, running without lights. Well, you didn't get something for nothing, an hour of icy sweat trying to see in the dark and wondering if the Coast Guard had routinely picked this night to run a check on the empty marina made the price about right. But definitely he had no intention of pushing his luck beyond tonight. It was the twilight of the coke era anyway. He knew that from information he'd picked up accessing hackers' bulletin boards on his computer. Any reasonably competent chemist could synthesize designer drugs that had a kick several thousand percent stronger than morphine; most of them weren't illegal yet and you could carry a billion dollars' worth around in a shoe box. With up to 15 percent of the population biogenetically disposed to drug addiction, designer drugs was the business of the future for an entrepreneur like himself. By dawn he'd have a total of a million six in cash packed away aboard the *Lolly*, where you'd have to tear the damn boat down to the waterline to find any of it. Next spring, a leisurely cruise to the Caymans, make the deposits in the corporate bank accounts his cousin Rollie had opened there. Then spread the money out carefully: to other banks in Panama, Curaçao, Hong Kong.

Unfortunately Carl had no way of knowing who Tomlin had spilled to, or if he'd opened his mouth at all. If he had any sense, after busting Wink's jaw he must have cooled down and realized he had gone as far as he could. Maybe he'd lay his suspicions on Anita. But Carl could handle that.

He still felt betrayed by Anita; living together for a year, it was almost like a marriage. But he had to get over the destructive feelings, the sick jealousy, because he knew without any doubt that he had the upper hand in this situation. It was within his power to move Anita and Tony away from the bayou, all he needed to do was convince the don it was necessary. And the family had already put him on alert. Look, he'd say, it's just a precaution until we know Angel's under lock and key again. Another move would cost some money, but the don had a conscience about this business, genuine regard for Anita. And there was little Tony, blood of his blood. In a way, much as Carl disliked dwelling on Anita's fling last night, Tomlin just might have done him a favor. Loosening Anita up, getting her juices flowing hot again. Oh, mama. Once he had Anita away from the bayou, Carl figured, maybe out on the West Coast somewhere— Santa Barbara was a great town—they'd settle back into the life they were all used to, but with a crucial difference. Anita would come to realize that family was what counted; nobody, especially this fly-boy, would ever care about her welfare as much as the family. She would find out how much Carl cared. He could afford to buy her some real nice things now. As for the sex, he'd been afraid to force her, thinking she really was frigid. Surprise. Next time he'd handle her just right. Getting rowdy with her in the bathroom yesterday morning, he'd seen more than a luscious cunt going to waste, he'd seen the urge slip in and out of her eyes. No wonder it'd been so easy for Tomlin. Carl was swelling up thinking about it. Jesus, all the broads he'd had, but none of them had affected him like Anita. Bare-legged in a pair of tight shorts, she blew them all away. The ass on her. Angel hadn't done her any damage where it really counted. Carl had finished his second drink without realizing how fast it was going down. He thirsted for another. His prick wouldn't stop throbbing. He threw his glass far over the side and opened his shorts, saying her name with a voluptuary's greed.

*   *   *

Anita went upstairs to Carl's bedroom to look around, returned to the parlor where Tomlin was waiting for her. She got a cigarette going before she spoke.

"He didn't pack much, if anything."

"Maybe he has enough clothes on board for a nice long trip."

Anita walked past him to the library doors, which were open a crack. Tony was playing a computer game inside, one called "Creepy Corridors." The remains of a peanut butter and jelly sandwich were on a plate near Tony. Big Dog looked up from his scrap of rug at her. Anita closed the doors all the way and went back to sit on the floor in front of Tomlin, wincing at the stiffness in her right hip. She put her head on his knee. He reached down and touched her nape, a shoulder.

"I wish you had said something to me before you accused Carl—"

"It wasn't just an accusation."

"I know, I know. You explained. I just can't believe that he—"

"How much do you really know about Carl?"

"Oh, not very much." Her voice a little tired tonight, the words not pronounced precisely, sliding into a coarse whisper.

"He was sort of assigned to you, is that it?"

"Yes. But if he's really gone—"

"Do you miss him?"

"That isn't fair! Whatever else he is, or may be, Carl did have compassion for us. He tried hard with Tony. I felt safe with him here."

"Safer than with a blind guy?"

She got up, pushing herself away from him in

exasperation. He heard her walking around the parlor. To the Ming dogs on the hearth, to the foyer door. He was getting better at tracking people by sound. It helped that the floor squeaked a little. Or maybe he was just more sensitively attuned to Anita than he would have been to a stranger in the house.

She came back quickly to where he was sitting and seized him by the shoulders.

"You're not blind, so stop feeling sorry for yourself."

Anita kissed him, and he pulled her into his lap. She had put the cigarette in an ashtray. He slid a hand inside her shirt, touched a nipple beneath her bra.

Inside the library there was a nasty, shrill scream from the computer as the little man in the creepy corridors got his. Still keeping her lips against Tomlin's, Anita slid his hand away from her breast. But held on to the hand.

After taking a deep and contented breath she said, "Tony likes you a lot, but—you and me, Clay, it's too much for him to absorb all at once. It wouldn't be good for him to wander into my room in the middle of the night, which he does sometimes, and find you there. Do you know what I mean?"

"I should take my time moving back into the house."

"Just give him a little longer to adjust to having you here."

Anita kissed him again, then got up quickly as Tomlin heard the library doors sliding apart. But she continued fingertip contact with his hand, behind her back.

"Hi, Tony! You're not going to play any more?"

Tomlin was sure, by the tone of her voice, that

Tony had caught her—them—in the act. He smiled a little.

"I'm bored," Tony said. "Could you fix me another peanut butter and jelly sandwich?"

"You can fix your own sandwich. Then on up to bed, it's already a quarter after nine."

"Good night, Tony," Tomlin said.

"Good night," the boy said after a few seconds, as he passed Tomlin's chair. Big Dog went panting after him. "How are you going to get outside?" Tony asked him.

"Your mother will help me."

Tony said to Anita, "Then are you coming upstairs? Right away?"

"Yes, I am."

Tony headed for the kitchen, and they heard him whistling.

"You've got a red face," Tomlin said.

"How do you know, you can't—oh, smart guy."

"Yeah," Tomlin said.

CHAPTER
TWENTY-ONE

Marilyn Anstedt's husband, Jack, a marketing analyst, was in Chicago on a business trip. Marilyn was late getting home herself, to the Colonial clapboard house on Birchall Road in Cherry Hill, New Jersey, so she had fifteen-month-old Larry out past his bedtime while she did a quick grocery shopping at the Pathmark near her house. The boy was teething, and fussy in the bright cavern of the supermarket; she gave him a cookie from one of the bins to munch on while she hurriedly piled the cart full of necessities, such as Pampers. With a faceful of chocolate-flecked crumbs Larry pointed out things of interest in an unintelligible language all his own.

Marilyn would have preferred not to be a working mother, at least until Larry was in prekinder, but the new house had cost them a little past the limit of what they could really afford, and all of the real estate agents had warned them that they'd better buy now, because next year mortgage rates and points could go to the moon. Jack was thirty-one, with at least three years left before he could hope to climb higher than middle management and eventually earn double the thirty-eight thousand he was bringing home now. Marilyn, who had gone to the Olympic trials when she was sixteen, worked as a gymnastics instructor at the local Y.

She was shopping now wearing a bulky cable-knit sweater with her green leotards and Capezios. She diligently checked off each item on a hastily written list. Had they moved the pet food again? They were always rearranging this store. She asked a stock clerk, and he pointed the way to the right aisle. Three cans of Tabby Treet. She had a coupon. And that did it.

The checkout girl had been in one of her classes recently. Good floor exercise, hopeless on the balance beam. Larry was fussing again, drooling, a mess. Marilyn picked him up and patted his baggy behind while the girl packed the groceries.

"Shorthanded tonight, Barbi?"

"It's the Bruce Springsteen concert. I wouldn't be here either, but I need the extra money to pay a speeding ticket. If you want to wait a minute, I'll find somebody to help you, Mrs. Anstedt."

"No problem, I can manage."

She carried her son in one arm and guided the cart with the other out to the well-lighted parking lot. Space was hard to find at night. There was a fourplex movie house on one side of the supermarket, a bowling alley on the other. Marilyn stopped behind her car, a late-model Toyota hatchback. Before unloading the groceries she fastened Larry into the child safety seat in back, and gave him another cookie, not caring about the crumbs: the seat was already dirty. Take the hatchback to the car wash Saturday, it would be time to buy gas then. Free wash job and vacuum with every fill-up. Squeeze each buck until it turned blue, someday they wouldn't have to worry . . . one of the sacks tore when she was a little careless lifting it out of the cart. Vegetables in plastic bags and canned goods spilled.

"Shit!" Marilyn said, seeing her vaporous breath against the dark hatch of the car. She realized then she was so tired she was close to tears. *Patience, Marilyn, patience.* She squatted to look for the scattered items and when she stood with her hands full she bumped into someone who had come up behind her and was holding out a bunch of broccoli. Quick impression of a black windbreaker, a flannel shirt. He had a squarish face and a short, dark haircut, a steady way of looking at her she didn't like one bit.

"Ohh, thanks—I guess that's everything. The way they make these bags . . ." He didn't speak. She quickly turned and dumped the cans into the car, the hell with it, let them roll around loose, she just wanted to get out of there. She reached for the broccoli he was holding out to her and his other hand came into view. He put a knife blade to her crotch, just under the hem of the long sweater. Marilyn drew a sharp cold breath that plunged almost as low as the cold point of the intrusive knife and went weak all over, felt her bones trying to knock together.

"Oh, God. Please. I have a baby."

"You drive," the Angel of Death said to her.

Anything would have been better than letting him into the car where Larry was, but she'd always been so terrified of knives. She didn't even like using them in the kitchen. All he had to do was push hard, and she would never have another child. She would die here in the parking lot she had been to a hundred times, it was as familiar as her own front yard. Her lower lip folded upward in a trembling arch, she tried to back up but the Toyota was in her way.

"No," he said, keeping the knife blade snug against her groin. "Turn around."

A car door slammed nearby, she heard laughter, she had an instant's hope. Somebody would see what was happening here, and help her.

He closed the hatch. "Come on," he said. He took her by the arm then and put the knife higher, beneath the sweater, near her navel, moved her around to the driver's side of the car. He opened the door and made her get in. He had taken her purse from the shopping cart. He went through it unhurriedly while she sat stiffly behind the wheel staring at the decorations for Halloween in the store windows. Pumpkins, black cats, witches. Make-believe terror. Beer bellies and bowling shirts a couple of rows away. Nobody paying attention to what was going on. But nothing was going on. She was sitting in her car and a man who might have been her husband was looking in her purse trying to locate the keys. She saw her face in the windshield glass and fought down the urge to scream. He would kill her if she screamed.

When he had the keys he jammed the back of the seat hard against her and got in beside the baby. Then he handed Marilyn the keys over her shoulder.

"Okay," he said.

She saw him in the rearview mirror, his dark head next to Larry's blond curls. Something shriveled tight in her, her womb dying where the blade had been poised. She said, "I don't think—I can drive." Her voice apologetic, but on the very edge of hysteria.

"I'm going to let you go in a little while. All I want is the car."

"Just take it now! Leave us alone."

"What's his name?"

"Larry."

"Do you want me to cut off his right hand?"

Marilyn put the key in the ignition and started the hatchback with the slow solemn precision of her first day in driving school. She backed out of the parking space carefully. She drove to an exit of the parking lot.

"What street is this?" he asked her. He was eating one of the apples Marilyn had bought at Pathmark.

"Haddonfield Berlin Road."

"Where's the turnpike?"

"To the right. About two miles. Is that where you'll let us—"

"Yes," he said.

She knew he was a liar. A good-for-nothing shit liar, he wasn't about to let them go. But what could she do? The baby was cranky. Tired. Him sitting back there going, "Shh. Shhh." What if he lost his temper with Larry?

Marilyn felt massive relief when he left the back seat and came up to sit beside her. He threw the apple core out the window and went through her handbag again, still holding his knife in one hand.

"I don't have—much money. I usually write— checks." Forewarned, he might not be angry. She could just hold back her tears, a storm of terror. To show that much weakness might be fatal. He didn't act very interested in her, seldom looked in her direction. But she sensed he was aware of everything she was doing, every thought of potential escape that crossed her mind. Cars going by them in both directions. Pull out suddenly, sideswipe someone. Larry's chances good, buckled into the child seat. But once the hatchback was out of control, a multiple crash could result. A fire. What chance would he have then?

The Angel of Death helped himself to the money she had, eleven dollars, and a gasoline credit card that belonged to Jack. Then he opened a soft leather case and took out her crucifix, which was hung from a strong chain of barrellike fourteen-karat gold beads. He held the crucifix up in his fist, studying the minute suffering Christ by the light of oncoming cars.

"Once there was a Perfect Man," he said. Something in the tone of his voice suggested that this apprehension made him happy.

"This is the turnpike."

"Keep going."

"Where?"

"Someplace. A park. A golf course. Woods."

Her mouth was stone-dry. She couldn't talk any more. She and Jack hadn't lived in Jersey for long, having moved from an apartment in Philadelphia the previous winter. She didn't know this area very well. It was mostly residential, the lots getting bigger and the expensive houses farther apart. Not so many well-lighted intersections any more, and little traffic.

"Take a right up ahead," he told her.

They went down a long country lane to a development that was just under way. Brick gateposts. *Hedgemoor.* A paved road into dark woods. He had her drive this road, past skeletal houses, the road winding around hillside homesites surveyed but not cleared. At the top of a modest rise they came to the edge of the sky and a field of stars, an unpaved turnaround with a tall fireplug and curbing in place.

"Here."

She stopped the car, the right front brake pad worn and screeching.

"Turn off the lights."

Marilyn did so. She looked into the back seat and saw that her son had gone to sleep, thumb in his sore mouth. The sight of him made her groan with love and dread.

The Angel of Death looked at her.

"Get out."

Marilyn stepped into the road under the bright stars, pressing her hands to her head, feeling faint. She kept her balance. She heard a farm dog bark a long way off. A commercial jet was descending to the west, landing lights on.

He got into the back seat again. Marilyn dropped to her knees on the hard clay road, still holding her head, afraid to see.

A little later she heard him getting out of the Toyota. At the sound of his foot on the road Marilyn spasmed, her bladder voided hotly.

He was holding the child seat, which he had cut loose from the anchors. Larry was still peacefully asleep, untouched by the madman.

Marilyn rose dumbly to take the heavy seat from him. Then she had to put it down, in her wobbly state of distress it was too much for her.

The Angel of Death got in behind the wheel of her hatchback, started the engine, turned the car around.

The headlights swept blindingly into her eyes. Then he drove past her, picked up moderate speed, went downhill and around a bend and kept going until she couldn't hear the sound of the engine any longer.

The frosty dark all around her; and silence.

Marilyn picked up the bulky child seat, not taking the time to unstrap Larry; the seat had cost a lot of money, she didn't want to have to buy another. The hatchback, that was insured. She was worried because Jack would have called from Chicago, and she wasn't home to answer the phone. Sharp stones sliced by a bulldozer blade and mashed into the road hurt her feet through the thin soles of the Capezios as she tried to run, thinking of the phone and how badly she wanted to talk to Jack. Soon she was breathing harshly through her mouth, not feeling the road all that well and stumbling. She had to slow down. Her leotards were soaked and cold. Hadn't wet herself since she was eight years old. The first of a series of houses framed in raw lumber loomed up between the tall trees.

A car was coming.

She stopped for a few moments, panting, listening, then began awkwardly to run again down the middle of the road. The car was traveling slowly, twenty long seconds passed before it topped the rise ahead of her and she had to turn her face away from the sudden glare. She stepped out of the way as the car began to slow even more, and then she heard the screech of the worn brake pad; her head jerked in shock as her own hatchback pulled a few feet past her with the face of the Angel of Death in the side window, eyes a virulent amber-yellow, the door opening and the rosary in his fist an unexpected menace, Christ dangling from a broad thumb. She knew he'd changed his mind about letting either of them live; and knew that horror behind definition would fill the dark of night before her final breath.

Marilyn screamed, which woke the baby she was carrying; a second later he began to scream too.

CHAPTER
TWENTY-TWO

Tomlin awoke in the dark as if he hadn't been asleep at all, his mind immediately clear, all of his senses except for sight functioning acutely. He'd heard something. The door, which he had double-locked, rattling. Wasn't just the wind, which he also heard, like surf lightly shaking the RV. He reached for the fish billy, a club with steel studs on the business end, that he'd placed on the floor by the bed. Then he relaxed at the sound of a muffled voice.

"Clay. Let me in. Clay."

He got up, still holding the fish billy. He was wearing white boxer shorts and a T-shirt. He felt his way through the dark to the door and unlocked it.

"Can I come in?"

"What are you doing out here, Tony?"

"Nothing. I couldn't sleep. C-could I stay with you for a little while?"

"Sure." It was cold in the doorway. Tomlin stepped up and back but Tony didn't follow him.

"Big Dog's with me. Can he come in too?"

"Why not? Wonder what time it's getting to be?"

"I don't know. I think it'll be daylight soon."

Big Dog was first inside, bounding up the step, his considerable weight rocking the RV a little on its shocks. Tony shut the door behind him. Then he locked it. Tomlin felt for the table lamp by the sofa and turned it on.

"Want something to drink? Hot chocolate?"

"Okay."

"You'll have to help me out. There's a carton of chocolate milk in the fridge, and I'll show you where the pans are."

"Do you drink chocolate milk?"

"All the time. Love the stuff."

Tony poured the milk into a pan and set it carefully on a burner. Tomlin turned on the gas. When he touched the boy he found that Tony was shivering in his flannel pajamas. He was wearing the Navy cap that Tomlin had given him. He stayed close to Tomlin's side.

"Would you like to sit up front in the driver's seat?" Tomlin asked him.

"No. Somebody could see in, couldn't they?"

"I suppose so. Who do you mean?"

"Somebody who could hurt you."

"Who wants to hurt me, Tony?" Tomlin asked, thinking about Carl.

"I don't know," the boy mumbled.

"Well, I wonder why you brought it up."

Tony didn't answer him. Big Dog walked by them, switching his tail, and went into the bedroom, just nosing around.

"The milk looks hot now."

Tomlin placed two mugs in the sink and picked Tony up to sit him on the counter. He turned off the front burner of the stove, found the handle of the pan by cautious touch. He put the pan into the sink near the mugs.

"Can you pour?" he asked Tony. "Doesn't matter if you spill some."

While Tony was filling the mugs to the brim he asked Tomlin, "Do you have any dog bones?"

"No. How would Big Dog like an Oreo cookie?"

"He'll eat anything." Tony put the pan down. "I spilled a lot."

"I would have spilled all of it." He lifted Tony down. "Cookies are in the cabinet opposite you." He picked up the mugs of chocolate from the steel bottom and slid one onto the counter where Tony had been sitting.

From the noisy gulping way Big Dog went after the cookies Tony handed him, Tomlin was glad it wasn't his shinbone. He and Tony went to sit on the sofa. Tony asked him if he would turn the cushions over first and check for snakes. Tomlin turned the cushions over. Then they sat down, Tony snuggled under a stadium blanket that had been thrown across the back of the sofa, his head against Tomlin's side. They drank their hot chocolate.

"What woke you up in the middle of the night?"

Tony leaned over to put his empty mug on the floor, then pulled the blanket closer around him. His skin was still cold.

"I was having—a bad dream. I dreamed he was in the computer."

"Who are you talking about?" Then Tomlin understood. "Your real father?"

"Yes. Him. Bad Angel. He wasn't there before I went to bed. But I looked. And—he's there now."

"Are you sure you didn't dream that too, Tony?"

Tony was slack and unresponsive, almost as if he'd gone to sleep against Tomlin. Then with no warning he went off like a bomb, hammering at Tomlin with his fists, screaming and crying in a paroxysm of fear. Big Dog began roaring. Tomlin wrapped both arms around Tony and hugged him close, hoping the wolfhound wouldn't read him wrong and go on the attack. It took him five minutes to quiet the boy down, until the explosiveness became random tics and twitches, the loud sobs turned to ragged breathing.

"All right. Easy now." Big Dog's head prodded him below one knee and the dog whined anxiously. "Okay, Tony. I believe you. He's in the computer. What I'll do is—I can't do anything until the sun comes up. Just hold on. When it's bright enough we'll see what this is all about."

Seven-fifteen by Tomlin's watch. After a long and restless hour, Tony lay fast asleep with his head in Tomlin's lap. Big Dog was stretched out at his feet. His right leg was numb, it felt like a keg of concrete from midthigh down, but he hadn't wanted to move and disturb the boy.

His vision—the morning light was toned down by the tinted glass of the windshield—was about 50 percent. By the time he made it over to the house he ought to be seeing well enough to check out what Tony had described.

The rhythm of Tony's breathing changed and faltered when he moved him to the other end of the sofa, but Tony didn't open his eyes. Big Dog was at the door. Tomlin let him out, then went back to the bedroom to pull on some clothes and step into his docksiders.

There was light mist hovering over the bayou, heavy dew on the lawn. He didn't see Carl's boat tied up at the dock. When he let himself into the house Opal looked down the center hall from the kitchen.

"Seen you comin' on the TV, Mist' Clay. Fix you some breakfast?"

"Thanks, Opal. Tony spent part of the night with me. He's still sleeping."

Tomlin walked through the parlor and opened the library doors all the way. He stared at the big projection-screen monitor, which was on. Something there, but he couldn't tell what. A face? He opened the veranda doors as well, letting in the sun.

Now he could make out the computer-generated image on the monitor. And the words printed beside that face, in the kind of balloon they drew in comic strips. The face appeared to ripple slightly, to move eerily on the screen. The mouth opened and closed. He didn't know how good the likeness was, but he felt sure from the reaction Tony had handed him a short time ago that it was close, frighteningly close, to the real Angel.

Do you love me? Do you love me?

"Son of a bitch," Tomlin said angrily. He went quickly to the computer desk and monitor. The modem light was on, which, he assumed, meant the image had been transmitted from another computer somewhere. Underneath the desk he tracked down the surge protector and yanked out all the plugs. The screen went blank and his nerves stopped fizzing.

The only question in his mind: who had put this grotesque greeting card on the screen for Tony to see? He didn't think Carl had the necessary talent for computer-generated graphics to pull it off, or, when it came down to it, the cruelty.

So there was a high probability Angel had done this. The hacker whiz and homicidal maniac. He had found out where his wife and child were, and he wanted them to know that he knew.

CHAPTER
TWENTY-THREE

Home from the hospital, where he'd undergone emergency surgery, Don Aldo Barzatti lay in his bed listening to the machines that reported on the fragile state of his life; he was surrounded by machines and sophisticated support systems, observed constantly by two nurses and intermittently by a priest. An ambulance was standing by in the courtyard of his house. But he had vowed to himself that he would not leave again except as a corpse. And although at times he had felt so detached from his own body it seemed to him that he was watching from a shadowy corner of the bedroom, his mother's strong fingers plucking at his sleeve from behind as he waited for the husk that was left of him to fail, he would slowly drift away from the embrace she wished to give him, drift through a silvery, bright fog and rejoin the body, feeling a jolt of pain and then a lot of discomfort, but no disappointment that his time was not yet over.

One of the nurses sponged perspiration from his forehead, and he smiled at her. She spoke a few words which he didn't quite understand. Then her face became the face of his beloved wife, a perfect heart from the sable peak of her hairline to her chin, lips so full and red they had never needed even a touch of paint. She didn't look like a ghost to Aldo, although he was well aware that she had died of childbirth fever in the stinking heat of their tenement·flat many years ago. She had lived in this country some fourteen years and understood more English than she let on, but she stubbornly refused to speak a word of the language. She spoke to him now in Sicilian.

"You have the final word, Aldo. Only you can tell them what must be done. Say it, so that we may all rest peacefully together in Eternity."

"Giuliana!" Don Aldo cried, ecstatic at hearing her voice again.

No one in the bedroom understood what he had said; it sounded like a raw gargle to them. Or, perhaps, "Greganti." So Mark Greganti was brought in, and kneeled at the bedside of his godfather. Mark kissed the papery fingers of Don Aldo's right hand, which had no tubes connected to it, and waited alertly for instructions. Don Aldo's eyes were open, but he didn't speak again until Mark thought to prompt him. He happened to find Don Aldo back in his body and temporarily lucid.

"You have news for me?" he said, tightening his grip on Mark's hand.

"Yes, Don Aldo. A young woman was killed last night in South Jersey. She was strangled with—I believe it was a rosary. Or her crucifix."

"Dominic's method," the old man sighed.

"The woman had a child with her. The child was found unharmed, strapped in a car seat near her body."

"Where is Dominic now?"

Mark had to lean over the bed with his ear an inch from Don Aldo's mouth in order to hear him.

"We don't know. But the woman's car was found abandoned two hours ago, at a truck stop near Augusta, Georgia."

"Georgia. He is traveling south. He knows, then. Knows where to find them."

"What do you want us to do, Don Aldo?"

"It is no use hoping for the best. Dominic will never be a normal human being. Tell Carlo to take Anita and her son away at once. Send a few good men to the bayou, to wait for Dominic. When he comes there, show him no mercy."

"All right. Is there anything else I can do for you now, Don Aldo?"

"I want the priest."

The priest was a bishop, an old friend of the family's. He had been keeping the death watch since shortly after midnight. He had administered the final sacrament hours ago. But Don Aldo probably didn't remember that. The two men linked hands.

"Casco."

"Aldo, my esteemed friend."

"I am timid before God."

"God has absolved you of your sins. You have nothing to fear."

"Did I mention doing the number on Toffo Magliotti?"

"I believe you did."

"Toffo was no good. He had sex with young girls. He stole money from his father, a hardworking man."

"Toffo Magliotti will burn in hell forever for his sins."

Don Aldo's eyes were fixed on something well past the grizzled head of the bishop.

"I see—is that God? No, I don't think so. It's somebody else."

There was a catch in his breathing, stress in his body. The tone of the chirping machines changed, and a nurse put a hand warningly on the shoulder of the bishop, who backed her up with a freezing glare.

"I have given—four million to the Church. Maybe that was not enough."

"You are blessed in your beneficence. But if you wish—shall I have someone come in?"

"Can't be too careful," Don Aldo said.

CHAPTER
TWENTY-FOUR

Tomlin went upstairs with a mug of coffee in one hand and knocked on Anita's door. She said to give her a couple of minutes, she was just out of the shower. When she let him in she was dressed, wearing a pair of dark gray wool slacks and a nappy sleeveless Norse sweater over a pin-striped shirt. She closed the door and they held each other for a few seconds and then Anita looked at his face and said, "What's the bad news?"

He told her.

Anita heard him out with only a little change of expression, a weariness settling upon her that in a way was worse than Tony's hysterical outburst. She turned from Tomlin and went to the windows, wretchedly rubbing the back of her neck with one hand.

"It had to be Angel. He'd think of something like that."

"I'm wondering how his mind works. If he's coming to see you, why warn you first?"

Anita looked around for her cigarettes, picked them up, dropped them. "It wasn't necessarily a warning. He might've been saying hello. Not that I'm an authority on his mental processes, and I lived with him for almost five years. He may well believe I'd be happy to see him again." She caught the shudders then, and crossed arms over her breasts to squeeze the tremors still. "He could be happy to see *me*. For five minutes. Then some little thing would go wrong, a load would shift in his head, and he'd do his best to throw me through a window. Uh-uh. I've had enough of that."

"Let's suppose all he wanted was to scare you. But he has to know you're under the don's protection. That might stop him from showing up here."

"Believe me, it isn't something Angel would worry about. He's coming. He'll be here. It's a matter of when, and what to do about him. But where's my protection now?"

"If you're staying, we'll work something out."

"If I'm staying—? Is that a polite request for me to get packed?"

"I thought you might want to go back to your family. Or, I don't know—"

"My father's had two heart attacks in the past year; the aggravation would kill him if Angel didn't do the job first. I don't know how to contact the don, I've already tried. Carl always took care of business with the family. I suppose I could book a hotel room. It's going to be summer in Argentina soon, isn't it? What the hell."

"You wouldn't like Argentina. You're with me, Anita. So let's circle the wagons."

"John Wayne lives," she said, with a smile that was admiring before it turned dismal.

"Brave but not foolish. Tony's down to breakfast. Have something to eat with him and then we'll drive into town. I need to start laying on extra help around here. Do you have a photo of Angel?"

"I threw them all out. No, wait, maybe he's in one or two snapshots with my family, back in the good old days. I'll look."

The two sheriff's deputies who came to Mace Lefevre's office in Port Bayonne were so similar in build they might have been twins: six-three, size 19 shirt collars, forty-six inches at the waist. Each man about thirty pounds over his playing weight at their respective institutions of higher learning. DeeJay Voisin had been a linebacker at Alabama in Bear Bryant's last year, and Shelby Burleson had toiled in the trenches as a nose guard for Mississippi State.

DeeJay had keen blue eyes, a baby face and a jaw like the business end of a front-loader, which he kept busy with a wad of gum. Shelby's features were all crowded in toward the middle of his face, as if an elephant had stepped squarely on his head. He had a petite nose, a tiny bow of a mouth, great expanses of cheekbone and brow and Dumbo ears. He outranked DeeJay, and did the talking after he'd heard what Tomlin and Anita had to say. He held a snapshot in one huge hand that showed Dominic "Angel" Barzatti at the fringe of a family group on an outing some years ago. DeeJay studied the county map on one wall of Mace's office and popped his chewing gum.

"If it's all right with you, ma'am, what I'll do is, I'll take the snapshot and have this here little area that shows your husband enlarged. We'll get a rap sheet on him and pass around the photo and the particulars to all the law enforcement agencies on the Gulf Coast."

"Will that do any good?"

"Oh, yes ma'am, you'd be surprised. From what I see of him here, and with your description, he wouldn't be all that hard to identify unless he made an attempt to disguise himself. Think he might do that?"

"I don't know."

DeeJay said, a finger on the map, "There's just the one road here that runs down to Lostman's. Other road branches off to the federal wetlands, but he couldn't get through from there to the west end of the bayou without having to wade through a hell of a lot of marsh. I'd say it's a practical impossibility; he'd need a boat of some kind."

"That's all open water between the Sound and my house," Tomlin said. "About half a mile, and no place to hide on the approach. The dock area is well lighted. He could swim. But *I* wouldn't want to try it."

"Lord, no," Shelby said. "With all the gators a man would have to be crazy—" He glanced at Anita, who didn't say anything. "We'll keep that possibility in mind, even though it is farfetched. Now, then. Do you people keep a dog?"

"Yes," Anita said.

"Big one?"

"He's an Irish wolfhound."

"That's a dog and a half. He'll bark some, won't he? Good 'nuff."

Mace Lefevre said, "So you boys think you can lend these folks a hand when you're off-duty?"

"Oh, sure, that won't be no problem. Let me have a look at the duty roster and make a few calls; and then there's air police we know over at Keesler wouldn't mind helping out for the extra pay. Me and DeeJay go off shift at four o'clock, so I'll tell you what, we'll cover the house ourselves tonight, say from about eight o'clock on."

"What I'd like to do," DeeJay said, studying the map, "is bring my camper down there and block the road. That way nobody gets in or out we don't know about, and we'll use your car, Shelby, to patrol the grounds."

"Yeah, we'll be a lot more comfortable with the camper," Shelby agreed. He smiled at Anita, crinkly around the eyes. "You get yourself a good night's sleep, and don't worry about a thing."

"I think—" Anita said, and stopped, and looked helplessly at Tomlin.

Tomlin said to the deputies, "After her husband ran her down, he tried to get into the hospital to see her, maybe to finish the job. He beat up a couple of private guards and some cops in the parking lot, one of them so bad he had to take early retirement with eighty percent disability."

"Some kind of wild man for sure," DeeJay said, not looking too impressed.

"Well, we know enough not to take any chances with him, if he comes our way," Shelby assured them. "Oh, one other thing. There's this battery-operated siren you can buy down at the hardware store, all you got to do is push the button and it'll honk like a mother up to a half hour's worth, hear it

for miles. You want to set that thing off for any
reason, we'll come a-runnin'."

"Appreciate you boys coming down this morning," Mace Lefevre said, and he showed the deputies
to the front door. When he came back Anita was
trying to smoke a cigarette and not looking much
more at ease. Her mind seemed to be caught in a
time warp. Mace was beaming. "Having a couple
like them on your team surely ought to help put your
problem in perspective," he said.

"I guess so. I can't help thinking—no matter what
we do, Angel will—there's no way to tell people
what he's like. No way to describe him."

"Mrs. Jeffords—"

"Anita. I never knew where to look when anyone
called me 'Jeffords.' "

"Anita, it's just possible you've overreacted to the
threat because of your terrible experiences. But what
I want to say is, it wouldn't be a bad idea if you and
your boy came on over to my place to stay for a
while, until we'd had us some kind of all-clear down
there on the bayou. Rainie would be tickled to have
company, she's a book reader like yourself, and I've
got three teenage daughters who are bound to spoil
Tony rotten."

Anita smiled gratefully, but she shook her head.
"Thank you, I couldn't do that. Until Angel is locked
up again, or—dead—I don't want to take the slight-
est chance of putting anyone else in jeopardy."

Tony came in then, having been down the street
with Mace's receptionist for an ice cream cone. Anita
gave him a hug so fierce it had him scowling, but
then in a sudden reversal of mood he kissed her,
leaving a strawberry smear next to her mouth.

"I'm bored," he said. "Can we go home?"

They did some shopping first. Tony was fascinated with the new battery-powered alarm, which was demonstrated for him in the hardware store. Anita bought a present for Opal's parents, who were about to celebrate their golden wedding anniversary and then, because Opal would be in Meridian for two days, they went to the supermarket.

"What would you like to eat tonight?" she asked Tomlin.

"Brisket of baby elf."

Tony stared at him, then recognized a joke and laughed loudly.

"So you don't want to be helpful," Anita said disapprovingly. "Your turn, Anthony."

"Cannelloni!"

"Yeah, cannelloni. The Sicilian way. And how about a side of baby artichokes—*carciofini sott' olio*. And maybe a nice home-style *cassata* for dessert, with plenty of pistachios and candied fruit?"

"Sounds terrific," Tomlin said, a hand on her elbow, then the small of her back, just keeping in touch. She would lean against him unobtrusively, return his touch, and Tony wasn't missing any of this. But he didn't try to butt in, to claim his mother's attention the way jealous kids usually do. He asked for permission to go look at the toys, which were in the same part of the store where they also sold house plants, motor oil, kitty litter and novels by Danielle Steel.

"So you think we're going to be all right," she said, not betraying any nerves about the situation but unable to stop thinking about it. Depending on him, wanting to be sure he had come up with the right answers.

"I like the looks of Burleson and Voisin, and I hope they have ten friends the same size. I wouldn't want Big Dog mad at me, even though he's not a trained fighter. It's a nice loud alarm, and you'll have it right beside you wherever you go. If I thought we were in any danger I'd be looking now for another place for all of us to live."

A note of finality in his voice; the briefing was completed. He was used to having his decisions accepted. She decided that she didn't mind that—his assurance, his authority. As long as he wasn't pompous, or tried to make all the rules.

"I'm going back to teaching," she said. "As soon as it's practical."

"Good."

She had been afraid he'd ask, "Why?" and then she'd have to say, "Because I'm not a goddamned housewife, that's why," and probably something would have cooled in the relationship, then and there. What else? Was he vain? Could she tease him?

"Did you ever wear a mustache?"

"Mustaches don't do a thing for me. I look older and unlucky and not with it. I look like I sell costume jewelry out of a suitcase."

Anita laughed. No, he wasn't vain. He had a firm sense of what was good for him, and a humorous way of of expressing it. "When's your birthday?"

"You're asking a lot of questions."

"I feel like asking a lot of questions."

"August 5th."

"August 5th!" She nearly ran the cart into a display of raisins in the middle of the aisle. "That's *my* birthday!"

"How about that? Do you suppose it's incestuous?"

Anita remembered that she needed raisins for the *cannelloni alla Siciliana*, and put a box of them in her shopping cart.

"Hmm. I guess it's too late to worry about that now, isn't it?"

CHAPTER
TWENTY-FIVE

In the afternoon Tomlin dismantled the trolling motor, cleaned and lubricated it. Opal's brother Roland and half brother Akeem were working around the yard and polishing up the RV before they all left for the family reunion in Meridian. At three o'clock Tony finished his schoolwork and came down to the dock to see what Tomlin was doing. The wind came off the Gulf in gusts strong enough to rattle the roof of the boat shed and set the dock to creaking; there were some thick dirty clouds building up like smoke from a dump fire. The weather might get rough in another couple of hours, Tomlin thought.

"Can we go fishing?"

"I don't know, Tony. Water's kicking up."

"Please?"

He decided it was better than just sitting around. Roland and Akeem would be on the place for a while. And deep inside the bayou there were little bays where the specs would congregate, away from the agitation of the wind.

He attached the trolling motor to the car battery in the johnboat and the motor started smoothly with one push of the button. He let Tony navigate down the main channel to a point three quarters of a mile west of the boat dock, where nothing could be seen of the house but a peak of the roof and a couple of lightning rods. They followed another long finger of the coffee-colored water, barely disturbing a flock of ducks newly arrived at this end of the Mississippi flyway and getting acclimated to the bayou. Tony asked him if he liked to hunt ducks. Tomlin said he hadn't cared much for shooting sports since a friend of his had been accidentally killed on a deer stand in the Homochitto National Forest.

"Any fool with a high-powered rifle can call himself a hunter," Tomlin said.

"Do you have any guns?"

"I own a .357 magnum I carried in Vietnam, in case my plane got shot down over NVA territory. I think the gun's in a trunk I left with a buddy of mine at Oceana. I haven't seen it for a while."

"What's Vietnam?"

"It's a country a long way from here where they had a war once."

"Oh. Did you ever get shot down?"

"No."

"What did you do in the war?"

"I blew up bridges that always seemed to get rebuilt overnight. It was an exercise in futility."

"What's—" Tony was distracted by a knob-eyed basker on the sunny bank less than six feet from them. "Look at the size of that one!"

Tomlin nodded. He saw it with no jog to his attention, just another gator, as familiar in these haunts as his own backbone. "Whopper, isn't he?"

"Did you ever kill any gators?"

"Had one come up to the veranda one time, he ate a puppy dog of mine. That made me mad, so I jumped him and wired his jaws together."

"You jumped on an *alligator*?"

"They aren't much of a threat out of the water. And their jaws aren't all that powerful, once they're closed. You can hold them shut with one hand. Just have to watch out for the tail."

They were in less than six feet of water, the channel wide but broken by numerous hummocks, some barely submerged and covered with grasses, others solid enough to support tall cypress trees. Stumps were sticking up in many places. The wind was at their backs, and Tony kept pulling down on the bill of his cap to make sure he didn't lose it. Tomlin broke out the fishing rods and opened the tackle box. Not the right time of day, he thought, but sometimes an imminent change in the weather could get the fish to biting.

They caught three nice-size specs, all around two pounds, in a few minutes of casting near a collection of snags. Tomlin threw them all back; they had plenty of filets in the freezer already.

Tony said, coming out of left field as he often did, "Do you like Mom a lot?"

"Well, you caught me kissing her. How do you feel about that?"

"I guess it's okay. I'm glad it's you."

The action had stopped at their particular location. The sun disappeared, the wind was still rising. Tomlin was about to move on when he looked around and saw Carl's sportfisherman nosing into the channel, looking huge and out of place there as it came toward them. Because of the wind he hadn't heard the engines. Carl was at the controls on the flying bridge and he blasted the siren at them, a really dumb thing to do. Tony, oblivious of the *Lolly*, almost lost his pole and fell overboard. Tomlin grabbed him as the johnboat rocked and shipped some water. The roots of his hair were sizzling, which always happened when he was instantly outraged about something.

"Steady." Carl had throttled back, but he was taking big risks with the *Lolly* at this depth, there were snags that could damage a propeller shaft just out of sight beneath the surface. He kept coming, cutting his engines abeam of the johnboat, creating swells that threatened to swamp them.

"What do you want, Carl?" Tomlin called up to him.

"Tie up alongside and put Tony aboard."

"Why?"

Carl lifted something up from the bridge deck. A shotgun, judging from the size of the bore, but Tomlin had never seen one quite like it.

"Just do it."

"*No*," Tony said, huddled against Tomlin's side in the middle of the johnboat.

"Don't worry, Tony. Carl's not going to hurt you." He didn't know what Carl had in mind. The shotgun was a ridiculous touch, what could he do with it? Blow them out of the water? Take a chance on hurting Tony? Carl's face was serious, and as far as Tomlin could tell he wasn't drunk.

"What's the point of scaring the boy?" he said to Carl.

"He's not scared. Tony knows he can trust me. I'm taking him to his mother. We're all going on a trip."

The johnboat was two feet from the starboard side of the *Lolly*, drifting closer. Tomlin quickly sorted through his options. There were times when you could say no to people who held guns on you, and get away with it. So push the button on the trolling motor and slowly ride away, down a branch of the bayou with two feet of draft where Carl couldn't hope to follow. Arrange a truce with some distance between them. Try to talk to Carl, explain that precautions had been taken and Anita and Tony would be safe at the house. *You* take a trip, Carl. Bimini was nice, this season of the year.

But there was a problem with this stand-off scheme. The sky was much darker, and Tomlin's vision was noticeably worsening. Carl's face hard to make out, up there on the bridge. He didn't want to be on Lostman's an hour from now with no vision at all, trying to talk Carl into behaving like a reasonable human being. Once he was aboard the *Lolly* the odds would be more in his favor, since Carl couldn't throw down on him with a shotgun and keep his boat out of serious trouble at the same time.

Tomlin said to Tony, keeping his voice down, his tone casual, even a little bored, "Tell you what. Maybe it'll be best just to let him play his game for a while. Okay?"

Tony's teeth were chattering. "He's got a *gun*."

"Yeah, that's some piece. Maybe he'll let us blast a couple of stumps with it."

Tony looked up at his face and Tomlin smiled to show that he wasn't in the least intimidated by Carl. Then he picked up an oar and dipped it into the water, bringing the stern around to bump against the side of the *Lolly*. He reached up with one hand to hold them in place while Tony crept over the seat and handed him a line. Tomlin tied the line to a stanchion on the starboard side of the *Lolly*'s transom.

"Now pick him up," Carl said. "Help him aboard."

Wide-eyed, Tony looked at Tomlin, the wind billowing his jacket and fluffing his dark hair. Tomlin lifted him from the johnboat and swung him over the transom to the cockpit of the *Lolly*. He started to climb in after Tony, but heard the slide action of the shotgun and froze, staring at the bridge.

"Not you, Tomlin. Over the side. Find yourself a tree to spend the night in, where the gators can't get at you."

Tomlin didn't believe him, but he hesitated a moment too long looking at the muzzle of the shotgun. Carl altered his aim slightly and fired three booming shots so fast it sounded like one report echoing back across the bayou. He was shooting at a stump in the water astern but at least one fistful of choked shot was so close Tomlin could feel the heat of the pellets flying past his head.

With his other hand Carl hit the throttles and the *Lolly* surged forward, yanking the line taut and dumping Tomlin in a cartwheel sprawl to splash down in the smoky wake of the yacht.

His left shoulder hit something hard and jagged just under the surface and when he came up choking he saw the *Lolly* making a slow turn with the johnboat in tow. Within reach if he could swim but his shoulder hurt too bad, he couldn't lift the arm and was barely able to keep himself off the bottom of the bayou by treading water. Tony was looking back at him, yelling something, but Tomlin couldn't make out the words over the noise of the diesel inboards. God, his shoulder hurt him, he was afraid it was broken. Carl now completing his careful turn to port, he would have to come very close to Tomlin again to get out of there, but that knowledge didn't do Tomlin much good with only one wing available. And there was Carl again on the bridge in natty whites, his image ghosting, steering with one hand, a tough grin on his face, aiming the shotgun, whether for effect or not Tomlin couldn't say but he remembered the brush-back of lead pellets zinging like hornets and took a deep breath and went under, diving for the mucky bottom, hearing the *Lolly*'s powerful screws and feeling the turbulence as the boat rumbled past him.

When he broke to the surface again, dragging his left arm along, he made a futile grab with the right hand for the gunwale of the johnboat and missed by at least a foot. Then he was swamped in a big wake and they were gone, Tony still yelling. This time with the wind in his face Tomlin could hear the boy pleading with Carl.

"No! Don't leave him here! It's getting dark! He won't be able to *see*!"

Sad but true, Tomlin thought, with more immediate problems than his slowly failing eyesight: he needed to get out of the water, and right now. The alternative was to swim back to the house, maybe a mile and a quarter, with his left arm all but useless. Angry and frustrated, he tried to get his bearings while the wind blew fiercely and the slopping of the bayou gradually subsided.

Anita brought the gift out to Opal as her housekeeper was about to get into Roland's Buick for the drive to Meridian. Opal, deeply touched, told her she shouldn't have gone to all that bother.

"A fiftieth wedding anniversary is pretty special. Give them my best wishes."

They drove off and Anita looked at the threatening sky, then at the dock where the johnboat was still missing. The bayou was gray as gunmetal with little licks of whitecaps here and there. She saw Big Dog trotting along at the edge of the marsh on the trail of something, raccoon or muskrat, but when she called to him he ignored her. She was alone and didn't like it. The wind moaning around the house, the light of day fading fast. That was something else to worry about, she thought, piqued at Tomlin. Out there with a squall coming on, in that boat with the low freeboard. Tony could swim only a little, probably not at all in a panic. She stared at the bayou, willing the johnboat to appear. No reason for him to take Tony out in the first place . . . that was just plain fooling around, on very little margin. If he didn't show up in the next five minutes then he was going to encounter an Anita he didn't know existed. Majestically wroth, to borrow Dickens' fine description of Sir Leicester Dedlock.

The appearance of the *Lollapalooza* was not a happy surprise. Nor was the fact that Carl was towing an apparently empty johnboat. *Oh, God!* She ran frantically toward the dock but stopped short when

she saw Tony aboard and unharmed. But he looked
as if he was crying.

Anita was waiting when Carl cut the engines of the
Lolly and it bumped against the fenders of the slip.
She reached under the grab rail and took line from
the foredeck cleat to snub the boat to the dock.

"He left Clay! He left Clay in the bayou! We gotta
go get him, Mom!"

She gathered Tony in as he ran to her, and looked
at Carl coming down from the bridge of the *Lolly*.

"What happened to Clay?"

"Tomlin's camping out tonight. What difference
does he make? I'm getting you and Tony out of
here."

"No, you're not!"

Tony was sobbing. "He shot at Clay with his
gun!"

Stunned, Anita said, "Carl, have you lost your—"

"Anita, Angel's on his way. I've got my orders.
The don wants you and Tony out of here, right
now."

"Where's Clay? Is he hurt?"

"No. Pack up just what you need for tonight, and
for Christ's sake let's go." Carl hunched his shoulders, absorbed the hostility in her stare for a few
moments, then walked off the dock.

"I want you to tell me where Clay is!" Carl just
shook his head and kept going, up the slope to the
house. Anita took Tony by the hand and followed
him.

"Carl, you lowlife—!"

He whirled on her, leveling a strict finger. "Hey,
don't ever call me that again! No wonder the boy
doesn't have respect for me. So what're you—you're

worried about *him*? Tomlin was born in this fucking swamp. Angel, *Angel* is the one you'd better be thinking about.''

Tony's head jerked up.

Anita said, ''Clay hired some guards. Off-duty sheriff's deputies.''

''Yeah? That so?'' Carl had a look around. A little rain was spitting down. The wind was high, buffeting them. ''Where are they?''

''They're coming later.''

''Yeah, later? How much later? After Angel's been here and gone, and you with your throat cut—''

Tony left his mother's side and swarmed all over Carl, furiously shoving him, then swinging his fists. Carl couldn't get a grip on him. He stepped back and slapped Tony sharply. Tony came to a full stop, mouth open, blinking, face going white except for the mark of Carl's hand on his cheek.

''You *bastard*!'' Anita yelled.

''Listen, I don't have time for this shit, I mean it.'' He went down on one knee in front of the shocked boy, taking him gently by the shoulders and looking at his cheek. ''I didn't hurt you that bad, did I? You got to try to control yourself, not have so many tantrums—''

''Carl, let's get back on the boat, all of us, and go back to where you left Clay. He's blind at night. He can't defend himself out there!''

Carl looked up at Anita, still holding Tony. ''You're the one's blind, and you must be deaf too. You're acting like you don't remember the last time you saw Angel.''

Tony rubbed his smarting cheek, making an incoherent, strangled sound that resolved into speech.

"Bad Angel . . ."

Carl nodded, looking him in the eye.

"Yeah, that's right. *Bad* Angel, Tony. He hurt your mother. He'll do it again too if he finds her here. So what do you say, let's get your clothes and—"

"The Magic Ring." Tony twisted frantically toward his mother. His voice rose shrilly. "The Magic Ring!"

Carl gave him a little affirmative shake, and Tony turned his attention back to him.

"You'd better go get the Magic Ring," Carl said.

Confused and terrified, Tony glanced at his mother again, then broke away from Carl and ran toward the house. Big Dog, ambling toward them from somewhere, saw Tony running and changed direction to follow him, barking playfully.

"Look what you did to him!"

Carl got sullenly to his feet.

"I wish somebody would give me a little credit around here," he complained. "I'm just trying to save your life."

CHAPTER
TWENTY-SIX

Wolfdaddy came riding back from town on his bicycle about six-thirty, the headlamp clamped to the handlebar throwing a little light on the patchy blacktop road that led to his tree house. It was almost full dark and riding against the wind gave him the wobbles, but most of the rain had held off. Just enough of it to make the going slick. He was wearing his top hat with the mirrors on it and a ratty Boy Scout knapsack, which contained his Bible and two Big Macs in Styrofoam cartons which the family of the woman he'd been visiting on a sick call had generously provided for his supper. Tied to the knapsack was a woven leather scabbard which held a cane knife, the handle a thick wrap of dirty adhesive tape, the blade worked narrow and sharp from years of hard usage.

A lot of leaves from the live oak were blowing his way by the time he was home. He chained his rusty bike to a ring bolt screwed into the trunk, so it wouldn't sail off into the bayou. On the platform above his head a low branch, moving up and down with the wind, picked at random keys on his piano. Sure was likely to storm before the night ended, he needed to cover that old piano with the plastic stuff he'd scavenged from the dumpsters behind Kroger's and taped into a waterproof tent. Weight it down with a few bricks. He saw a gleam of animal eyes off in the marsh grass and heard a forlorn meow, but there was a notable absence of cats hanging around the rickety steps up to his house.

"Kitty?" Wolfdaddy called. "Kitty? Where all my kitties gone to?"

Oh, well. Wolfdaddy trudged up to the platform, where he paused to shrug off his knapsack. He ran his hands over the piano keys, trying to revive a hymn that had come vaguely to mind. But he was too hungry to think about music right now, hadn't had a bite all day. Needed to fetch that plastic tarp first, then—

Wolfdaddy opened the door to his shack and started back in surprise, as the man who had been standing just inside, waiting, came at him fiercely with the binoculars raised in one hand.

He slugged Wolfdaddy backhanded with the binoculars; it stung like sin.

Wolfdaddy's hat fell off and he tottered helplessly, reaching out to grab hold of something. His fingers slipped off the nylon of the black windbreaker in front of him and his left foot found nothing but air. He fell in a twisting way, landing hard on the packed ground amid a scattering of folding chairs. The fall broke his hip, wrenched his back severely and knocked the breath out of him.

Wolfdaddy stirred weakly but couldn't raise up. He saw the branches of the tree lashed by the wind and the frightening eyes of the Angel of Death contemplating his doom from on high. Then his own eyes teared, he struggled to breathe and lost consciousness for a few seconds.

When he came out of it, breath in his body and rasping through his parted lips, pain everywhere, he saw, mistily, something moving on the platform above his head. Couldn't make out what it was at first. Then he heard a discordance of keys and realized, with a great flash of fear that momentarily obscured his pain, that it was the piano being shoved to the very edge of the platform, teetering there as the wind howled and a groan was torn from his throat . . .

No, mains! I hurts bad 'nuff already! Please don't drop that pianna on me!

Tomlin had used his time since hauling himself out of the murky bayou by preparing for a long and uncomfortable night, although he still hoped someone was going to come looking for him. He wondered if Anita had cooperated with Carl; or was there any question of cooperation when the Cosa Nostra *pistolero* was wearing his black hat and carrying a persuader? They might already be gone, and he would never be able to find them. His sense of loss was intensified by his anger at himself for letting this happen, never mind that he'd had no alternatives, Carl had been at the top of his game.

Anita, he thought, would have sent help if she'd had the chance. When it was too dark for him to read his watch any longer Tomlin had pried off the watertight crystal with the tip of his fish knife and kept track through touch. Twenty minutes to seven now. Too early for Burleson and Voisin to be there. No one else was within shouting distance except, possibly, Wolfdaddy; but Tomlin knew he couldn't make himself heard against the wind.

His father had taught him always to carry a few waterproof matches whenever he went out in a boat, even if he didn't plan to go more than forty feet from the dock. That precaution had paid off after all these years: he had a good fire going on his hummock. But the pile of debris he'd collected while he could see was dwindling fast. Soon he'd be down to mostly green stuff that would smolder and smoke but not give much flame. Another hour, at best, and he would really be in the dark.

But his clothes were nearly dry, from the wind and the fire, and there was another plus—his shoulder wasn't broken or dislocated, though it still pained him. He had diagnosed a deep muscle bruise or a slight separation. He had the use of his left hand, but he couldn't lift the arm very high.

There was company nearby, a couple of bull alligators snorting at each other, but the gators didn't worry him. He was tense but not anxious, bored when he wasn't angry. Nothing to do but pile on the deadwood, keep track of the time and hope the south wind kept blowing like this. Because if it slacked off or stopped, then it was going to rain. Hard.

CHAPTER
TWENTY-SEVEN

Anita had spent a lot of time with Tony, holding him, talking to him. He had been sitting on his bed in his room for more than an hour, clutching the Magic Ring, before he said a word. Carl at least had the sense to leave them alone, after scaring Tony so heartlessly. The boy was lethargic, unresponsive. But when Anita tried to leave the room for a couple of minutes to get something for her headache he screamed, in a chilling way, for her to stay. He seemed to have regressed to about the age of four, which was how old he was the summer Angel ran her down on Flatbush Avenue.

But gradually, as she loved him, rocked with him and reassured him, Tony responded in a more normal tone of voice, although he wouldn't let go of the ring with the blue stone and he wouldn't get off the bed.

"Tony, I need to pack your things," Anita said finally.

"Okay." He watched her as she took his suitcase from the closet shelf and began opening drawers.

"I want my Garbage Pail Kids."

"I know."

"Can I take my aircraft carrier?"

"Anything you want, sweetheart."

Staring at his aircraft carrier, Tony was reminded of the unpleasantness on the bayou, Tomlin in the water after Carl had fired a shotgun at him. He began to shudder.

"Are we going to leave Clay?"

"Tony, you know I won't do that." She straightened up from emptying a drawer and held her head tightly, feeling dizzy and nauseated.

"What are you going to do?" he demanded, not believing her.

She made herself smile at him. "As soon as we're all packed and on the *Lolly*, we'll go and get him."

"Carl won't do that!" Tony said, angry with her.

"Yes, he will. I can make a deal with Carl." *God help me*, she thought. But it didn't matter now. What mattered was rescuing Clay, then Carl could take her and Tony to wherever the don thought they would be safe. And if Carl insisted on his bed time with her, a sexual reward for his year of faithful service, that didn't matter so much now, either; because sooner or later she was determined that she and Tony would find their way back to Lostman's Bayou and to Clay Tomlin, if he still wanted them.

She was holding on to the confident smile pretty well but feeling the pressure of tears behind her eyes when the lights flickered, sank low, stayed dim for a few moments and then went out as the wind assaulted the house. The only illumination in the bedroom was the mellow glow of Mickey Mouse's face on the oversized alarm clock on Tony's dresser.

"Mommm!"

"It's—don't worry, I think it's the generator." Her blood was freezing. She knew they couldn't be out of fuel, Roland had checked the reserve storage tank today. She kept her tone casual. "Carl will see what the problem is. I'll light the hurricane lamps in a minute."

"Where are you going?"

"To the kitchen. I don't know where I left my cigarettes, and I don't have any matches. Look, Mickey's all lit up. And here's the alarm we bought this morning." She took it from the desk and put it beside him on the bed. "Remember how it works?"

"Uh-huh."

"It's *loud.*"

"Will it scare Bad Angel?"

"Bad Angel isn't here, Tony. If he was, Big Dog would jump all over him, and then Carl would tie Angel up. So you don't have to worry."

Tony didn't think to ask, if it was that simple, then why did they have to leave? "I wish Big Dog was here. Where is he?"

"Oh, outside roving around. Maybe he's down at the boat with Carl."

"Come right back," Tony said to his mother.

"I will," she said, and gave him kisses.

Carl was deep in the engine room of the *Lollapalooza* trying to figure out why the portside diesel had started coughing on him when the shore power failed and his work light blinked off.

For several seconds he was absolutely still in the

dark, visualizing exactly where he had placed the emergency flashlight, not wanting to make too many moves without it, because he was sure to bang his head on something in the tight quarters belowdecks.

When he had located the MagLite with a groping hand and turned it on, he squeezed up into the cockpit and flashed the beam on the swaying, 220-volt line that ran from the deck to the generator shed behind the house seventy-five yards away. The cable was still connected to the boat. The floods around the veranda were off too, which meant the generator had shut down. That made him a little uneasy; and the wind cuffing the boat in the slip, causing the wooden walkways to creak as they rose and fell with the movement of the bayou waters, was getting on his nerves.

He went forward to the saloon to turn on auxiliary power, then decided he'd better not put a strain on the batteries. Just run the other diesel until he had a chance to check out the generator. He wondered if Roland had been doing the required maintenance. But the nigger never did anything until Carl told him at least three times.

The key ring was not on the main deck console, where he was sure he had left it. Well, he had a lot on his mind, so maybe— Carl went through the many pockets of the bush jacket he was wearing, which only served to convince him he'd been right, definitely he had left the engine key in the ignition.

Lights out, no keys. The coincidences didn't please him. Was friend Tomlin back from wherever it was Carl had dumped him? Carl didn't see how he could have pulled *that* off, but if he'd managed to swim home, then obviously he was not in a very good mood right now.

Carl went straight to the fly bridge, hurrying, nervous, thinking, The goddamned shotgun better *be* there.

It was. Picking up the Jackhammer, Carl was instantly soothed.

He hadn't reloaded after winging those shots in Tomlin's general direction, but there were a few shells in a cargo pocket of his jacket. Number 4 standard shot. He decided he wouldn't mind switching to double-O for extra whup tonight, just in case. He returned to the saloon and found the shells he was looking for in the false bottom of the stowage locker under the couch, emptied the plastic cylinder of the lightweight charges and reloaded it with the closest thing to dynamite you could find in a hand-held weapon.

With the gun in his grip and his morale greatly improved, Carl thought he'd better go up to the house, have a look at the genny and get Anita stirring, if this little interval of lights-out hadn't jolted her into gear yet.

When he stepped down onto the dock there was a momentary lull in the rip-snorting wind; he heard a jingling sound that couldn't be anything else but keys. Maybe he'd dropped them earlier on the boardwalk, and had just kicked them into the water. *Damn.* he aimed the powerful beam of the MagLite—too powerful; when he looked away from the light he was all but blind—at the boardwalk, but picked up nothing metallic. The wind rose again; and the johnboat he had untied from the stern of the *Lolly* earlier, then moored on the other side of the slip where he was standing, bumped hard against the oil drums supporting the boardwalk.

He heard the jingling again.

Almost as if someone was standing a little way off in the dark, holding the keys and shaking them.

See about that, he thought.

Carl moved the big flashlight in smooth arcs, lighting up every inch of the dock, the boat shed, the lawn that came down to the edge of the rippling marsh grass. He didn't see anyone, but the jingling persisted, hard to tell where it was coming from because of the pressure of the wind on his ears.

Then he thought to look up, and discovered five feet away the key ring hanging from a nail on one of the floodlight posts, near the cable that usually carried current to his boat. The keys were not within easy reach.

Someone had come aboard the *Lolly* while he was down in the engine room leafing through a maintenance manual, had taken the keys from the ignition of the console in the cabin, hung them on the post and then gone up to the house, probably to kill the generator.

Carl couldn't see any point to all that. From what he knew of Clay Tomlin, it wasn't the man's style to be devious.

But who could tell what went on in the mind of Angel Barzatti?

Carl grinned, but his throat was tight enough to hurt. He held the shotgun where he could shoot from the hip if he had to. With the MagLite he made a quick sweep of the boat behind him, but the decks were clear. What the hell, if Angel was hiding aboard the *Lolly* he'd had plenty of chances to jump Carl

already, in worse circumstances than Carl found himself in now.

Assuming the crazy bastard was here, what did he
want?

Carl knew he wanted his keys back. Badly. He
couldn't come up with a reason why he shouldn't
have them, although, the way they were dangling
near the top of the four-by-four post, they seemed to
be a kind of bait.

Carl took another careful look around, and was
convinced he was absolutely alone on the dock.

Shotgun in his right hand, finger on the trigger.
Flashlight in his left hand. He would have to reach up
and hook the key ring with his little finger and lift it
down. Two seconds. Easy. What was he worried
about?

The shiny dangle of keys had become the focus of
his universe. The keys to his boat, with all of his
cash hidden aboard, and also the keys to the swank
Mercedes. Stealing his keys was almost like stealing
his manhood. Hanging them on the post was an
obscure gesture of contempt. Some complex meaning
to it all, perhaps—in the mind of a madman.

Carl took two steps, flashlight beam aimed upward, and reached for the keys, all of his weight on
the toes of his right foot.

The razor-edged blade of Wolfdaddy's cane knife
drove straight up through a narrow gap in the boardwalk, sliced through the rubber weld of Carl's canvas
boat shoe and cut off all but the big toe of his foot.
Deprived of four toes, he lost his balance instantly
and toppled forward, left shoulder glancing off the
post, deflecting him down into the johnboat. He fell
hard on his shotgun and triggered it.

The explosion was muffled by the thickness of his body. The force of the blast, and the damage, was similar to that he might have suffered falling on an antipersonnel mine. And the brilliant beam of the MagLite, sinking in the water off the bow of the johnboat, briefly illuminated the face of the Angel of Death as he swam out from beneath the drums that floated the boardwalk and also provided airspace under it.

"Mommmmmmm!"

Anita finished lighting the second of two hurricane lamps in the kitchen, went to the back steps and called up to Tony.

"Okay! I'm coming right now!"

The wind had gotten in between the screen and the back door and was making a shrill moaning sound by vibrating a thin piece of metal weather stripping. It set her teeth on edge. She started out of the kitchen with the lamp, then became aware of the odor of the rich cannelloni sauce, which she had prepared and left to simmer on a back burner of the stove and totally forgotten about. She retraced her steps across the kitchen to turn the gas off. No thought of eating anything now, but she knew she should take something to Tony. A glass of milk. She set the lamp down and opened the refrigerator.

Outside Big Dog yelped, and she heard something heavy thump down on the floor of the veranda. Anita nearly went up the wall. With the refrigerator door still open she turned, listening, heart beating wildly. But she heard only the harrowing whine of the loose metal along the edge of the door.

She poured a glass of milk for Tony and picked up

the lamp again, intending to go straight upstairs. But she couldn't stand not knowing what had happened on the veranda. Had a limb been torn from a tree and hit Big Dog? He should have been scraping and scratching at the screen door by now to be let in.

She left the milk on the counter between the refrigerator and stove and crossed to the door. Ruffled curtains hid the glass, and whatever was in the dark beyond. Anita pulled the curtains aside but couldn't see a thing. She hesitated, then touched the knob of the dead-bolt lock and turned it. Dropped her hand to the doorknob. She intended opening the door slowly, just a little, but the pressure of the wind expanded into the kitchen through the crack she allowed, tearing the door from her hand, knocking the chimney off the hurricane lamp. The thin glass shattered on the tile floor and the exposed flame swiftly guttered out.

"Carl!" Anita yelled. "Carl, where are you?"

The wind returned no human voice to her, but somewhere on the long veranda she heard Big Dog whimper.

Anita went back to the kitchen table for the other hurricane lamp. Behind her back the screen door opened and closed quickly, with a sharp slap. She turned, gasping, but no one was there: the devilish wind had done it.

The screen yawned open again as she got to it. Big Dog appeared from the darkness, turning her skin to scales of ice; he lunged as if he were walking on something slippery and forced his body through the opening. She almost dropped the extra lamp.

"Oh! God!"

Big Dog was filthy, matted and mired as if he'd

been wading through the marsh. He padded wearily by her and flopped on a rag rug in front of the sink, lying on his side. He had a frothy red gash in his chest about an inch and a half long. He was struggling to suck air through the deep wound.

When she knelt beside him and tearfully touched the side of his head her fingers came away bloody; his ear had been slashed as well.

Anita left the lamp on the floor, leaped to the door, threw her weight against it and shot the dead bolt home.

Big Dog was hyperventilating, saliva dripping from his grimacing mouth.

She needed Carl, badly. But she wasn't opening the door again.

The wind made its drawn-out, metallic humming sound.

Shock had slowed her, dulled her perceptions. She looked at the blood on her hand. If it had happened to Big Dog, then maybe it was happening to Carl too.

She realized that it had been three or four minutes since she had heard anything from Tony.

Anita grabbed the lamp and went to the foot of the stairs. The darkness of the second floor reached down to stifle light.

"Tony!"

The absence of a reply was like a wall of intimidation. She broke through it, running up the steps. Shadows leapt and fell along the hall like half-wild children playing.

She stopped in the doorway to his room with the lamp thrust forward and glowing hotly, illuminating the rumpled bedcovers where he had sat. The bed empty now, he wasn't there. The mouse clock grinned as her terror filled the room like a fog, as her scalp crawled and blood backed up in her throat, leaving her faint. The lamp chimney rattled against the doorjamb. *Tick-tock too-bad*, said Mickey.

"Mom?"

Anita's head jerked toward the bathroom door, which was closed.

"Tony? Are you all right?"

He said in a small voice, "I had to go. I've got cramps."

She felt it too, a sympathetic cramp. But the sound of his voice had revived her miraculously, her heart was pumping again.

"Tony, listen. We're going to take the car and drive into town. Right away."

"What about Clay?" Tony said, sounding as if he was about to cry. "Don't you care about him?"

She pressed the hand that was sticky with Big Dog's blood against her cheek, trying to hold herself together for a few crucial minutes longer.

"Yes—you know I do. I'll ask Mr. Lefevre or someone else to come and find him, but—we—you, I want you to stay right here and wait for me, I need to get my purse and keys. Tony? Lock the door."

"I did already."

Anita left Tony's room and headed for her own. But she paused at Carl's door. Trying to concentrate on just one thing, which was getting herself and Tony safely out of the house. For that, maybe, she needed assistance.

She opened the door to Carl's room.

It was warm, almost stuffy, inside. A pane in one window rattled. Anita smelled his strong cologne, but Carl wasn't there. His luggage, half packed, was in disarray on the bed. The wardrobe doors stood open. Anita put the lamp on a marble tabletop next to the door and went to the bed with the dark high headboard, began ransacking Carl's luggage, tossing underwear and shirts and black socks aside. She didn't find what she needed in either of the pigskin bags. His attaché case was on the floor beside the writing desk and she seized that next, turned it upside down. The last thing to fall out was a Detonics .380-caliber automatic pistol in a suede leather holster.

The bedroom door slammed shut behind her, and as she was coming up from the floor, turning, yanking the pistol from the leather, the lamp chimney was smashed, the flame leaped thinly and went out.

Anita pressed against the wall beside the writing desk, regretting how uninterested she'd been when Carl was trying to instruct her in the proper use of firearms. But she'd fired a few dozen rounds anyway, from this particular weapon. She knew how it worked, and she made ready to shoot without having to think about it. Thumb the safety down, pull the slide back smartly, release it—a satisfying sound in the black trap of Carl's room. Wind slam-banging the house, but she was breathing even more loudly than the wind. She caught a runaway breath and held it. The automatic up and steadying in her two hands. Finger on the trigger and near the point of maximum tension. But where was he?

She listened. Blood storming in her ears, the bugaboo wind distracting. Listened for the giveaway creak of floorboards beneath a heavy tread.

Instead she smelled him.

A different odor in the room, stronger than Carl's

favorite Roman cologne. Morbid, spunky odor, collapsing on her like a spider's dense web.

Come at last, the Angel of Death.

His name on her lips released her at last from the frozen crypt of hatred to which he had consigned her.

"Angel?

"Not *this* time, Angel!"

Methodically Anita began to fire the automatic, emptying the magazine into the dark around her, going blessedly deaf after the first couple of rounds and falling over in a cold faint once the chamber was empty, the hammer clicking futilely as she pulled the trigger one last time.

CHAPTER
TWENTY-EIGHT

When Tony heard the gunshots, he got off the toilet, clutching the Magic Ring, opened the door to the linen closet and huddled inside under the bottom shelf, trembling.

He waited for his mother to come back, but was afraid she wouldn't. He rubbed the stone of the Magic Ring until his fingers were hot. Gradually his violent trembling ceased and to his eyes the stone in darkness took on a pale, ethereal glow.

Then, somewhere in the house, Big Dog barked weakly.

Tony was elated; he didn't have to hide any more.

He buttoned his jeans and pushed open the door of the linen closet. He heard the slam-bang wind and a rising vibrato moan that he knew was from the wind, because he had often listened to it, lying in his bed sleepless on stormy bayou nights. He wasn't afraid of the wind.

But his mother had taken the lamp from his room,

267

which he now found more threatening than familiar. With one hand he covered the stone of the Magic Ring, not wanting to use its power until he needed the Ring to explode Bad Angel into a million billion pieces, which his mother had assured him would happen.

"Mom?" he said quietly. Seeing very little of his room except for the face of Mickey Mouse on the loudly ticking clock, and the ten-watt battery-powered night-light that took the place of Mickey's nose in the dark.

He slid the hand with the Magic Ring into a side pocket of his jeans, then picked up the clock and carried it before him like a lantern to the stairs.

He heard the wolfhound again, not a bark this time but a whimper.

Where?

"Big Dog?" Tony called timidly. Then he called his mother, with a little more strength in his voice. The wind was in the house, damp and drafty, but that didn't bother him as much as the fact that there had been gunshots, and his mother wasn't answering him.

He was starting to tremble again; he needed to cry.

"Carl! Did you shoot something? Where did everybody *go*?"

Hard to hold back the tears as the silence continued, finally they just poured down his face. He was more mad than scared, thinking that they had just gone away, forgetting about him, not caring any more. Trying not to think that something unimaginable but awful had happened.

Tony went down the remaining steps faster, now more accustomed to seeing by the meager glow of the clock face. The loud ticking had a faintly sedative effect on him. He had fallen asleep so many nights in this house, listening to his cheerful clock, awakening in the morning to odors of breakfast from the kitchen, perhaps to see his mother sitting on the side of his bed.

Okay, sleepyhead. School day. Wash your face. Time to get cracking.

Get cracking. For some reason, when she said that, he always thought of the picture of Humpty-Dumpty in one of his books.

He reached the foyer, and stopped there, looking around, a strong draft in his face.

The doors to the library across the parlor were closed but rattling, almost as if Big Dog was inside and throwing his weight against the doors in an effort to get out. He'd been about to go down the hall to the kitchen but he crossed the parlor instead, the tiny light of the clock in his hand bringing out the protruding, mildly glowing eyes of the Ming dogs on the hearth; it was easy to imagine they were about to come to life and spring at him. He hurried.

"Big Dog! Mom! Are you in there?"

No one opened the library doors for him. Tony had to leave the Magic Ring deep in his pocket, set the clock down and open the doors himself.

A fierce blast of wind lifted the hair on his head. The doors to the veranda were wide open, the wraithlike curtains blowing as high as the coffered ceiling. Someone had lighted the hurricane lamp that always stood at one end of a trestle-style map table. Tony looked around quickly but saw only the saturnine face of a hawk-nosed British admiral in an oil painting on one wall. His own face screwed up in disappointment and fear.

The lamp cast some light outside on the veranda. Behind him were the dark parlor and the porcelain dogs he had seen, that had eyes to see *him*. He could not force himself to go back through empty rooms to look for his mother, or Big Dog.

If she had left the lamp here, he thought, then she might be just outside; only she hadn't heard him because of the wind.

Tony walked slowly to the threshold of the veranda, his shadow appearing and thrusting through the doorway, three times larger than he was. The Magic Ring was a hard lump in his tight jeans pocket.

There was a lull in the wind; the blowing curtains fell down around him and he panicked, stumbling outside. He heard an unexpected sound, like the bell of a bicycle.

"Who's that?" But he could see almost nothing, and maybe he was just hearing things. He wanted to walk away, then run to the RV—but Clay wasn't there. His throat closed tightly at the thought of Clay alone, and unable to see. Maybe a gator was going to eat him, right now. Tony couldn't move his feet. He was suffering, and the nightmare that had gone on for too long now affected his ability to make any kind of decision, to react to threatening circumstances.

He heard the sprightly bell again, and from around the back of the house the Angel of Death appeared in Wolfdaddy's top hat and frock coat, clumsily mounted on Wolfdaddy's rusted old Schwinn with the fat tires, the headlamp on the handlebar throwing out splintered rays of yellow light.

He pedaled slowly into Tony's nightmare. Tony could only stare, slack-jawed, at this hunched-over apparition.

The Angel of Death was having a little trouble keeping his balance in the humdinger wind, but he bore down steadily on the dumbstruck boy. He had to steer with one hand, because with the other he was reaching back over his shoulder for the cane knife in the scabbard tied to Wolfdaddy's Boy Scout knapsack.

In the reflected light from the bicycle headlamp, and the outlying glow from the lamp in the library, the many mirrors of the top hat twinkled like a starry sky. But his face was filled with darkness, dark as the death he had brought to the bayou.

Tony got his feet unstuck from the mire of nightmare and backed off; almost too late, he remembered the Magic Ring.

He dug frantically in his jeans pocket and put his hand on the Ring; backed up a little more. He lowered his head and held the Ring, protruding from one small finger, straight out in front of him.

The cane knife flicked free of the scabbard as the Angel of Death pedaled into the light shining across the threshold of the doorway.

The bike was only five feet away from the crouching boy when Big Dog came leaping through the tangle of windblown curtains, hitting the Angel of Death broadside. The bicycle veered off into the railing around the veranda; both the man and the dog fell into the yard below as the cane knife went flying.

Tony looked up at the sound of the impact, and Big Dog's throaty snarl. He saw them struggling in the yard. Big Dog outweighed the Angel of Death by more than thirty pounds, but he had been severely weakened by blood loss; he had been near to dying when alerted to come to Tony's defense.

The Angel of Death punched the dog in the face

and kicked him; he crawled after the cane knife. Tony saw Big Dog get up unsteadily, but he went on the attack again as the Angel of Death picked up the long knife.

Then Tony had to look away because he knew what was going to happen. He heard the wet chopping of the blade and Big Dog's pathetic howling. Tony didn't think about what to do next, he just did it. He ran to the end of the veranda and jumped over the railing, landing in the backyard and hurting an ankle, which slowed but didn't stop him. He left Big Dog dying behind him and ran for the dock.

The Angel of Death heard Tony cry out as he landed wrong, and paused with the cane knife raised over the laid-out wolfhound. Then he caught a glimpse of the boy, dimly visible against the slightly reflectant darkness of the bayou, and gave chase.

Tony found the mooring line of the johnboat and frantically untied it, knowing the Angel of Death was after him. Because he heard him breathing, louder than the wind.

With the line free he jumped down into the johnboat and squealed in fright. He had landed on the back of Carl, and Carl was a swamp of blood and tattered bush jacket.

The johnboat, propelled by the momentum of Tony's body, drifted away from the dock.

The Angel of Death shook the boardwalk, making the drums heave and suck in the water; he went down flat and reached out, hooking his fingers over the gunwale. He started to pull the boat back to him.

Tony picked up the only weapon he could find, a splintery old oar. He thrust it full into Angel's face, hitting him across the eyes and the bridge of his nose.

Angel let go of the johnboat and jerked back, pawing at his nose and a partially blinded eye stuck full of splinters.

Tony scrambled over the facedown corpse of Carlo Buffano and punched the starter button of the trolling motor, which kicked right over. Drifting, with a push from the wind, the johnboat was now sideways to and eight feet from the dock; when he looked he could no longer see the Angel of Death, but was fearful that Bad Angel was now in the water, moving invisibly toward him.

Tony was cold from shock, and sweating. He got the boat turned around and moving farther from the dock, before the now-cooperative wind could turn on him and push him back. The low-powered motor made so little sound he couldn't hear it, but he knew by touch that it was still running. A little water splashed over the gunwale, getting him wet. He had lost his bearings. He thought he was heading up the bayou, where they had left Clay stranded that afternoon; but he might as easily have been going straight out to sea. He sat hunched in the stern of the johnboat with his hand on the tiller, one of Carl's boat shoes pressing against his thigh. He wasn't positive it *was* Carl, but he didn't know how to make sure. The shudders hit him again, followed by a form of lockjaw. Tremble, lock; tremble, lock: he wanted to yell and maybe Clay would hear him, but he couldn't manage it.

More water splashed across the boat, wetting his face this time. Now he was really scared, because he had lost Big Dog and he was alone with a dead man.

The Magic Ring had brought Big Dog to save him. But why did Big Dog have to die? he thought, overwhelmed by sorrow and bitterness. That wasn't the way it was supposed to be, his mother was a *liar*.

He realized then he had lost the Magic Ring in his mad scramble to get to the boat; so what could save him now?

CHAPTER TWENTY-NINE

Shelby Burleson followed DeeJay Voisin down to Lostman's Bayou, and they arrived at the fork in the road a few minutes after eight. DeeJay parked his camper, mounted on the bed of a Bronco, across the road to the house. Shelby was driving his wife's car, a blue Cougar. He had brought his Smith & Wesson .44 magnum, which he carried upside down in a shoulder holster under his red nylon jacket with all the bass tournament patches on it.

DeeJay had switched from chewing gum to Red Man now that he was off duty. He got out of the camper and unloaded a stream of tobacco juice downwind and said to Shelby, "Reckon we ought to have a look around, let 'em know we're here."

"Yeah."

DeeJay took his semiautomatic shotgun from the rack in the cab of his truck. It was a police-issue model called the Roadblocker. He also carried his off-duty piece, a .38 revolver, in a holster on his belt. He wore a sweatshirt with a hood. Both men had flashlights and handcuffs with them. They got into the Cougar, which had side-mounted spots, and went slowly down the road.

"Wind's a bitch tonight," DeeJay said.

"Yeah."

"You like 'Bama and six on Saturday?"

"I don't like it any better than the last time you brought it up."

"How about the Dogs and eight at LSU?"

"I'll just give that'un some thought," Shelby advised him.

DeeJay grinned, then leaned forward a little in the seat and said, "Hold it." But Shelby was already slowing down. "What's that under the live oak there? Isn't that Wolfdaddy's tree? Sure it is."

"Looks like his piano fell down."

"It's a good wind tonight, but it's not that good."

DeeJay put some extra light on the piano, and they saw the body under it. Cats' eyes glowed all around at the edges of the light, and a big striped tom went leaping down from atop the piano, which was angled into the ground like a sinking ship.

"Well, shit," DeeJay said tensely. "This ain't gonna be such a quiet night as I thought."

They got out of the car cautiously. Shelby left the motor running. DeeJay had the Roadblocker across his chest ready to rumble, and Shelby walked with the long-barreled .44 straight up by his right shoulder. They approached the wrecked piano well apart, Dee-Jay turning a slow circle every few feet, trying to avoid looking into the spotlight, which was aimed low at the ground and Wolfdaddy's glistening pate.

"Yeah, it's Wolfdaddy," Shelby said, going down on one knee.

DeeJay just kept moving, looking up, looking around, circling the piano with his back to Shelby. The wind hurting his ears a little. He pulled up the hood of his sweatshirt. Shelby placed two fingers against Wolfdaddy's throat, feeling no heat and no flutter.

"He's long gone, DeeJay."

"How long?" DeeJay let loose some tobacco juice but misjudged the cornering wind and got almost all of it back in his face. He grimaced and wiped his cheek on a sleeve of the sweatshirt.

Shelby looked at the blood, now dried, that had leaked from Wolfdaddy's yawning mouth.

"Maybe a hour."

He got to his feet and looked up at the platform, which didn't look as if it had fallen in. The light-weight door to Wolfdaddy's shack was flopping, open and shut.

"I don't believe that piano just fell off from up there. Unless Wolfdaddy was trying to rearrange all his furniture, find him a spot for the king-size bed."

"No, I don't buy that explanation at all," DeeJay said, still moving, trying to peer into the depths of the dark all around them, feeling bulky and uncomfortable and overexposed.

"Well, we'd better call it in."

"Let's go down to the house first, partner. Won't make a particle of difference to Wolfdaddy. We'll use their phone."

"Thinking the same thing," Shelby told him.

DeeJay backed off to the Cougar and waited for Shelby to join him. Shelby got in quick behind the

wheel, then DeeJay ducked in and Shelby let go of
the brake, turning off all but the parking lights as he
drove toward the bayou.

"So who'd want to kill Wolfdaddy?" DeeJay spec-
ulated, trying to scrub the rest of the Red Man off his
face with a spitty handkerchief.

"Kind who don't leave no witnesses. Nobody.
That kind of operator."

"I hope I'm not gonna wish we got ourselves
down here a tad sooner."

"You see the house yet? Can't make out a damn
thing."

"There's no lights," DeeJay said. "Well, shit.
How we gonna do this?"

"Slow and quiet."

"If I remember correctly, there's a decent grade
from the gate to the house. You could shut the
engine and coast down from there."

"Thought of that already," Shelby said.

"He must have a car stashed somewhere. Pulled it
off the road into the piney woods."

They were nearly on top of the house on the bayou
before they began to see it. The wind was washing
up against the Cougar, rocking it a little in spite of
their combined weight in the front seat. They passed
through the gate and coasted the rest of the way to
the carriage house.

There was a Mercedes sports coupe in the drive,
and Shelby stopped a few feet behind it. He turned
off the parking lights then. They got out, having to
force the doors open against the wind, closed them
gently. Shelby flicked his flashlight sideways, having
a look at the bulk of the RV parked on the slab.

DeeJay put his light into the Mercedes to make sure it was empty, two seconds and then off.

They stood a few feet apart studying the house.

"There's a light," DeeJay said to Shelby, just loud enough for him to hear.

"Around there by the side? Might be a hurricane lamp. Power's down, for sure."

"Maybe they're okay then."

"Let's walk around that way."

"You circle out there on the lawn," DeeJay suggested, "and I'll go on up to the veranda."

"DeeJay?"

"Yeah?"

"Reckon this is the way Eastwood would do it?"

"He ought to be here now, find out what the real thing is like." DeeJay grinned. "Eastwood'd take the Tide and six, he's no pussy."

" 'Nuff talk," Shelby told him, and they separated.

DeeJay went running in his Nikes up to the veranda, trying to retain a sense of where Shelby was, off to his left, as he walked slowly around the corner of the big house. DeeJay tested the flooring of the veranda, but the boards were reasonably tight. Something in the way there: oh, a porch swing. He ducked soundlessly around it. He didn't want to turn his flashlight on; there were a lot of windows and French doors and somebody could be standing just inside watching, might throw lead instead of a piano this time. Right now he'd just as soon listen than look, although the high wind made it hard to hear anything, even the squeaking of the chain-hung porch swing behind him.

The library doors off the veranda were open, the curtains all tangled like ropes and thrown over the tops of the doors. He saw the lamp inside, at one corner of a big table. He glanced down at the yard and found Shelby moving slowly out there. Near the other end of the veranda a bicycle was lying with one wheel half under the railing.

DeeJay went through the formula routine for entering an unfamiliar room in which someone might be waiting to blow him away; but once he was inside with his back to an outer wall he saw no one, nothing except another, darker room next to the library.

"DeeJay?" Shelby called from the yard.

DeeJay rolled out through the library doors, crouching, made one sweep with his leveled shotgun, then vaulted over the railing. He joined Shelby, continuing to sweep the house and grounds.

"What've you got?" he said, his back still to Shelby.

"Fuckin' dead dog. So chopped up, hell I don't know, maybe it's those people's wolfhound they were talking about."

DeeJay had a look for himself, but couldn't tell much. "Chopped up?"

"Yeah."

"This is getting good," DeeJay said, expectorating.

"See a fuckin' phone in the house?"

"Yeah, sure did."

"Let's us go in."

"You too?"

"No, I'll just stay here in the great outdoors and guard the fuckin' dead dog."

They went up over the railing to the veranda and entered the library with as much care and caution as DeeJay had shown before.

"Over there," DeeJay said, pointing out the phone;

he decided to have a look in the parlor. He approached the doorway from one side, then entered the parlor with an easy stealth and more agility than he'd shown in years. He drew no fire. He didn't find any bodies. Beyond the parlor was an entrance hall, stairs; he decided to pass up the tour of the rest of the house for now and went back to join Shelby, always keeping the doorways on both sides of the library in view, and his shotgun on the level.

Shelby held the receiver of the telephone to his ear with a pained expression.

"Dead?" DeeJay asked him.

"You got it."

"What do you want to do now?"

"Check the outside of the house, then go through back to front, first floor. I'll flush; you sit in the blind."

"Okay, partner."

DeeJay and Shelby left the library by the veranda doors. DeeJay went quickly, with the Roadblocker at port arms, to the Cougar in the drive. Checked inside with his flash, then opened the door on the driver's side and rolled the window down, hunkered behind the door with the shotgun on the sill, within easy reach of the headlights if he suddenly needed to turn them up full on the front of the house. Now all he had to do was keep in mind that his back was vulnerable and try not to let the wind drive him nuts while he waited. But it was better than even that the perpetrator they thought they were stalking was long gone from here, leaving God only knew what kind of homicidal mess somewhere in that dark house.

He hadn't been waiting long when he heard Shelby yelling for him.

DeeJay rose and went hustling to the back of the house.

He saw Shelby standing at the corner of the veranda with his .44 in one hand and flashlight in the other, illuminating something he'd come across.

"Body?"

"I don't believe this. I just fuckin' *don't believe it.*"

DeeJay had a look.

There was a man on the rear veranda, sitting up high on the top step near the kitchen door. In the sizzle of the long-distance beam his unswollen eye was full and glassy, the reddish yellow of a classic Halloween moon. He paid no attention to the light, in fact he was facing somewhat away from it, staring off in the direction of the bayou. He was completely naked. His body rigid, fists thrust down below his muscular, alabaster thighs. He was the color of hot bleached bone except for the dark nap of his hair and inky brow shelf, smears of blood on his face and forearms, the faint purple bulb of his upstanding cock.

"Who I think it is?" DeeJay said in an awed tone of voice.

"Has to be. I put the light on him, he didn't react, but I just about dropped a load. You ever see anything like this?"

"That's what I was like every night for six months after I got married, waiting for Myrna to get home from the 7-Eleven."

"He must be a—what do you call it? Cat-uh, something."

"Cataplectic? I don't know. You talk to him?"

"Yeah, and he won't take 'Bama and six neither."

"So let's put the cuffs on him, and find out if anybody's alive inside."

"Watch it. He's maybe sitting there like that now, but—"

"You go up behind him with the cuffs, and if he twitches I'll just blow his right foot off at the ankle."

"You know something, DeeJay, there's times I think you're gonna be a success at this job. Make it his balls instead of his foot."

DeeJay switched on his own flashlight and Shelby climbed up over the railing to the veranda, grunting a little from the effort. He did not attract the notice of the Angel of Death as he walked slowly toward the steps, gun holstered now because he needed to reach behind him to his hip pocket for handcuffs. Below the veranda DeeJay matched Shelby stride for stride, keeping a lot of light on the subject, who he saw was drooling like a baby. And bloodier than he appeared to be from a distance. He had an odor, too, as the wind came around in DeeJay's face. Fetid, gory, disgusting. DeeJay's bulging jaw worked; he squirted tobacco juice to the ground.

As he came around in front of the Angel of Death, with the top of his head at about the level of the naked man's crotch, he was paying more attention to what Shelby was doing and that proved to be fatal for DeeJay.

He had only a glimpse of the automatic shotgun wedged in tight behind the broken latticework of the riser beneath the step on which the Angel of Death was sitting, and recognized too late that the wire looped around one finger of his clenched right hand probably was attached to the taut trigger of the concealed gun. *Fuck*. It was DeeJay's last earthly thought;

before he could make a move to dodge out of the line of fire the Angel of Death stood straight up, pulling hard on the trigger wire, and the Jackhammer went off like a string of dynamite charges, lighting up a big cloud of blood and tumbling DeeJay's now headless body backward down the slope to the bayou.

Shelby Burleson was thrown off balance by Angel's unexpectedly violent action and so shocked by DeeJay's simultaneous demise that he made only a clumsy, fumbling effort to draw his revolver before the Angel of Death, shedding the loop of wire, smashed him in the breadbasket with a low shoulder, drove him back eight feet and through a kitchen window. Shelby was struggling breathlessly to free himself from the shards in the window frame, which held him like pincers, when the Angel of Death stepped away from him, reached down to pick up the dropped revolver, and backed up coolly.

Shelby, all out of time and knowing it, bleeding from a dozen cuts, righted himself and took two stumbling steps toward Angel, reaching for him. Several bullets went through his palms, and he was dead before his sprawling momentum took out a section of the railing around the veranda and he joined DeeJay down in the yard.

CHAPTER
THIRTY

Tomlin's fire, in spite of his best efforts, was steadily dwindling. He had heaped everything he could find, working his way around on hands and knees within a radius of fifteen feet, onto the ash and low flames. Now there was nothing left to burn.

He had company, there on the little island: a couple of alligators—at least two that he knew of—who had sluggishly crept near the warmth of his fire. They hadn't bothered him, and probably wouldn't; gators rarely attacked men, particularly on land, and this wasn't their season to be aggressive anyway, with the nights growing nippier. Soon the gators of Lostman's would spend days at a time on the bottom of the bayou, where the water stayed warm the year around; they would go for several months without eating.

He wasn't in desperate trouble. But he was cold and still angry. Thinking about Anita and Tony, wondering if the boy had told her about his predicament.

Of course he had, which meant Anita was in no position to do anything about it.

Talking to himself was a bore and he couldn't exercise; he might trip over a gator lying low and fall into his own fire. A real comedown for a man who had his pride. But he needed to do something to relieve the tension and the tedium, to get his blood moving a little more briskly. He imagined how good it was going to feel when finally he was standing in a steaming hot shower, once he got off this island. And the thought of a shower started him singing.

> "When I heard the crash
> on the highway
> I knew what it was
> from the start.
> I went to the scene
> of destruction
> A picture was stamped
> on my heart."

Pretty fair, Tomlin thought. Of course it lacked the powerful pathos Roy Acuff could bring to one of his trademark songs, and Tomlin didn't have Wilma Lee or Maybelle Carter alongside him, playing lead guitar or autoharp. But maybe the gators were entertained. Like it, fellas? This is the refrain that gets me, every time.

> "I heard the groans
> of the dying, but
> I didn't hear nobody
> pray."

On a bright Pacific afternoon during what now seemed to be another lifetime, he had concluded a routine operation with a sudden drop in the A-7's oil pressure and corresponding loss of power before his carrier was in sight. With the air boss recommending blue water ops he had elected to try to deck his bird and pulled it off, though he landed powerless, and missing the cable would have meant, probably, going to the bottom of the sea. But he felt confident, even happy, as he went into his break, and he'd entertained the bridge with a few choruses of "Wreck on the Highway" before touching down safely. The admiral had chewed him out privately for this touch of macabre humor, but when you were wing commander you could get away with a little show of bravado, as long as it didn't encourage the younger hotshots to act recklessly the next time they found themselves in a jam. Sing it again, Tomlin.

> "Who did you say it was,
>   brother
>   Who was it fell by
>   the way?
>   When whiskey and blood
>   ran together
>   Did you hear anyone
>   pray?"

Better than all right, he decided, wondering if he still remembered all the verses to "Gathering Flowers from the Hillside." That was a song you could really throw your heart into. The way Wilma Lee and Stoney Cooper did it, with that Dobro fading in and out, sending mournful chills up the spine: outstanding. Tomlin gave it a shot.

> "I know that you have seen
> troubles
> But never hang down your
> head
> Your love for me is like
> the flowers
> Your love for me is dead."

How about that for a lyric, punk rockers? Tomlin got to his feet, really belting out the last verse.

> "I shot and killed my
> darling;
> And what will be my doom?"

"Clay! Clay!"

Tomlin, astonished, shut up and listened. So faint and far-off the cry, was he just hearing things? Or could it have been Tony?

"Clay, where are you?"

"Tony?" He broke into a big smile and began to bellow. "Hey! Big guy! Where are you?"

That wasn't much use. Tony's small voice came back to him on the wind.

"Here! But where are *you?"*

Tomlin looked around blindly, laughing.

"I don't know! Who's with you?"

He fully expected to hear Anita answer this time. But Tony called, "Nobody! Carl is. But he's dead."

Jesus Christ. Tomlin cupped his hands to his mouth and shouted, "Tony, I made a fire! Look for my fire!

Are you in the johnboat? Steer toward the sound of my voice!"

"Sing something! Not about people dying!"

Tomlin just shook his head, temporarily without inspiration. Then he remembered the spiritual Wolf-daddy had been playing and singing not too many nights ago, at the Next-Thing-to-Heaven Church.

> "Lord, Lord, you sure
> been good to me
> Lord, Lord, Lord, you sure
> been good to me
> 'Cause I'm a soldier, a
> soldier of the cross!"

It was a pretty good approximation of Wolfdaddy's bluesy, rasping style. Tomlin wondered how the fire was doing. He still smelled it, and could feel a little heat. You son of a bitch, don't go out on me now. He wondered if he could still imitate that muted horn sound, mouth against his cupped hands. Just keep making a lot of noise, and hope the boy would locate him.

"Tony! Tony! Tony!"

"Clay!" Now sounding hopeful, stronger, nearer. "I think I see the fire. I'm coming!"

"Come on, Tonnnnyyyy!" Tomlin cheered. "You're doing great! You're right on course!"

"Sing!"

Tomlin sang, trying to pitch his voice above the keening of the wind. He was nearly out of breath, beginning to feel exhausted.

"I see you!" His voice rose a notch. "Clay!"

"What?"

"Don't move! There's gators!"

"Oh, them. How many?"

"One, two, three—uh, four. No, *five!*"

Tomlin looked around again, smiling at the unseen alligators.

"Thanks, guys. You've been a wonderful audience, I mean that sincerely. Next week, Liza Minnelli." He took a deep breath, with no more interest in tomfoolery. "Tony, you here yet?"

"Yes." Not sounding very far away.

"You'll have to come get me."

"Won't they bite?"

"No."

"I'm afraid to."

"Well—I'll meet you halfway."

"There's one lying right in front of you."

Tomlin nudged the alligator with his foot. "Do I have heads or tails?"

"Tails."

Tomlin stepped over the oblivious gator and walked slowly toward the sound of Tony's voice.

"Okay now?"

"I'm coming."

He heard the boy splash into shallow water.

"Don't let the boat drift away."

"I've got the line."

"How far away am I?"

"Just keep walking."

"Tony, are you all right?"

"Y-yes, but I'm cold."

"So am I."

"Here's my hand."

Tomlin reached out; Tony seized his fingers and held on tight. Tomlin took the line from him and followed it to the boat, sinking into the water, gas bubbles rising from the disturbed bottom. He reached into the boat and located the sprawled body inside.

"Is that Carl?" he asked Tony.

Tony began to sob.

"Okay, okay, you're doing great so far, Tony. Don't—honest to God, you're the greatest kid I've ever met in my life. Now we need to—we want to think about what we're going to do next. Can you steer the boat? That's a dumb question, you got here, didn't you?" He waited for Tony to say something, afraid that the boy wouldn't climb into the boat again as long as the body was there. He didn't know how Carl had died, but from touching his perforated back Tomlin knew Carl was a mess. "You—you have to talk to me, Tony. I can't see you. Tell me how you feel."

"*Mom—*"

Tomlin shivered in a flood of fear. He held tightly to the gunwale of the boat with both hands.

"Where's your mother?"

Tony sniveled and couldn't, or didn't, want to answer the question.

"Tony. Please tell me."

"I—I don't know where she is. I think Bad Angel's got her."

CHAPTER
THIRTY-ONE

Even before she knew where she was or what had happened to her, Anita glimpsed the face of the Angel of Death and felt, not frightened, but terribly wronged. Because she knew she must have shot him, there in Carl's dark room. Couldn't have missed. Yet he was sitting just a few feet away, face mostly in shadow, as expressionless as a clumsy woodcut. Her eyes felt puffy and her vision was blurred; she blinked monotonously, finally bringing him into focus. His mouth moved, was he talking to her? No, he was chewing. Eating.

Not much light in this room, wherever she was. Anita felt a strong cold draft, as if a window was open. She saw a gaslight glaze on Angel's forehead, the Italianate bridge of his nose, one bald shoulder. He ate steadily, raking his spoon across the plate. She smelled the cannelloni sauce she'd been preparing and was instantly nauseated, choking back the distasteful fluid that spurted up from her stomach.

He heard the sound she made and looked at her. His right eye was a bulging shiner, as if he'd been in a fight. There was a cut on his nose, other scribbles of dried blood; he was generally unclean, he might recently have dug himself out of an untight grave. His hairline, she noticed, had receded drastically. Otherwise, the same old Angel.

Anita realized they must be in the kitchen, with the table between them. Shiny things lay on the table near Angel's plate. A knife with a long blade. A whetstone.

She raised her head and discovered that the tightness at her throat was a rope. Her knees were pressed together. She could move her toes but couldn't spread her feet. All trussed up with her hands somewhere behind her back, no feeling in them. She was helpless, when Angel should be dead.

"Shot you," Anita croaked.

He studied her again while tearing into half a loaf of Italian bread, crumbs sprinkling like snow down his hairless chest. He shook his head but didn't say anything. He didn't have to.

She'd missed, that's all. Six shots in the dark—no, seven. Missed him. Then fainted dead away as the climax to her incompetence, leaving Tony defenseless in the—

"Did you hurt Tony?"

White teeth gnawing a crust. He'd always had wonderful teeth. He shook his head again, the stingiest of gestures. Thank God . . . but could she believe him?

"Why did you come, Angel? Why do you want to hurt me again? Because I failed you?" He allowed nothing; seemed not to have heard her. "All right.

Maybe I did. But I—I'll try again, Angel. If that's what you want. Is it?''

His chair scraped back. He stood up. He was naked. Worse, he had an erection. The indecency of his dick dismayed her. Had he used it on her yet? She still had her clothes on. She didn't feel as if she'd been violated. But that was coming, without a doubt. Anita was choked with loathing.

The Angel of Death moved briefly out of her line of sight, then returned to the table with an opened bottle of Valpolicella. He drank from the bottle, holding it by the neck, not taking his eyes off her. She was so thirsty. She would die before she asked him for anything. *She would die*.

"What are you—going to do with me?"

He put the wine bottle down and came around the table. She felt his soiled, profane body close behind the chair in which she was bound, and gasped. He picked her up easily, turned the chair, put her down again facing the stove. Anita saw that all of the gas jets were on. She stared at the rosettes of flame for several seconds, slow to comprehend what was on his mind.

Then she understood. And tried, unsuccessfully, to scream.

The chair rocked, then tipped over backward. Anita's head hit the kitchen floor. The rope around her throat tightened, choking her cruelly. As she passed out again she had a whiff of something, the death-fragrance of cooking gas. The last thing she saw was Angel standing astride her, wearing Wolfdaddy's eccentric hat with the mirrors, the whetted, freshened knife swinging like a pendulum in his hand.

CHAPTER
THIRTY-TWO

"Where are we, Tony?"

"Coming to the dock."

"Do you see him anywhere?"

"No."

"That's good. Is Carl's boat there?"

"Yes."

"Any lights?"

"No. There was a hurricane lamp in the library, but I don't see it now. Wait!"

Tomlin felt him leaning forward, as if he were straining to make out something in the darkness ahead. He had a hand on Tony's shoulder. The boy was still trembling, big husky spasms, but he hadn't given up like a lot of kids would have done, drifted off to never-never land with a thumb tucked in his mouth. Tomlin thought about how much his father would have admired Tony. *So it's hard. But you're harder.*

"What is it, Tony?"

"I think there's a light in the kitchen."

"Okay. Tony, we want to go aboard Carl's boat and use the radio. Do you know where it is?"

"Yes."

"I don't want to turn on any of the boat lights. How far are we from the dock?"

"Almost there." A few seconds later the johnboat bumped against an oil drum. Without having to be told, Tony scrambled out, a line in one hand. Tomlin shut off the motor, grasped the edge of the boardwalk for a few seconds, visualizing the move he was going to make before he stepped out of the boat. Finding it difficult, after being hunkered down in the boat, to keep his balance.

"Tony?"

He felt a tug from behind on his sleeve.

"There you are. Is Carl's boat in the slip?"

"Yes."

"Help me aboard."

"What are you going to do?"

"Mayday call. That should bring a Coast Guard chopper and cutter, and the sheriff."

"Give me your hand," Tony said, and led him a few steps down the boardwalk. Tomlin, groping, found the grab rail on the stern gunwale of the *Lolly*. He jumped aboard and turned, holding out both hands for Tony, lifted him down to the cockpit deck.

"Hey, we're doing all right."

"Mom's not doing all right," Tony reminded him.

"Let's get to the radio."

Tony guided him slowly through the saloon to the main cabin console. Tomlin sat down in the pilot's seat, running his hands over the board until he located the microphone.

"Do you know how to turn the radio on?" he asked Tony.

"Carl showed me once. What if it doesn't work?"

"It'll work if the batteries are charged," Tomlin assured him.

"I think this switch is the one—"

"Go ahead. You should have a red light showing now—"

"It's on!"

Tomlin thumbed the mike button to *transmit*. He didn't care what channel they were tuned to, although they would get faster action on 16.

"Mayday! Mayday! Mayday! This is the *Lollapalooza* at Lostman's Bayou. Repeat. The *Lollapalooza* at Lostman's Bayou. There has been a shooting aboard. We are under attack by a man who is armed and dangerous. Need immediate medical assistance. Request anyone monitoring this channel to contact the Port Bayonne police and the Jackson County sheriff. Repeat—"

"Clay!"

"Mayday! Mayday! Mayday!"

"No! He cut it! They can't hear you!"

Tomlin lowered the microphone. With his other hand he touched the end of the cord, sliced off three inches below the mike.

"What do we do now?"

Tony had screamed; almost immediately they heard a faraway scream from Anita, as if she were answering his distress with an even more unbearable anguish.

Tony held Tomlin tightly, his face against Tomlin's chest.

"He's hurting her!"

"There's a CB radio in the RV—but he probably

took care of that one, too. Carl was a gun nut, he must have guns aboard somewhere. Tony, where did Carl keep the guns?''

"I don't know! *Do something!*"

"Tony, I'm trying—I need—I've got to have—"

He stood, pushing the boy away from him, hands searching for the console locker. Found it. Not locked, fortunately. He began taking inventory of the contents. Flashlight, that was no good. A tool of some kind, like a pry bar. *Maybe.* He was beginning to get a few ideas, some of which were crazy, others merely reckless. A big socket wrench. *Keep it.* He was filling up with tools at the beltline. So much depended on Tony. If the boy didn't keep his nerve, do exactly as he was told, they could all die. He was almost to the bottom of the locker, *where the hell was it?*

"What are you looking for?" Tony asked. Scared, but no longer sounding so close to panic.

"We have to take him on, Tony. You and me. But I can't try it without some kind of—"

Tomlin caught his breath, and was very still for a few seconds. Tony touched the nape of his neck with cold fingers. Tomlin slowly withdrew his hand from the locker.

"What's that?"

"It's one shot, Tony. One goddamned shot! But it's better than nothing."

Tomlin opened the breech of the flare pistol he had taken from the locker, making sure it was loaded. Sweat was dripping off his chin. He snapped the pistol shut and tucked it inside his waistband with the tools.

He turned around and took the boy in his arms.

"Tony, you spend a lot of time playing those computer games, don't you? Well, now we're going to play a game like one of those, only for real. Angel—"

"*Bad* Angel."

"Bad Angel's the—the dragon. The monster at the end of the corridor. Understand?" He put a hand on Tony's head; the boy nodded solemnly.

"What's the game like?"

"I'll teach you how to play, right now. It's easy. There's only a couple of things you need to do. But I want you to tell me something first. Do you know which is your right hand, and which is your left?"

"Yes."

Tomlin held up his right hand, palm out.

"Put your left hand against mine."

Tony did so, without hesitating. Good. Any hesitation, later, might be fatal. But Tomlin felt encouraged.

"I think it'll work," he said. "Don't worry, we'll get your mother out of there."

In the kitchen, Angel had finished knotting some Dacron clothesline to the refrigerator door handles. He tested the tautness of the line, which was wrapped around Anita's upper body, going across her breasts and under her arms. He had turned off the burners of the stove after bringing in the hurricane lamp from the library.

Anita was spread-eagle on her back on top of the stove, arms pulled back over her head and anchored to the ceiling fan. He had tied her feet together, then lashed that line to the sink faucet. She could move her head, but that was all. Already the heat from the pilot light of the stove was painful, burning the small of her back. But that was nothing, compared to what she would feel when Angel turned the four jets back on.

"Angel, please don't do it! Please!"

She had screamed; she had pleaded with him until her throat was raw and she tasted blood from her bitten tongue. He had not said a word as he went about his chores. Now he stood back, somewhere near the center of the kitchen, shadowy, contemplative, but not static—spinning scarily as a buzzsaw spins from the pure force of his irrationality. Watching her as her head snapped frantically side to side (fright a kind of ecstasy), no resources left but the power of speech, a desperate need to appease and persuade.

"It won't make things better for you, Angel. Why do you have to kill me? Can't we talk about it? I don't want to die! Is that what you wanted to hear me say? I—we—have a *son*. Think about Tony. You must think about him *sometimes*."

The Angel of Death reached behind him and picked up the cane knife from the kitchen table. He walked to the stove and stood there with the edge of the knife level, an inch above her forehead, his hands too patient. Anita stared at it, afraid to move her head any more. At the touch of the blade against her sensitive temple she snorted insanely, blood foaming at the corners of her mouth.

Painstakingly he shaved a lock of her hair from her head and carried it back to the table in the palm of one hand, looking at it thoughtfully.

When the surge of blood from her furious heart subsided, Anita's ears unblocked and she could hear the wind again, the graveyard wind.

"I hope you enjoyed that, you son of a bitch," she said, just able to say it. Almost, but not yet broken.

He turned to look at her again and as he did glass shattered somewhere in the house, distracting him. At first Anita thought it was just the wind; but there was something rhythmic, even purposeful, in the continued breaking of panes.

Then she heard Clay Tomlin, calling.

"Angel! Come here, Angel! We want you!"

And Tony's voice, a high-pitched chant: "Angel! Angel! Angel! Angel!"

Anita sobbed, thrilled and terrified. So brave. And Angel would kill them both.

Cane knife in one hand, naked and priapic, the Angel of Death picked up the hurricane lamp and moved away from her toward the dining room door, which was wavering in a strong draft. The brittle splintering of glass continued.

"Look out!" Anita shouted. "Look out, he's coming!"

"Come out, Angel! We want you!"

"We want you! We want you!" Tony echoed.

No, run! she thought, too feeble and out of breath to shout again. She saw Angel hesitate at the dining room door, listening as glass was broken in the French doors that opened on the veranda. Then the destruction stopped. Angel moved the swinging door a little and looked into the dining room, holding the lamp above his head, the cane knife twitching like a predator's tail. He stepped quickly into the dining room, the door swinging shut behind him, and Anita groaned.

He was going after them.

*   *   *

They sat together in the porch glider at the front of the veranda, sixty feet from the French doors of the dining room, which hung open, shards of glass picking up the light from the hurricane lamp as Angel approached the veranda. Tomlin's right hand was thrown casually over the back of the glider. He had his left arm around Tony, who was kneeling on the seat, jittery, pressed against him, hiding his face. The boy seemed to have less and less flesh on his frame as the night piled on terror. They were both breathing hard; they had broken a lot of windows. Tony's left ear, nicked by a splinter of flying glass, was leaking blood.

"Is he coming?" Tomlin asked.

Tony took a fast look. "He's in the dining room. I see the lamp." Then he saw the Angel of Death, forbiddingly, reflected in half a pane of cracked glass as the wind swung one of the doors toward the dining room. "There he is!"

"Outside?"

"Not yet."

"Hey, *Ain-gel*," Tomlin called, a lot of scorn in his voice. "What's the matter with you? Scared of something? A blind guy and a kid? Come on out here, I want to talk to you. That's what I said, *move it,* chickenguts!"

"He hasn't got any clothes on," Tony said, fascinated.

"Is he on the veranda yet?"

"No, I can see his reflection."

"Angel, name's Tomlin. This is my house. I don't remember inviting you. So I want you to get the hell out!"

Tony, looking back over his shoulder, said worriedly, "He isn't coming!"

"Anita doesn't want you here either. She doesn't give a damn about you, Angel, you're just wasting your time. You want to know what Anita told me? I'm a hell of a lot more man in bed than you ever were!"

"What does that mean?" Tony said.

"I'll explain later, Tony. What's happening?"

"*Nothing*. He's just standing there in the—no, he looked out! But now he's—"

"Being cautious." Tomlin raised his voice in exasperation. "Peek-a-boo, Angel! My, but you're sweet! Don't worry, I won't hurt you, sweetums, long as you do what I say. But if you don't do it, I'll kick your balls off and feed them to the gators."

The Angel of Death stepped carefully over the threshold of the veranda, a big step to avoid the litter of broken glass.

"Here he comes!" Tony whispered, and buried his face again.

"How fast?"

"He's barefoot. There's a lot of glass."

"Let's just keep him coming."

"He looks funny. His peepee's big, real big."

"Hey, Angel! Tony says you've got a hard-on! I bet I had one bigger than that when I was twelve years old!" He gave Tony a squeeze. "Start reading him for me. Remember what I told you."

Tony took a fast look around. "On glide path. On course."

"Angel, I'm not waiting all night for you to get over here—"

"He's got a knife!"

"You hurt women! You scare little kids, huh? But a man, yeah, you're afraid of a man, right? Even one who can't see."

Angel was moving now closer to the outside of the veranda, one careful step at a time.

"Right of course!" Tony whispered frantically. "He's going to the railing."

"Remember what I told you—when I say go you run, run as fast as you can and don't look back until you know you're safe."

The Angel of Death hesitated, his right foot on a floorboard that Tomlin had loosened with the pry bar. He stepped back, away from the railing, moving closer to the center of the veranda, holding the lamp up, the cane knife in his fist out front now. Watching Tomlin's eyes, he moved the lamp back and forth.

"*Coming!* On glide path."

"I'll bet you're even uglier than Anita said you were, Angel! Yeah, she's told me all about you. Your big thing is whores, right? You like to get them from behind. They probably wouldn't take you on if they had to look at your ugly face."

"On glide path!"

"*Where?*"

"The library—!"

"Anita's happy with me, Angel; so I'm taking her away from you. Think you can do something about it? Well, why don't you try me, you motherrrrrrrr-fuckerrrrrrrr!"

Roaring, Angel sprang at Tomlin and Tony in the glider, the cane knife raised high.

"Now, now!" Tony screamed.

Tomlin stood in Angel's path, almost hurling Tony away from him, to the floor of the veranda. He leveled the flare pistol he had concealed behind the glider.

Angel dodged toward the house, leaving Tomlin aiming at empty space.

Rolling over on the veranda, Tony saw him moving and called out, "No, left of course!"

Tomlin altered his aim a steady three inches to the right, now or never. He pulled the trigger of the flare pistol.

The magnesium flare, a crucial comet bright enough to restore precious vision to Tomlin's eyes, was off the mark as Angel stepped quickly toward Tomlin, the cane knife at an angle to disembowel him. The lantern was in Angel's left hand, well away from his body.

Tomlin had a glimpse of eldritch eyes and the oncoming tip of the knife just as the flare hit the lamp dead-center and exploded it. Instantly half of Angel's body was a billowing sheet of flame. His foot cracked through another booby-trapped floorboard and he was hung up inches short of eviscerating Tomlin.

Tomlin backed away from the searing heat on his face. Tony was screaming.

The wind fanned the flames wildly over the Angel of Death. He dropped the cane knife, the taped handle on fire, and bent over, grasping his trapped ankle with roasting hands. He pulled himself free and glanced at Tomlin, indifferent now, preoccupied with burning. With his head blackening to a nugget within a flame of blue brilliance, licking almost to the roof of the veranda, the Angel of Death danced three steps to the railing, perhaps thinking of the soothing black waters of the bayou. He fell over the railing, leaving little flickering clots of himself behind, struggled to his feet impassionedly.

Then, as Tony watched, covering his ears in an attempt to shut out the shrieks, the Angel of Death went running down the lawn, a dragon's tail of flame in his wake. He never came close to making it to the water.

CHAPTER
THIRTY-THREE

They came to the bayou at first light, four men in a late-model Chevrolet sedan. They stopped at the Next-Thing-to-Heaven Church for a look, just one man getting out to make sure that the black man under the piano was dead, then drove on to the house and parked behind the blue Cougar. They got out of the car with guns and looked around through the ground mist. The smut on the veranda, bodies in the yard already attracting blizzards of flies.

In the parlor, Clay Tomlin woke up to the sound of muted voices, footsteps on his veranda. He was sitting up on the sofa with Anita on one side of him, Tony on the other, both asleep. Tony with his fists clenched. None of them had taken a bath, or changed clothes. Just held each other, through the remainder of the night.

"What is it?" Anita said with a little jump, not opening her eyes. Wanting to keep them shut.

"Somebody's here." He kissed her bloodless cheek, to show he wasn't concerned. "I'll go."

He walked outside through the wrecked library doors and found himself facing Uzis and other potent weapons. He looked the men over, seeing flesh tones but not faces too well, despite a streak of sunrise at the tree line.

"Who are you?" one of them said.

"Tomlin. This is my house." Burnt odors, and the veranda streaked nastily black in places; but the clean smell of the sea already was at his door. It could still be a good place to live. "What's your name?" he asked the spokesman.

"Vic."

"Police?"

"No. Angel was here?"

Tomlin laughed harshly. "He's still here. If you found something that looks like left-over barbecue, it's Angel."

They lowered their guns. Vic said, "He gave you a little trouble, huh?"

Tomlin leaned against the side of the house and folded his arms, not caring about Angel any more. Only Anita mattered now. And Tony.

"I guess you won't be needing us," Vic said.

"If you're who I think you are—Carl's down there in the johnboat at the dock. I think he's dead."

Vic shrugged. "Not our business. Call the cops."

"Phone's out of order."

"We'll call them for you, on our way out."

They were walking away, toward the rental Chevy, when Vic hesitated and then came back toward Tomlin.

"The don will want to know how Anita is."

"I need to tidy the place up a little. After that we're getting married."

Vic cocked his head, then he grinned. "I'll tell him."

Tomlin watched until the Chevy had turned around and was heading for the gate. He heard a crunch of glass in the doorway and looked over his shoulder. Anita was standing there, tight-shouldered from the morning chill, face bleak. Then her face turned, caught a flash of sun, revived shockingly; her cheeks filled in a pretty way and she said, daring him to verify it, "*Who's* getting married?"

Tomlin laughed at her expression. Then he put an arm around her, and walked her back into the house.

ALSO AVAILABLE FROM
HODDER AND STOUGHTON PAPERBACKS

All these books are available at your local bookshop or newsagent, or can be ordered direct from the publisher. Just tick the titles you want and fill in the form below.

Prices and availability subject to change without notice.

Hodder & Stoughton Paperbacks, P.O. Box 11, Falmouth, Cornwall.

Please send cheque or postal order, and allow the following for postage and packing:

U.K. – 55p for one book, plus 22p for the second book, and 14p for each additional book ordered up to a £1.75 maximum.

B.F.P.O. and EIRE – 55p for the first book, plus 22p for the second book, and 14p per copy for the next 7 books, 8p per book thereafter.

OTHER OVERSEAS CUSTOMERS – £1.00 for the first book, plus 25p per copy for each additional book.

Name ....

Address ....

....